Killer Green Tomatoes

Also by Lynn Cahoon

The Farm-to-Fork Mysteries
Who Moved My Goat Cheese?

The Tourist Trap Mysteries
Rockets' Dead Glare
Killer Party
Hospitality and Homicide
Tea Cups and Carnage
Murder on Wheels
Killer Run
Dressed to Kill
If the Shoe Kills
Mission to Murder
Guidebook to Murder

The Cat Latimer Mysteries
Of Murder and Men
Fatality by Firelight
A Story to Kill

Killer Green Tomatoes

A Farm-to-Fork Mystery

Lynn Cahoon

LYRICAL UNDERGROUND
Kensington Publishing Corp.
www.kensingtonbooks.com

LYRICAL UNDERGROUND BOOKS are published by

Kensington Publishing Corp.
119 West 40th Street
New York, NY 10018

All Kensington titles, imprints, and distributed lines are available at special quantity discounts for bulk purchases for sales promotion, premiums, fund-raising, educational, or institutional use.

Special book excerpts or customized printings can also be created to fit specific needs. For details, write or phone the office of the Kensington Sales Manager: Kensington Publishing Corp., 119 West 40th Street, New York, NY 10018. Attn. Sales Department. Phone: 1-800-221-2647.

First Electronic Edition: July 2018
eISBN-13: 978-1-5161-0383-6
eISBN-10: 1-5161-0383-1

First Print Edition: July 2018
ISBN-13: 978-1-5161-0384-3
ISBN-10: 1-5161-0384-X

Printed in the United States of America

To my crazy family. When I say a variety of spices makes the best sauces, I think of all of you.

Acknowledgments

Soups, stews, and sauces are all made better with a little heat, time to develop the seasonings, and a nice mixture of seasonings and ingredients. The same can be said for families. It's the people who came into and out of my life over the past several years who have made me who I am. They also affect the products that come out of this author's mind. There are too many of you to thank by name, but know you're in my thoughts.

Thank you to Kensington for building my cozy career and welcoming me to their family. I'd also like to thank my agent, Jill Marshal, for pushing me to do better with each draft.

Chapter 1

A good sauce is like a strong family. Mixing all the elements together in a hot pot, letting it steep and boil, gives you the deeper flavors. Flavors that make each ingredient more than what it was alone. And that family bonding stays with you forever. Even when the actual people are gone, random memories can hit at any time. Memories about settings, or laughter, or even food. Bits and pieces can be almost in our grasp, then float away as quickly as a puff of smoke. Today was one of those days.

The aromas of three different sauces filled the kitchen of the County Seat and mixed together into a pleasant cacophony of the sweet, tangy, and tart. Angie Turner, head chef and co-owner, and the rest of her kitchen staff experimented with what might be Angie's favorite summertime treat ever, fried green tomatoes. A dish she planned on elevating to be able to put the appetizer on the menu, just as soon as they found the right recipe. They'd been working on their recipes all morning, and it was almost time for the taste testing. Angie knew she was trying to create a memory from when her Nona had fried up tomatoes straight from the garden. But just because it was a vague and distant food memory didn't mean it wasn't worth pursuing.

Angie grabbed a bottle of water from the fridge and glanced at her team. They'd only been together about a month, but the chemistry was working. Nancy and Matt worked together on one dish, with Nancy clearly taking the lead and Matt following her directions like they were cooking for the White House. Angie wondered if there was a romance brewing between the two, and if so, if it would mess up her kitchen if it got serious or imploded.

On the other side of the kitchen, Estebe Blackstone, her sous chef and second in command, walked Hope through the knife cuts. Hope was actually their dishwasher, but she was attending culinary school, so she jumped at any chance she got to actually cook. Angie watched as Hope practiced the chop she'd just been shown, then looked up at Estebe for guidance. This was the kind of kitchen she'd dreamed of running. One where people were engaged and willing to help each other. She'd worked in a few places where the competition took main stage and the food was more of a sideline. She like this environment much better.

"Wrap it up, people. We've got a taste testing to serve." Angie started plating her own dish. The taste test would be the first order of business at the staff meeting that Felicia had already started with her servers and the bartender. The kitchen staff was expected in less than ten minutes. "And remember, no lobbying for votes. This is about the food, not about who cooked it."

"Yeah, but we are so going to kick butt in this." Matt high-fived Nancy.

His partner shook her head at his exuberance. She glanced over at Angie. "Sorry, he's a little bit wired on coffee this morning."

"I'd say he's delusional." Estebe set the family-style plate of tomatoes on the expediting station. "Especially since it's clear that the recipe Hope and I developed is clearly superior."

Angie laughed as she finished her own plating and took the dish forward. "You all forget, the boss always wins."

"Not when it's a blind taste test." Hope joined in the banter. Her face beamed from the heat of the kitchen and the joy she always seemed to radiate. "I love cooking with you guys. It almost feels like I'm a part of the team."

"You are a part of the team." Nancy hugged her. "Now, let's get cleaned up and go join the front of the house. I've got a date tonight with a bathtub and a bottle of wine. Man, my upper body takes a beating at the grocery store."

Nancy worked a second job on Mondays, Tuesdays, and Thursdays. With her shifts at the County Seat, Nancy was working every day of the week. Angie knew her prep cook/pastry chef needed the money, but she couldn't move the team to a more full-time schedule until fall, although they were getting closer to running that as bookings were filling up quickly.

They left the dishes under the warming lights and went into the dining room where Felicia and her crew were just wrapping up their weekly meeting. At Felicia's nod, two of the servers stood and headed back to the kitchen to bring out the food.

"Welcome to the party. We just finished going over this month's menu and any changes in the service. Anything you want to add?" Felicia poured a glass of water as she sat at one end of the table. They called their meetings family meals, and as a tradition, Felicia, as head of the front of house, sat at one end of the table. Angie took the opposite end. Angie liked the family feel. For too many years after her parents had died, it had been just her and Nona at the table. She'd never had the big, gather-around-the-table kind of meals, so she'd made her own family. Her work family.

"I'm interested in any comments, good or bad, you may overhear from the guests. Just because they don't tell you up front they don't like something doesn't mean everything is all right. Look for unfinished plates or unhappy looks on their faces. If they don't like what they ordered, offer them something else to replace it. We want every guest to want to make the County Seat a regular in their dining-out schedule." Angie glanced over the other notes and decided to leave them for the next meeting. She didn't want her main message to be diluted. "We are playing with some interesting flavor combinations here in the kitchen. Not everyone is going to like what we serve. But we can find something on the menu they will like, or I'll make them something off menu that they will like. No one goes home hungry."

"You sound like a commercial," Jeorge, the bartender, joked.

Angie shrugged. "There's worse mottos for a restaurant. I want people to think of us first when they're making plans. Or a dish we had that they can't get out of their head."

"That's a tall order." One of the servers set a plate of fried green tomatoes in front of her and then took his seat. "But with my off-the-chart serving skills, I'm sure everyone will be coming back, just to sit in my section."

"Conceited much?" Nancy took the plate Angie offered her and put a slice on the tasting plate in front of her. Then she passed the platter on to Matt. "Servers come and go, but people come back to a restaurant because of the food."

"Not always true." Jeorge winked at Nancy as he poured himself a glass of water. "A lot of the time guests come back because of the people. Yes, you have to have good food, but you also have to have great people working. And Felicia and Angie have hired wisely. We're all amazing at our jobs."

"And I thought chefs were full of themselves." Hope glanced at Estebe. "Present company excepted, of course."

The people gathered around the table laughed at Hope's attempt to back out of the insult she'd just thrown her idol. Estebe either hadn't understood the jab or agreed with the description. Either way, Hope was in the clear.

As all three platters had been passed around the entire table, Angie held up a hand. "Let's get this started. I'm looking for a fried green tomato recipe that will fit in with our August menu. The kitchen staff and I have made three different dishes, each highlighting a different Southern twist on the basic idea. When we're done, we'll vote on which one wowed your taste buds."

The room grew quiet as the team dug into the three different appetizers. The sauce Estebe and Hope had made to go with their tomatoes made Angie think of a trip to New Orleans she'd made when she was still in culinary school. She hadn't met Felicia yet so she took the trip solo, mostly just to eat as much Cajun food as possible in a weekend. Nancy and Matt's offering brought back memories of a trip to the North Carolina shore where she'd eaten seafood every night for a week. And finally, her own offering tasted like home. Not quite the recipe Nona had made for her so many years ago, but close. Memories flooded through her as she finished the sampling.

When the vote tally was finally counted, all three dishes came in tied. Angie shook her head. Groans came from the kitchen staff. "You've got to be kidding me. I'm trying to make an informed decision here, and this is all I get?"

"The good news is any of them would be worthy of putting on the menu." Felicia went back to her agenda, and within a few minutes she'd gone through the rest of the items. "Anyone got anything before we break?"

Estebe stood. With a nod toward Felicia, he started. "You all know that I won't be here the last weekend of the month. I'm volunteering for the festival of San Ignazio held annually down at the Basque Cultural Center. I know you all can't come and enjoy the festivities since you'll be working, so I have two tickets for all of you to the volunteer breakfast next Thursday. It's our annual dry run with food, dancing, and a maybe a few adult beverages. Please come as my guest and I'll show you my heritage."

He handed out the tickets, then sat down.

Angie glanced at Felicia, who seemed as overwhelmed by the offer as she felt. "That was very nice of you, Estebe. I'm sure a lot of us will take advantage of your lovely offer."

"I can't, I'm working." Nancy held out her two tickets. "Someone want these? Someone who doesn't work twenty-four-seven like this crazy girl?"

Hope held up her hand. "I'll take them. That way I can take my mom, dad, and baby brother. This will be rad. Thanks, Estebe!"

Shock filled Estebe's face as Hope jumped up and gave him a quick peck on the cheek. Angie stood at the end of the table and excused the group. "I want to thank Estebe for his kind invitation. I'll see everyone Friday afternoon for prep. Let's make this a great week, everyone."

As the group dispersed, Estebe came over to her. "I have someone you need to meet."

"If you want to bring family members to the restaurant, just let Felicia know and we'll book the chef table for them." Angie made some notes in her staff notebook for next week's meeting. When she looked up, he was still standing, waiting for her to finish. She hadn't personally thanked him. That was probably what he was waiting for. The man had his traditions. "Oh, and thank you for the invitations to the festival. I'm sure the team will enjoy it."

Estebe's cheeks turned red and he waved away her words with his hands. "That's not what I'm talking about. Javier Easterly has a farm outside of River Vista. He's been the produce supplier for the festival for years, and I think you'd like his product. Can you come with me to visit him tomorrow?"

Angie liked her current supplier, but it never hurt to make more connections in the area. Especially with produce. You never knew what would happen, so she needed options. She glanced down at the calendar where she kept all of her appointments. "I'm free tomorrow morning. What time and where do you want to meet?"

They made arrangements for Estebe to meet her in front of the County Seat and they'd drive over together. When he left, Felicia came over and sat next to Angie, bringing two glasses of ice water to the table. The dining room had emptied out quickly once the meeting was over, and Estebe had been the last one to leave.

"So, what was that about? Are you going out on a date?" Felicia shook a finger at her. "You're such a loose woman. Ian's going to be heartbroken."

Angie looked up from her notebook. "What are you talking about?"

"Your conversation with Estebe. I overheard you talking about meeting him here tomorrow." Felicia sipped her water, her blue eyes dancing with humor and interest.

"You should have eavesdropped better. We're going out to meet a friend of his who runs a farm nearby. Estebe thought I might like his produce." Angie closed the notebook and picked up the glass, taking a sip before she spoke again. "I can't believe the tomato question is still up in the air. I wanted to get a start on August's menu."

"All three dishes were great. Choose any of them. You should be proud that the staff is so talented." Felicia leaned back in her chair. "You like my front staff, right?"

Angie sat her glass back down before answering. Felicia didn't like conflict, so this might be an indication that she was having trouble with one or more of her staff. "What's going on?"

A twitch of a grin teased over Felicia's lips as she looked back at Angie. "Oh, no. You aren't going to use my probing investigative questioning back on me. I just want your opinion on the staff, not just your half."

That seemed fair. Angie thought of the interactions she'd had with the crew over the last month. Mostly positive. She'd had to correct a couple, as they hadn't been following Felicia's protocol dish presentation as they delivered the food to the tables, but some of that was just a learning curve. Finally, not finding fault in any of them, Angie shrugged. "I guess they're fine. I mean, no one sticks out as a troublemaker, and they all seem to take correction well. What are you concerned about?"

"They seem too perfect. Like Stepford Wives perfect." Felicia pushed her hair behind her ears and sighed. "In California, I was hiring and firing a server every other month. Here, they seem to like their jobs."

"Don't sound so surprised. We pay a higher-than-average wage for the area. Tips might not be as big as they could get in Boise, but we keep the place and their stations filled with paying customers. They should be happy." In California, they hadn't even been close in payroll to any of the higher-end places in town. And they still paid out almost all their gross profit in wages. Idaho had a lower cost of living, and she could see them actually being profitable in one to two years, rather than the ten years el pescado, her first restaurant, had taken. "Relax. Things are going amazing."

Felicia side-eyed her as she stood. "I'm heading off to a yoga class down at the church. A group of stay-at-home moms meets every Wednesday at two. I've gotten over a dozen bookings from the group. You should come. They'd love to meet a real chef."

"No, thanks. I've got to get home and check on Dom. You go on your way to enlightenment and lighten up a little. We're doing great. Nothing is going to go wrong." Angie closed down her office, making a mental note to work on accounting tomorrow. The numbers were the only thing she really hated to do, but she felt she needed to understand what the business was doing before she hired an accountant to take over this part of her duties. She wouldn't be sad when she could actually give it up. Ten minutes later, she was home, and she had a visitor sitting on her porch.

"I'm so glad you came home. I've got a favor to ask you." Erica, Mrs. Potter's granddaughter who lived across the street, stood to greet Angie as she came up on the porch.

Angie unlocked the door into the kitchen. "Come in. How long have you been waiting out here?"

"Just a few minutes. Granny's taking a nap, so I wanted to catch you now, before she finds me gone. She'd tell me to not bother you with this."

Erica followed her into the cool kitchen. The Potters had been her Nona's neighbors ever since the two women graduated from high school so many years ago. They'd both raised their families and lost their husbands since those promise-filled days. Even though Nona was gone, Angie felt compelled to continue the relationship. Mrs. Potter was more like family rather than just being a neighbor.

Angie leaned down to give Dom some attention as she talked to Erica. The baby St. Bernard wasn't much of a baby anymore. The dog was close to a hundred pounds as of his last vet appointment. She nodded to a chair at the table. "Sit down. I was going to warm up some tomato bisque for lunch. Maybe a ham sandwich to go with it? Have you eaten? You can tell me what's going on over a meal."

Erica shook her head. "I've been too upset to eat."

Angie stood and took Erica's arm, leading her to the chair. "Now you have to stay for lunch. What is wrong?"

Instead of answering her, Erica laid her head on the table between her arms and started sobbing.

Chapter 2

It took a while, but Angie finally got Erica calmed down and eating the proper lunch set in front of her. Dom had added his comfort by laying his big head on Erica's lap and staring at her with his big brown eyes. Angie knew the power petting Dom's soft coat could have on lightening her own mood. She sat down at the table and picked up a spoon, took a sip, and sighed, hoping the action would cause Erica to follow suit. It did, and in a few minutes, Angie noticed some color coming back into the young woman's face. The power of food.

"So, what did you need to ask me?" Angie tried to make the question seem casual, hoping not to send Erica into waterworks again.

"I told you about my study group, right? They have a trip planned for next week to Cabo. I know, Mexico in the summer, not prime vacation time, but I've never been and it's really cheap." Erica looked at her with pleading in her eyes.

Angie felt her heart sink. As much as she liked the young woman sitting in front of her, she just didn't have the money to lend her for even a cheap vacation. Every dime she had was sunk into the County Seat. She decided to put Erica out of her misery quickly. "That sounds wonderful, but I really..."

"I know it would be a terrible imposition to ask, but honestly, I can't see letting her stay in that house all by herself. She's fallen three times in the last few months. I've talked to her about getting one of those alarm systems, but she says she doesn't need it." Erica rushed through her words as if she needed to get them all out before Angie turned her down.

"Wait, what exactly do you want from me?" Clearly it wasn't money, but she couldn't see how much of an imposition checking in with Mrs.

Potter would be for a week. "I'd be glad to help in any way you need. You should go with your group."

Erica clapped her hands together in delight. "I knew I could count on you. I'll have her over here on Monday morning before I leave for the airport."

"Over here?" Angie's eyes widened. What had she just agreed to?

"She'll need a room on the bottom floor to sleep. I'd have you stay over there, but Dom wouldn't be comfortable at our house. I know you work a lot, but she's really not much trouble. She'll watch television or read most of the time. I just want to make sure someone is watching out for her while I'm gone. I'll make sure to pack her favorite books." She glanced at her watch. "I've been gone too long. She'll be looking for me. Thank you so much for your kind offer. I'll be back early Sunday night, so I'll come and get her as soon as I can. You're the best."

Actually, Angie thought as she cleaned up the lunch dishes, she was a complete fool. She'd been so worried that Erica needed money that she failed to determine the real reason for her distress until after she'd offered to help. Her words to Felicia, just a few hours ago, popped into her mind. What could go wrong?

"This will be fine," she told Dom, who was watching Mabel, the lone surviving black-and-white chicken from her grandmother's flock, out the screen door. "It will be like having a sleepover."

Angie hadn't had a roommate since college. She liked her quiet time where she could read or work on recipes, or sometimes, just chill. "Buck it up, it's only a week," she told herself as she went out to the barn to feed Precious. The baby goat was growing up, but Angie thought she'd always be small. As soon as she walked through the door, she heard Precious's bleating welcome. The goat watched for her. For a while, Angie thought she cried all the time, but one day she'd turned on the baby monitor she'd installed for safety issues and realized the goat only talked when she entered the barn. After filling up the food and water dish, Angie sat inside the goat's pen on the stool she'd bought for the barn and talked to her. Precious loved getting scratched under the chin and was surprisingly a good listener, watching Angie's face as she talked, rubbing her head against Angie's leg. Her way of showing her support, she assumed.

Dom made a chuffing sound as he lay outside the pen watching them. He didn't like the goat, but at least he wasn't scared of Precious as he had been when he first met her. Angie hadn't meant to add the goat to her mini farm, but things happened and now she had a growing puppy, an elderly chicken, and a baby goat. She brushed off the straw from her pants and gave Precious a last rub on her head. "I guess life happens when you're not looking."

After feeding Mabel, Angie stopped at her garden and pulled out a couple large, firm green tomatoes. She'd missed something in the recipe this morning, she was sure of it. Maybe cooking at home would help her remember the steps as she sorted through her memories of Nona cooking. Of course, this wasn't included in the recipes her grandmother had written down, because she'd thought it had been too simple. And yet, it was the one recipe Angie craved to replicate.

A text from Ian welcomed her when she returned to the kitchen. She read it aloud to Dom. "Teaching a group of fourth graders how a goat dairy works tonight. You sure you don't want to come join in the fun?"

She sat the table and texted back. *Working on a recipe. You want to come over afterward?*

She took out a piece of paper and started playing with the recipe, writing out what she'd done earlier and considering changes to the breading mixture as she waited for a response.

When it came, she wasn't surprised. They both had busy lives. But she was a tad bit disappointed reading it aloud to Dom. "Mildred wants to go over the dairy records. She thinks something's off with the output. Breakfast tomorrow?"

She had a sneaking suspicion that Mildred Platt was lonely and just liked spending time with Ian. Angie texted a quick *I've got plans to visit a farm. Have fun and talk soon*, then put the phone down. She needed to be more open minded. More charitable. Mildred had just taken over the goat farm after last month's events. She was still trying to get a hold of what she needed to do as well as continue her daytime job at the Cheese Commission. And Ian, well, the boy was a helper. He was always volunteering for one thing or the other. Community organizer and activist in a totally down-home, acceptable format for the more conservative River Vista townsfolk.

Besides, her life with getting the restaurant up and going was busy too. Maybe they were both too busy for a relationship at this time.

Feeling a little put out, she started cooking. She overcooked the first batch, the crunchy breading too brown and the tomato undercooked, hard and crunchy when it should be warm and almost melting. She put that batch aside and made another batch of flour mixture, this time backing out the sugar, which probably caused it to brown too fast.

The second batch turned out better, and before she turned in for the night, she had a recipe that although it didn't match the taste of Nona's tomatoes, at least looked like the ones from her childhood. Frustrated, she cleaned up the kitchen and grabbed a memoir she'd been reading to take up to bed. She'd take a long bath, read, and have a glass or two of the wine she'd opened a few nights ago for dinner with Ian.

* * * *

Thursday morning she'd typically go into the office at the restaurant, but she'd mostly finished the paperwork yesterday, and the accounting could wait. She wasn't meeting Estebe until later that morning, so after feeding the circus, she pulled out her waffle maker and tried a few different recipes. When she finally looked at the clock, she had just enough time to shower and get into town. She bagged up the waffles in three sections. One for the freezer for her, one to drop off with Mrs. Potter and Erica, and one for Felicia. Angie had a bad habit: She couldn't cook for just one. Ever. Good thing she ran a restaurant.

When she was ready, she gave Dom a hug, telling him to guard the house. He leaned into her like she'd just said she was leaving him forever and ever. Hopefully he'd be gentle with Mrs. Potter in the house next week. Angie couldn't be here all of the time, but she could adjust her schedule to make sure Mrs. Potter was safe.

As she drove, she turned her thoughts to the farm she was visiting. What did she need at the restaurant that the other suppliers didn't have? Sweet corn would be coming on soon, and she wanted to do a multitreatment that highlighted the sweetness of the vegetable. Around here, corn on the cob was a summer tradition. Maybe she could play with that idea. She'd started to wrap her head around a possible dish when she reached Main Street. Estebe stood in front of a black Hummer, arms crossed and watching down the street for her. She went past the restaurant, pulled a U-turn in the middle of the deserted street, and parked behind him. Her newer SUV looked tiny compared to the military-style vehicle he drove. He moved to the passenger-side door and opened it for her.

"I'll drive." He didn't say anything else for a couple of blocks while they drove out of town. Then he looked at her. "You look very nice today."

Angie glanced down at the sundress she'd thrown on. She tried to dress up when she met new suppliers. The act of courtesy seemed to be appreciated by the more traditional farmers she met with. Besides, it was supposed to get in the nineties today. It was either shorts and a tank or a light cotton dress. She realized he was waiting for an answer. "Thanks."

He reached for the radio, then paused. "Do you like music?"

Angie pushed away the nagging thoughts Felicia had stuck in her head. Estebe was trying to be kind. Any discomfort she felt must be double for him, since she was his boss. "I do. Play whatever you like. I like a wide variety of stuff."

When classical music filled the vehicle, Angie was surprised. She'd expected maybe classic rock or even a band from his cultural roots, but not an exquisite baroque symphony. She nodded. "This is lovely."

They didn't talk again until he reached the farm. "I have to warn you, my cousin fancies himself a ladies' man. He may turn his attentions on you for more than just the chance to sell his produce to the County Seat."

"Oh, I didn't realize this was your cousin's farm. Anyway, warning taken, but you have to realize I can take care of myself. I don't fall easily for pickup lines." She pulled her phone out of her purse. "Do you think he'd mind if I snapped some pictures? I like to photo document where our food starts."

"Take as many as you like. Javier is very proud of his farm."

Estebe's tone told her there was more of a story behind the words than he was letting out. She tried to read his face, but she saw no emotion before he turned away and climbed out of the vehicle. As she reached to open her door, he was there, his hand reaching for hers to help her out onto the dirt driveway.

A man came out of the brightly painted red barn with a large *PF* inside a circle, painted in black on the doors. A matching charm hung around his neck on a silver chain. The man's smile lit his face. Where Estebe could be classified as broodingly handsome, his cousin was a lighter version, maybe not as handsome, but more open, friendlier.

"Estebe, my cousin. How are you?" Javier pulled Estebe into a bear hug that even Angie could tell felt fake but required.

"I am fine." Estebe stepped back and turned toward Angie. "This is Angie Turner, owner and head chef of the County Seat. I told her you had the best produce in the area."

"And you didn't lie." Javier turned toward Angie, holding out his hand. "But you didn't tell me how breathtakingly beautiful your boss is. What, are you trying to keep her to yourself?"

Angie wondered how she should play this. She didn't want Javier to have the wrong impression, but she also didn't want to insult the man, especially if she wanted to forge a business relationship with him. She settled for a noncommittal response. "Thank you for inviting me over today. I'd love to see what you're growing."

Javier apparently took the hint, as he laughed and slapped Estebe on the back. "All business, then? We'll talk more at the festival at the end of the month. You've been way too quiet lately." He turned to Angie. "Follow me." As they walked toward the barn, Javier talked about the farm and its beginnings. He told her how he inherited it from his father, whose own father had built the area from a small acreage to the multiacre farm it was now. As they got closer, a young woman burst out of the house that sat next to the barn and called his name.

Anger turned Javier's handsome face into something cruel and hard. For a second, Angie thought he was going to yell at the woman. Instead, she saw his face soften. "I've got business to deal with, Heather. Go back inside."

Heather looked from Javier to Angie and then to Estebe and pulled the flimsy short robe she wore closer to her chest. She didn't answer, just nodded and disappeared back into the house.

Javier went on with his story like he hadn't even been interrupted. "Of course, now we pasture our sheep close to home, no open range for us anymore. One of the traditions I was more than happy to give up. Spending summer at the sheep camp was difficult for a young man."

Estebe snorted. "You survived. Some boys would love to spend their summers out on the range, no one to tell them what to do. Being able to ride all day."

"You were always in love with the romantic notion of our cultural heritage." Javier turned away from his cousin and toward Angie. "The old stories do give me an excellent opening when I'm courting a new woman to my bed."

The disgusted sound coming from Estebe made Angie's lips curve. If anything, this visit had been a great font of information about her sous chef. "So, what's in season now?"

"We've added a small watermelon to our fields this year. They are just starting to ripen, not like the traditional melon that will be ready in late August. And of course, we're producing more Roma tomatoes than we have demand for. Those plants just keep on giving fruit. Maybe you would like to see what we have available this week?"

"That is why we came," Estebe grumbled.

Javier just laughed, ignoring the tone, and opened the barn door. "Then come on in. We're open to the public on Fridays and Saturdays, but the community frowns on us selling on Sunday, so we stay closed."

"And being closed lets you go drink on Saturday night without concern," Estebe added, his tone low.

Angie wasn't sure Javier had heard the comment until she saw his face turn to stone for a second, and his eyes narrow toward his cousin. Apparently, there was no love lost between the two men. Just what Angie didn't need was to stumble into a family feud. She snapped a picture of the display stands, then went over to where the gleaming red tomatoes were set up. Picking one up, she smelled the sweetness before even taking a bite.

A vision of a fresh marinara sauce—or no, bruschetta with garlic butter on the toasted bread and the tomatoes and roasted peppers on top. She glanced around the rest of the vegetables and found the pepper section. Gleaming green and yellow peppers from jalapeños to sweet banana filled the section. She turned to Estebe and started listing what she wanted and in what quantity, her mind already on the recipes she'd add to Friday's menu as a special, then depending on the new items' reception with patrons, she would keep them on until the season changed up or she found something new to highlight.

She'd almost forgot about the hard feelings between the men as she made arrangements for Javier to deliver to the restaurant tomorrow morning and boxed up a small selection to take home and play with tonight. She'd have to bake some focaccia bread as soon as she got home, but she thought the dish would highlight the ingredients perfectly.

Angie was still lost in her head as they returned to the Hummer. She let Estebe open her door and then grabbed a notebook and started scribbling notes. As he pulled out of the driveway, he turned down the music. "You were happy with Javier's selection, then?"

"Happy? I'm over the moon. It's what I've been looking for, a small farm that focuses on specialty produce. I'm going to open one of the watermelons tonight and see if I can come up with a small salad for the weekend. After I get the bruschetta just right. If you have any ideas, let me know."

Estebe smiled then. "I am glad you enjoyed your visit."

He turned the music back up and left Angie to work in her notebook, lost in her thoughts about the perfect dish. When they arrived back at the restaurant, Estebe parked behind her car. "I can keep driving if you need more time to work."

Angie glanced up from her notes, realizing they were outside the restaurant. A woman passing by on the sidewalk with a Yorkie paused to look at the car and its inhabitants. Angie waved at her and the woman hurried off. Weird. She tucked her notebook into her tote and turned to Estebe. "Thank you so much for the introduction to your cousin and his farm. I'm sure his produce will be a great addition to the menu."

This time she didn't wait for Estebe to open her door. She slid out and unlocked her own car by remote. Before she could grab the produce she'd brought back, Estebe was already standing at the back of her car with the box waiting for her to open the hatchback. He sat the box down in the car and closed the rear door. "Thank you for coming with me. Javier has been asking for an introduction for weeks. He believes he is the only produce farmer in the area."

Angie smiled. "It's good to have a business you want to support. I enjoyed our morning. Thank you for taking me there."

"My cousin has many more responsibilities than just the farm. He should take life more seriously." Estebe looked flustered with his announcement. He closed his eyes and took a breath. "I should be more charitable. I will see you tomorrow."

Angie watched as he climbed back into his Hummer and drove slowly away. She realized she didn't even know where he lived. She'd assumed Boise, but since his cousin was just on the outskirts of River Vista, maybe that wasn't true.

As she drove home she thought about the tension between the two men. Family ties. They wrapped you up in emotions you didn't even know were there. She pushed the thoughts away and instead thought about the dishes she'd create as soon as she arrived home. Food was about family too. And food always had good memories attached.

Chapter 3

Someone rapped twice on her door first thing Friday morning. Angie had already fed Mabel and Precious. She set Dom's breakfast down on the floor and went to see who was visiting. She suspected she'd find Mrs. Potter on the other side, but Ian McNeal stood there with a large pastry bag. "What are you doing here?"

"Do you have coffee made to go with the donuts? The bakery in the local store makes them fresh each morning. I had to stand in line for a good three minutes." He walked through the doorway as Angie opened the screen door and set the bag down on the table. Crouching down, he rubbed Dom's chest. The St. Bernard was beside himself with wiggles. Angie suspected Dom loved Ian almost as much as he did her. "Hey, who's a good boy?"

"He's in trouble with me. He tried to knock Precious's food bucket out of my hand this morning." Angie went to the counter and poured a cup of coffee for Ian. He preferred a good Irish breakfast tea, but she noted if she had a pot already made, he'd ask for coffee. "Plates or napkins for the donuts?"

"Why dirty a plate?" He glanced around the kitchen. "It smells wonderful in here. Have you been creating?"

Angie refilled her own cup and brought over several napkins. "I'm too easy to read, aren't I?"

"Well, I kind of got a call from Missy at the Farm Store." He took out a donut and offered her one.

"You have a maple bar in there?" Peering into the bag, she ignored the offered treat and grabbed the one she was craving. It was probably too early in their relationship for him to actually know what kind of donuts she preferred, but at least he came with a good variety. She'd eaten half of the doughy goodness before his words sank in. "How would Missy know I've been working on recipes? Does she live out here?"

He sipped his coffee, obviously considering his words carefully. Finally, he set the cup down. "You're not going to like this, but it's part of living in a small town."

A pit formed in Angie's stomach. "Rip off the Band-Aid."

Ian shook his head. "I've never understood that American saying, but I know what you mean. Missy called me to tell me she saw you getting out of Estebe's Hummer yesterday and asked if I knew you were stepping out on me."

Angie spat out part of the sip of coffee she'd just taken to slow down the sugar rush. "Stepping out on you? Because I rode in a car with another man? What is this, the 1960s?"

"I told you. Small town." He handed her a napkin. "When I moved here, because I ordered tea at the diner instead of coffee, there were concerns about what exactly I was doing here, and someone called Allen."

"They sent the sheriff over to talk to you because you moved into a small town? What, did they think that everyone had to be born here to like living in River Vista?"

Ian finished his donut. "Actually, they were more concerned about my intentions regarding the town. I might have been someone who didn't like the slower lifestyle. They wanted to make sure I'd fit in. And now I do. Heck, they're even protecting me from my wanton girlfriend."

"And you decided to come out here and check to make sure Estebe wasn't having breakfast with me?" She studied him, wondering what his reaction had been when the town busybody had called.

"I came out here with breakfast because we didn't get to see much of each other this week. You've been busy with the restaurant. And Mildred's been clingy. I needed to get away from her before I said something that would hurt her feelings." He stood and went to refill his coffee cup. As he brought the pot to the table and refilled her cup, he added, "And to make sure Estebe wasn't having breakfast with you."

"Ian!" Angie glanced up into those impossibly blue eyes and saw the humor in his reaction.

"You have to admit, we've never talked about this thing between us being exclusive. And with you straight out of California, you may not be as traditional as I am. So I thought I should come and ask you straight out. Angie Turner, would you be my girlfriend?"

"Which means I don't date someone else, or I don't drive in a car with a man?" Angie sipped her coffee, wondering how they'd gotten in so deep so quickly.

Ian pulled a second donut out and tossed the bag to her. "What it means to me is we're exclusive in the softer side of the relationship. I have no problem with you being with anyone else as long as it's not a date."

"Or a hookup. I hear those loose California women like to just have random encounters with strange men." She noticed he'd left the last maple glazed donut for her. This having a boyfriend thing was working in her favor.

He was staring at her.

"What? I was kidding. Or did you want the maple donut?" She held it toward him.

"Sometimes the things you say..." He paused. "Just don't be saying that around Missy. I don't think she has the same sense of humor as you do."

Angie snorted. "I don't think the woman has any sense of humor at all. Okay, fine, I'll be your girlfriend. Does this mean you're giving me your class ring?"

"Not sure what that is, but I bought you breakfast this morning. Isn't that enough?" Ian stood and took his cup to the sink. "I better get going. I've got a meeting with the board for the farmers market this morning. Thank you for breakfast."

"You brought the donuts, all I supplied was coffee." She stood and took her own cup over to the sink. "I've got to get ready to go in too. There's always so much to do the first night we're open each week. Besides, I really want to check out Estebe's cousin's produce. I've got some killer ideas if he can actually deliver consistent quality like I got yesterday."

"From what I've heard about Javier, I'm not sure he spends a lot of time at the farm. He's more of the sales department for the younger brother, who does all the work." Ian pulled her into an embrace and kissed her. "Bye, girlfriend."

"You just like saying that word, don't you?" Angie brushed a donut crumb off the corner of his lips.

"Funny, but I really do." He gave Dom a rub between the ears and went outside to his car. The guy was whistling. Angie shook her head. He really was sweet, and apparently, he had been at least concerned when Missy told him about her ride in Estebe's Hummer. The gossip train had just better learn to ignore her actions because she wasn't changing who she was just because some woman had an antiquated idea of what was proper.

As she drove into River Vista, she thought about what Ian had said about Javier's younger brother. She'd have to ask Estebe about the guy and if he thought the brother was dedicated enough to provide product. She'd hate to have to redo a menu in the middle of the month, but she guessed she needed to take a chance on the farm, for her sous chef's sake. He'd trusted her enough to share this part of his life with her. She could trust him.

When service started Friday night, Angie was surprised to see Missy Stockwell and her husband seated at a table near the door. Felicia had just seated the couple and waved Angie over.

"I'm sure you both know our head chef, but Angie likes to get out and talk with our guests." Felicia set out menus in front of each diner. "Angie, this is Herbert and Missy Stockwell. They own the Farm Store. Did you know that?"

"I think they owned it back when I went to school at River Vista High." Angie furrowed her brow. "Don't you have a daughter?"

"Tina. Our daughter was in your class, I believe." Missy's voice sounded tight and her nose twitched like she smelled something rotten.

Herbert looked up at Angie. "I remember you. You're Margaret's granddaughter. When Missy got these reservations a month ago, I wasn't sure I wanted to come. I like places a little less stuffy, like Cracker Barrel. You never need a reservation there. But I told her we'd come, if she insisted. I'm sure if you're Margaret's kin, the food is going to be amazing. That woman brought the best potato salad to the church picnic I'd ever had."

Missy glared at her husband, but he waved her off.

"Now, Mother, I'm not saying your food is bad, but boy, Margaret could cook." He patted Angie's arm. "I'm sure you have more important things to do than listen to an old man talk, but Margaret Turner was one of a kind. She's sorely missed around here."

"Thank you for saying so." Angie felt the tears form behind her eyes. That had been the hardest thing about coming home, all the memories of Nona. "I hope you enjoy your meal."

She stepped away from the table with Felicia, who led her over to the bar. "What the heck was that? I swear Missy Stockwell was trying to burn a hole through you with her eyes."

"She saw me getting out of Estebe's car yesterday and told Ian I was cheating on him." Angie saw no reason to hold the truth back from her friend.

To her surprise, Felicia laughed. "Boy, she doesn't know you at all, does she?" She added a garnish to one of the drinks waiting for a server to pick up the tray. "Although I did tell you that it felt like a date."

"It was not a date. We went out to visit a farm that hopefully will work out as a regular supplier for the restaurant." She straightened her chef jacket. "Ian understands business. Why don't you?"

"Oh, I understand business." Felicia frowned at the bartender, who had forgotten the garnish on a second drink. "I just also understand men."

Angie held up a hand. "Whatever. I need to get back into the kitchen, where things make sense. You people out here are all about rumors and innuendos."

Felicia called after her. "Just because it's not true doesn't mean it's not a good story."

Going back into the kitchen, Angie relaxed and started expediting the tickets. By the end of the night, her body ached and yet she felt amazing. She loved working at the County Seat. Her kitchen team worked as a real team, pitching in wherever they were needed. She had been lucky in her hires. One bad apple did spoil an entire bunch. She sank into a chair at the chef table with a plate of trout and mashed potatoes. Matt and Nancy joined her with their own plates. But Estebe stood over at the dishwashing station, helping Hope finish up the last of the evening's cleanup.

"Come on over and eat. We can finish those up after the meal," Angie called over.

Estebe shook his head. "We're almost finished. We'll be right there." He looked at Hope. "I've made you a special plate. We'll test your palate as you eat."

Angie turned toward Matt and Nancy. "Great job tonight. You guys look like you have been cooking here for years."

"Nancy makes it easy," Matt told Angie, causing Nancy to blush at his words. "It's hard for me to remember tickets, but she just tells me what to do next and I don't get frustrated."

Nancy quickly changed the subject and told a story about a past job where the owner thought he knew how to cook, but his plates kept coming back with complaints. "So finally, he throws up his hands and announces to the kitchen, if they don't like his food, he'll just go mind the bar."

"What did you say?"

Nancy shrugged. "The staff had the good sense not to cheer until he actually left. Then I took over expediting and we pumped out the tickets. I started looking for another gig as soon as I got home, and that's when I saw your ad. Luck comes to those who are open to change."

"And work hard." Estebe and Hope had joined the group at the table during Nancy's retelling of the story. He glanced around the table, his fork in hand. "What? You only get lucky when you're working your backside off. And then it doesn't always come to you. I've known many people who are successful when they shouldn't even be able to do a simple task. Luck doesn't always happen."

Angie wondered if he was thinking about his cousin. "Well, here's to another successful night where we cooked our behinds off and the customers loved the meal."

As the group disbanded for the evening, Angie went into the dining room to check in on Felicia. "How'd it go out here?"

"Besides having a bartender I had to watch constantly because he was too proud to look at the drink book Jeorge developed for training? I guess okay." Felicia rolled her shoulders. "I'll be glad when Jeorge gets back from Mexico. I don't think I'm ever approving vacation requests for him again."

Angie grabbed a bottle of water from the fridge. "Is the new guy scheduled to work tomorrow?"

"Unfortunately, yes. I can't get a new temp that quickly, and the guy said he understood when I went through all the drinks just now with him." Felicia covered a yawn. "I'm beat and going up to bed. Unless you need to talk about something?"

"Nope, just checking in. Let's plan on having a late lunch together tomorrow and we can talk about the business stuff. I feel like things are going well, but let's look at the numbers when you're not so tired."

"See you then." Felicia headed upstairs, turning off lights as she went.

Angie made sure the front doors were locked, then left through the kitchen door that opened out onto the small parking lot behind the building. Locking the door with her key, she turned and stopped short when she saw the shape of a man standing by her car. There was only one light in the parking lot. The music from the live band from the bar down the street echoed in the alley. Country rock. Angie searched her mind for the name of the original band but came up empty. She stared at the man, turning her keys over in her hand and wondering if she had time to turn around, unlock the kitchen door, and get back inside before he caught up with her.

"Are you all right, Angie?" Estebe's voice called out from the darkened lot.

She took a deep breath and forced her hands to stop shaking. The man by her car worked for her. She really needed to get more light out here, especially since she apparently was prone to jumping to conclusions. She started down the few steps. She tried to keep the tremor out of her voice as she lied. "I'm fine. I was just trying to remember if I turned off all the stoves."

"I checked the stoves before I left the kitchen. I walked Hope out to her car and then waited for you to leave so you would be safe as well." He nodded to her car. "I'll wait for you to get in and get it started, then I will head home. I have a few things to get done tonight."

"You don't have to wait for me. I'll be perfectly safe." She didn't mention that he had frightened her by trying to keep her safe.

"A woman shouldn't be out alone at night." He stepped away from her car so she could unlock it. Then he opened the door for her. "You don't have your guard dog to protect you. I don't mind stepping in for him."

He shut the door, then walked to his Hummer that was parked on the street. True to his word, he didn't leave until she'd pulled out of the parking lot and was back on Main Street. She turned west toward home and Estebe turned east.

So many people taking care of her. She felt at home.

* * * *

Saturday morning, she quickly fed the circus, then sat down to write out the recipes from the trials she'd made on Thursday. Angie wanted to bring at least one of the dishes to her crew and see if they could add a special to tonight's menu. She'd make all of them for Felicia today for lunch and see which one she liked best. A knock on the kitchen door made her look up.

Erica stood at the door. She had a notebook in her hand. "Hey, do you have a minute?"

"Come on in. Can I get you a glass of iced tea?" Angie stood and took her own glass to the counter. When Erica nodded, she poured a second glass over ice and refilled her own. She returned to the table with the drinks. "What's up?"

"I wanted to bring you this notebook. It has all of Granny's medications, when she takes them, her doctors' names and phone numbers, and Delores's information. I didn't want to give it to her when I bring her over Monday morning, it seems so, I don't know, childish? Like you're babysitting or something?"

"That's nice of you trying to keep her dignity." Angie took the notebook and flipped through the pages. "You have a lot of information here."

"It makes it easier. Besides, I can take that to school with me, and if something happens, I have all the phone numbers I need." Erica sipped her tea, not meeting Angie's gaze. "I feel guilty leaving her just to have fun."

"Everyone needs a break now and then. Don't worry. She'll be fine over here. I'm here most of the day. And when I'm working, most of that time she'll be asleep." Angie put the notebook in her tote. "She'll never know I have this."

Erica laughed. "I really appreciate the help."

After Erica left, Angie wondered if she really knew what she'd got herself into. She didn't have any training dealing with the elderly. Nona hadn't called her home when she'd gotten ill. She'd hired a live-in caretaker. Maybe she had known something that Angie didn't know about herself. *Or maybe*, the internal voice of reason spoke up, *she knew you were busy building a life and a career.*

Angie knew the voice was rational and probably true, but it didn't keep her from second-guessing her choices. She returned to her work, and by the time she needed to leave for town to meet Felicia at the County Seat, she had two new recipes ready.

Felicia was already downstairs, working on her laptop when Angie arrived. When the door opened, she looked up, worry creasing her brow. "Hey, I was about to call you. Everything okay?"

"I got stuck behind a line of cars following a tractor. I know it's Saturday, but some people work weekends, right? I don't know why they don't move those machines on a day that's not busy." Angie dumped her tote out on the counter, looking for the recipe notebook she carried around at all times.

Felicia walked over, picked up the spiral notebook Erica had given Angie that morning, and opened the cover. "Is this instructions for Mrs. Potter? I thought you were going to tell Erica you couldn't do it?"

Angie couldn't meet her friend's gaze. "Don't judge. I know I told you I was uncomfortable with the whole thing, but I want to do this."

"You don't owe this to Nona."

Her friend's words struck home, and finally, Angie looked straight at her. "Maybe not, but I can be a good neighbor and a friend to Erica when she needs help. Anyway, how much trouble can one woman cause in a week? By the time Erica gets back, we'll be best friends."

"Doubtful." But Felicia didn't press the issue. "What can I do to help?"

They cooked lunch together, adding the two appetizers that Angie had developed that week. When they sat down to eat, the discussion turned to staffing and restaurant business. Like Angie's kitchen team, Felicia was happy with her front-of-the-house staff. "Although Jeorge's vacation has taught me that we're too dependent on too few people. I'd like to hire a part-time server who could also be trained in bartending. That way, if someone calls in sick or vacations, we don't have to settle for who the temp agency sends us."

"It's a great idea. We kind of have that built in with Hope. The week Estebe's gone, I'm moving her out of her dishwasher duties and into a prep chef. Nancy will cover for Estebe, but I'll need a temp dishwasher. That shouldn't be hard to find."

They had just finished the meal and were beginning to look at the numbers when Angie's phone rang. She looked down at the caller ID and groaned. There was only one reason he'd be calling her. Estebe wasn't showing up for work tonight. She tried to keep her disappointment out of her tone when she answered. "Hey, Estebe, what's going on?"

She watched as Felicia started cleaning the dishes from the chef table. The table was cleared and the dishes were probably stacked in the dishwasher, waiting to be run, by the time Angie had finished the conversation.

Felicia returned to the table and studied her. "Do we need to call the temp agency?"

"Yes." Angie considered the recipe she'd been planning on adding to tonight's dinner menu. "We might need to hold back on adding the bruschetta."

"Why? Just because Estebe called in sick?" Felicia shook her head. "I think you count on him too much. I'm sure Nancy can run his station fine."

"Estebe's not sick." Angie took a deep breath. "His cousin asked him to go out to the farm. He doesn't know when he'll be done there."

"Seriously? He's ditching us for a family meeting?" Felicia sank into her chair next to Angie. "He needs to set some priorities. No wonder he hadn't worked in a real kitchen for years."

"It's not that." Angie held up a hand, stopping Felicia from continuing her tirade. "His cousin's girlfriend was found dead this morning."

"OMG. Did she have a heart attack?" Felicia's eyes narrowed. "Wait, is this the player cousin? I thought you said that girl was Hope's age. What did she die from?"

"She was killed outside the Red Eye Saloon down the street late last night. Heather, that's her name, was found in the alley behind the bar just after closing."

"I must have been out. I didn't hear any of the commotion." Felicia shook her head. "That poor girl. So Estebe's helping Javier with the funeral arrangements?"

"Actually, he's trying to bail him out of jail." Angie leaned back into her chair. "They think Javier killed her."

Chapter 4

Before service started, Angie brought the kitchen team together and explained Estebe's absence. The temp Felicia had hired wasn't expected for a couple of hours. Angie didn't know what all to say, but it turned out she didn't need to fill in the details because Matt already had told them.

"Heather and Javier Easterly were at the Red Eye drinking most of the night. They got in a big fight when Javier started dancing with some other girl." He glanced around. "I know, the guy was a jerk with women, but that doesn't mean he killed her. The guy already had a new one on the line, why would he care?"

"Heather was in love with him." Hope spoke up for the first time since she'd heard the news. Everyone turned to look at her and she shrank back from the attention. "I knew her from high school. We were in a Young Leaders community service club. We stayed in touch after we graduated. She was a good person and didn't deserve to die like this."

"I'm sorry for your loss." Angie hadn't realized Hope had known the girl. "Do you need some time? We can drop down to a three-person team for the night."

"I can do it. Heather and I weren't close, we were more like Facebook friends. She talked about Javier and how wonderful he was for the last month. She'd fallen hard." Hope shook her head. "She always fell for the guys who were never going to work out. Even in high school, she went for the players. I'll visit her parents tomorrow. They must be heartbroken."

"If you change your mind, you let me know." Something in Hope's tone made her question the relationship, but it wasn't her business. Angie glanced around the room. The team looked sad at the tragic news but not wiped out. In a small community like River Vista, the death of one of its own had to make an impression on everyone. "We okay? I was going to add a new item, but I think we'll hold off until next week. Let's go over the menu."

As they prepped for the upcoming service, the kitchen was quiet, each person lost in their own thoughts. Angie turned on the CD player and classical music poured out. Estebe must have left one of his discs in the machine. Somehow the music felt right and the team started working together, talking quietly. When the temp hire showed up, Hope took him over to the dishwasher stand and explained his job and how to work the machine.

Felicia came into the room a few minutes before opening. She stood near Angie, taking in the quiet kitchen. "Everyone all right?"

"We'll be fine. Are we ready to open?" Angie glanced around the room and realized her words were true. The group had been shocked at the news, but they'd bounced back and stepped into Estebe's absence well.

"The first table just got seated." Felicia followed Angie's glance around the room. "That didn't take long."

"What do you mean?"

Felicia smiled as she stepped away toward the front. "You have a team here, not just employees."

As she cooked, Angie realized Felicia was right. When times were good or tough, the kitchen crew would get through it. Not for the first time, she felt like she was exactly where she needed to be.

* * * *

On most Sundays, Angie liked to sleep in, but for many reasons, today her mind was running a mile a minute. She'd thought about calling Estebe more than once, but she always set the phone down, knowing it sent the wrong message. She might not see their relationship as more than friends, but she didn't need to throw any more gas on that flame for others in town, especially Missy Stockwell. At least her husband had been nice, even though he'd compared her restaurant to a chain. Maybe she'd make up a dessert and take it over to the Farm Store tomorrow. She could say it was to thank them for coming in, but that made a bad precedent for other townies who she didn't bake a personal thank-you for. She really just wanted to give Missy a piece of her mind, not a piece of pie.

"Hey, are you decent?" Ian's voice called through the house. She'd been upstairs, gathering laundry to start her chores.

"Depends on what you call decent." She called back. Glancing in the mirror, she pulled her hair back behind her ears. She looked fine. For a Sunday morning. "I'll be right down. Grab some coffee."

"That will work. I brought something to eat from the store."

By the time she'd gotten downstairs and put the laundry basket on top of the washer, Ian was sitting at the table talking to Dom and sipping his coffee. A zucchini bread sat sliced on a plate at the table, and she noticed her own cup had been refilled. "You don't have to bring food with every visit. I am a chef, you know."

"I like this zucchini bread. I know you probably have an amazing recipe, but I didn't want to ask you to bake on this lovely day." He gave Dom one last rub under his ear, then stood to wash his hands. "I take it you heard about Estebe's cousin?"

"He called me yesterday afternoon, as he couldn't come into work. Did Sheriff Brown really arrest Javier?" She slipped into her chair and took a slice of the bread. She sniffed it, then took a bite. Ian was right, it was good. But her recipe was better. She hadn't made zucchini bread in years. She'd need to pull it out. Maybe figure a way to make a dessert for the restaurant out of the moist bread.

"He didn't arrest him. He just brought him in for questioning. According to Allen, he sent them home about seven last night." Ian sipped on his coffee. "Allen's a mess. Two murders this summer and he's gone over twenty years without one. I think he's consulting with someone from the Idaho State Police in Meridian."

"It must be hard." Angie felt a twinge of guilt. She moves back, people start dying. Maybe she was a Typhoid Mary or something.

"Don't go there." Ian must have read the thought on her face. "Just because you're here doesn't mean you caused these things. Unless you're a vicious serial killer and I'm a completely bad judge of character."

"If I was, you wouldn't be spending all your free time with Mildred." Angie sipped her coffee. "You know, there was a weird vibe in the air Friday night. I left the building and thought someone was watching me."

"Did you see who it was?" Ian sat straighter, his gaze tight on her face.

Angie laughed. "Yeah. It was Estebe. He waited for me to leave to make sure I'd be safe. Who does that? Most of my crew takes off as soon as the shift's over. He hangs around because I don't have good lighting in the back parking lot."

"Well, that's good." Ian's face didn't match his words, but Angie let the comment go. They'd already had that conversation. No need to dig it up again.

"Anyway, it just felt weird. I don't think I've ever felt uncomfortable in that lot, and there were a lot of times when we were getting the restaurant ready that I didn't leave for home until after midnight." She picked up a piece of zucchini bread and sniffed it, trying to decide if there was cinnamon and nutmeg or maybe some other spice in the mix. "I'll call an electrician next week and get them to add some security lights. Even if I feel okay, Felicia lives there."

"And she likes to go to the Red Eye at night," Ian added.

"She's a single adult. She has a right to go to a bar if she wants to go." Angie didn't like the sharp tone in her voice.

Ian held up his hands, blocking the emotional assault. "I'm not saying anything against Felicia. I'm saying she should be safe walking in an alley in River Vista. It's not like we're a big city like New York, Los Angeles, or even St. Louis."

"Or Boise. I've heard on the news some surprising crimes that have been happening in their downtown area. Of course, it has way too many bars per city block down there. We're lucky we only have two." Angie, started doodling on a piece of paper, listing off what she thought were the ingredients in the bread.

"Three."

She looked up, frowning. She had already lost track of the conversation and wondered how he knew how many eggs were in the dish. "Three what?"

"Three bars. The Red Eye, the Rocking Rodeo, and the County Seat." Ian watched her react in surprise. "What? You have a liquor license, dear. Don't think that people won't come in just for a drink."

"It never occurred to me that they would. I only set up the bar for an extra waiting area. People won't really just come in to drink, right? We're not set up for that. And we close a lot earlier than the real bars." Angie thought about Jeorge and Felicia's unhappiness with the temp who had covered. If they lost their bartender, it would take weeks to get someone with that kind of training. "You're messing with me."

"I am not. And I can't believe this wasn't in your plan. You plan out everything, especially when it comes to that place of yours." He glanced at his watch. "Sorry, it's been fun messing with your head, but I've got to get into town."

"Another meeting? Tell Mildred hi." Angie couldn't help but tease him about his new BFF.

He leaned down and kissed her. "I do have an appointment, but not with Mildred. The laundromat down the street from my apartment is my destination. I don't have any clothes left for going back to work tomorrow.

And I don't think Allen would like it much if I started my own nudist colony here in River Vista." "I might." She stood up to follow him to the door. "Make sure you call me when you're heading outside. I'll bring the popcorn to watch the festivities."

After he left, she glanced around the house. She had her own chores to do, but she was curious about Javier. She picked up her phone, and hesitated. She should keep her nose out of other people's business. There was no way Sheriff Brown was going to question her on this murder. She'd been tucked in bed by the time the bars closed, worn out from working the Friday-night service. A good boss would check in on her employee, just to make sure he was okay. It was a stressful time. She hoped he didn't just assume she was looking for gossip. Which she probably was.

Hesitating for a second, finally, she pressed Estebe's number and let the chips fall as they might. When he answered, she took a breath. "I was just checking to see how you are doing. Do you need anything? More time off?"

"Angie, thank you for calling. I was just about to call you, in fact." He paused, talking to someone in the background. Finally, he came back on the line. "Could you meet me out at the River Vista park? I need a favor."

"The park? The one in town or the one by the river?" Angie wasn't sure why her sous chef was being so secretive, but she'd give him some leeway. His cousin's girlfriend had just been killed.

"The one by the river. I will be there in twenty minutes." He paused. "Thank you for not asking questions."

"I'm not sure what questions to ask yet." Angie glanced at the clock. It would take her ten minutes to get down to the park. "I'll be over by the sitting area by the bridge. We can take a walk. Dom loves that area."

Estebe's chuckle made her feel warm. "Leave it to you to put the needs of your dog first. How do you know what the animal likes?"

"You can tell. I guess you're not a pet owner?"

"Animals are put here for our use. Not for us to make them our friends." Estebe spoke with authority.

"Maybe being friends with humans is exactly the purpose of animals. Have you ever thought of that?" Angie countered.

"You are a surprising woman." He talked to someone again, then came back on the line. "Twenty minutes. Thank you again."

After the conversation, Angie sat her phone down and opened a notebook, listing out all the questions she'd like to ask Estebe. She'd probably not ask any of them, but she wanted to have an outline in her head before she met with him. She tucked the notebook into her tote, then grabbed her keys and Dom's leash. As soon as he saw her take it off the shelf, he positioned himself in front of her and lifted his chin.

"We'll put it on at the park. Do you want to go for a ride?" Angie held the door open for him. When she'd locked the kitchen door and walked to her SUV, Dom stood by his door, his tail wagging up a dust storm near the vehicle.

She opened his door and he jumped into the backseat. She slipped into the driver's seat and turned the vehicle around in the driveway. Mrs. Potter and Erica were sitting on their porch, and Angie waved as she pulled out onto the county road. Tomorrow she'd have a roommate for a week. Angie wasn't sure how she felt about it, but how hard could it be to have Mrs. Potter in the house? Of course, she'd have to cook, but that was a joy, not a problem.

Angie started menu planning in her head as she drove, and by the time she arrived at the park, she had a game plan. She pulled out her notebook and made a grocery list. She would have soup and sandwiches made up for Friday and Saturday dinners since she'd be too busy running the County Seat to make sure her new roomie ate. Oh, and Thursday morning Angie would be at this volunteer thing with Estebe. But other than that, she'd enjoy cooking for someone else for a week.

A tap on her window brought her out of her meal planning. Estebe stood outside her window. Dom stared at him, like he couldn't place how he knew this human, but he didn't bark. Angie returned the notebook to her tote, which she put on the floor, then she opened the door and let Dom out on a leash. When he was settled, she went to join Estebe on the bench where he sat waiting for her. "Sorry about that. I've got company next week and I needed to plan out a food strategy."

"Come sit by me. As I mentioned on the phone, I have a favor to ask." He patted the bench next to him.

Estebe's words were tight. And Angie saw his gaze dart to his car and then back at her. "I'll do whatever I can. But unless you tell me what's going on, I can't help you."

He looked at her, his eyes filled with pain. "I need you to talk to Javier. You must prove that he couldn't do this horrible thing they think he did. I need you to help clear my cousin's name."

Chapter 5

"I don't understand. How can I help your cousin?" Angie started to stand, but Estebe put his hand on her arm, stopping her movement.

"Wait. I told him he could plead his case with you. I know I shouldn't have agreed, but as he reminds me often, he is family. Besides, I don't agree with his request because Javier, well, he can be convincing, especially with women. So if you really don't want to help, just tell me and we will drive away and this conversation will have never happened."

"I don't know what you think I can do for Javier. I'm a chef, that's all."

Estebe shook his head. "That's definitely not all. I know how you found the killer for that goat man. You were the one who put together the clues."

"And almost got killed myself for the trouble. I'm not the police. You should go talk to Sheriff Brown. He probably knows a bunch of private detectives who can help you find out what really happened that night." Angie shook her head. She'd promised herself she'd stay out of any more investigations into a murder. Besides, she didn't have any authority to seek out justice for the guilty. "I'm sorry, I think you're confused about what really happened at Moss Farms."

"That is what I told Javier. That you are not a superwoman. That you can't just make this go away. He needs to learn to live with consequences. Sadly, those lessons have been missing from his life. His parents spoilt him since he was the oldest child." He stood. "I'm sorry to have bothered you."

"It's not a bother. Come walk with me and tell me what you know. Maybe I can give you some advice." *Like hire an attorney*, she thought as she stood and motioned toward the path. "Dom still needs some exercise. My Nona always said moving around helps solve what's bothering you. I used to walk miles and miles around the house after my parents died."

"Stay here, I'll be right back." He sighed as he walked to the car. As he approached, the passenger side door swung open and Javier climbed out. Angie was shocked at the changes in the man's appearance since last week. She didn't see the overwhelming confidence, just a man who seemed desperate for someone to believe him. He ran up to her, ignoring Estebe's outstretched hand trying to stop him. Dom growled as Javier approached, and she put a hand on his collar to control him.

"I'm so glad you agreed to help. This is all a terrible misunderstanding. Heather and I weren't even serious. There's no reason I'd kill her, for God's sake. I was the one who broke it off that night. The girl was way too clingy." He ignored Dom and took another step closer to Angie. "I knew you'd believe me."

As he reached out to put his hand on her arm or shoulder, Dom reacted to the movement and lunged at him, putting himself between Angie and Javier. Angie pulled him back to a sitting position. Between the barking and the screams coming out of Javier's mouth, Angie couldn't hear herself think. She pulled back on the collar and stepped a few steps away from Javier. "Dom, stop it."

"Buck up and act like a man." Estebe grabbed his cousin by the arm and shook him, pulling him a few steps away from Angie and Dom. "I can't believe you don't know how to approach someone with a large dog."

Angie thought Estebe was saying something else in his carefully worded statement, but she didn't have time to interpret his undertones. She needed to get Dom settled. "Look, why don't you come over to the house in about an hour and we'll talk. I need to get Dom calmed down, so I'll take him for a walk and you two go and get a cold drink."

"I don't know. I have a lot of things to do." Javier started to say something else, but he glanced up at Estebe and blanched white. "Okay, then."

Estebe nodded toward Angie. "We'll go pick up some soft drinks at the Whoa and Go down the street. We'll be at your house in an hour."

A car parked next to Estebe's, and as the couple got out, they stared at the odd threesome, trying to gauge the situation. Angie put on her best *I'm not being tortured by serial killers* smile and the woman took a step backward. So much for being welcoming, Angie thought. And for a moment, she thought about one of her first meetings with Ian, where he said she had a creepy killer smile.

Estebe and Javier started walking toward the parking lot, and Angie turned the other way with Dom. "You sure don't like Javier much, do you?"

Dom turned back toward the retreating men and huffed. Angie guessed that was her answer. She'd have to keep Dom in the kitchen while they talked in the living room. She tended to entertain most of her guests in the kitchen, probably because she was usually cooking or eating something. As they walked through the almost deserted park, Angie thought about Javier's situation. What could she really add to the conversation? But she had helped solve Mr. Moss's murder just last month. Maybe she had a knack for these things.

"More like a knack for getting into trouble." She rubbed Dom's head as he looked up at her, trying to understand her words. "Don't worry, boy, I'm going to be good and stay out of this investigation."

Now all she had to do was convince the two men she had invited over to her house of her new intention.

When she got back home, she decluttered the living room, moving her Nona's cookbook project over to a table on the side rather than the coffee table. Then she ran a sticky roller over the couch to get off at least some of the dog hair. She glanced at the clock. Estebe and Javier should have been here by now. She took her phone out of her tote and saw she'd somehow missed a call. She played back the voice mail.

"We are heading back into town. Javier has a meeting with Papa Diaz that he didn't tell me about. I will come by tomorrow if that's all right." The phone message ended without a goodbye or sign-off. Angie didn't know who this Papa Diaz was, but from the way Estebe sounded, she didn't think Javier was going to be happy after the meeting.

She glanced around at the now-clean living room, sank into the couch, and grabbed the remote. Dom jumped up next to her and laid his head on her lap with a loud sigh. She found the Food Channel and leaned back into a television coma.

* * * *

Angie rubbed Precious's head through the gate to her pen. The goat was growing fast, but she still enjoyed getting some attention every morning. As she watched, the goat stared out the barn door, then bleated a welcome to the car that had just pulled in.

"I swear, you're a better guard dog than Dom." Angie looked around to make sure her pup wasn't in earshot. She stood and gave Precious one last rub behind her ear. "Just don't tell him I said that."

In Dom's defense, he was taking a nap in the kitchen. He didn't like coming out and helping her with the morning chores anymore. Mostly, Angie knew it was because he didn't like the goat. She'd hoped they'd start getting along, more out of familiarity than anything, but so far, that hadn't been the case. She walked around Mabel, who was pecking at her own breakfast, and went out to meet her new roommate. A week really wasn't that long.

Erica was helping her grandmother out the passenger side and had set up her walker. Mrs. Potter swiped at her hands. "I'm not an invalid. Let me be."

"Welcome. I'm looking forward to our week together." Angie tried to defuse the tension. "Come inside, I've got breakfast ready for all of us."

Erica smiled, grabbing the bags out of the back of the car. "Isn't that nice. Granny, I'm sure you're hungry since you've barely eaten the last few days."

Mrs. Potter was on the porch, struggling with the screen door. "I'm not hungry. I suppose I'm being set up in Margaret's sewing room?"

"I took that stuff out, but yeah, there's a bed with an attached bath." Angie glanced at Erica, who shook her head. "Do you want me to show you?"

"I think I know my way around this house a little better than you since I visited Margaret for years before you were even born. In fact, before your father was born." She swatted at Dom. "You move over, I don't want to run over you with my walker."

And with that, she disappeared into the house. Erica handed Angie a bag. "Those are her meds. I set up her weekly box, so all she has to do is take them with meals."

"Should I put this in her room?" Angie jiggled the plastic box with letters on the top of twenty-one sections. Morning, noon, and night. The plan seemed easy enough.

"The way she's acting, if you do that, you might not see her all week." Erica grabbed the last bag and walked with Angie to the house. "I'd set them up on the kitchen counter. I'm sorry she's being such a problem. I would have thought she'd be over her tiff by now."

"Not your fault. And, no," Angie added when she saw the haunted look in the young woman's eyes, "it's not wrong for you to want some normal time off. You deserve a week alone having fun. She'll get over it."

"You may not be so supportive when I leave and you have to deal with the fallout." Erica held open the screen door. "I'm going back to put these in her room and hang up her clothes. I'll be right back out, but then I need to leave. My plane takes off in a few hours, and I still have to get to Boise."

"We'll be fine," Angie called after the retreating Erica. She looked down at Dom. "Right, boy? We'll be fine. What kind of problems can an elderly woman give us?"

Dom looked at her like he couldn't believe she asked the question. Angie made herself a plate from all the food on the counter and sat down at the table to eat.

When Erica came back, she nodded to the spread. "You sure you don't want to grab something to take with you?"

She glanced at her watch, then grabbed a plate. "I'm mostly packed anyway."

Erica filled her plate with eggs, bacon, and hash brown potatoes. "So, did you hear about the dead girl? I knew Heather from school. I mean, she wasn't in my class or anything, but she was attending Boise State. Nursing school, I think."

"I did hear. I met her over at Pamplona Farms last week. I guess she was dating Javier?"

Erica shrugged and, between bites, told what she knew. "Javier doesn't really date. He's all about the one-night stands. So when Heather started talking about them like they were a couple, I knew she was going to have a bad fall when he dumped her. The girl was nice, but really naïve."

"Did you date him?" Angie decided to keep using the word, even though Erica had been clear that Javier's intentions were more of the gigolo variety.

Erica brayed a laugh. "Me? Sorry, I'm not quite his type. He likes them young, blond, and missing a few brain cells. I always thought Heather was too smart for him, but I guess she hid that side of her when they were together."

"Maybe Heather was seeing someone else too?"

"No way. That girl had wedding bells in her head." Erica glanced at the clock. "Crap. I've got to run. If you need me, you have my cell. I'll fly back if you can't handle her or if something happens."

"Nothing's going to happen, and you are not cutting your vacation short just because I can't handle your grandmother." Angie stood and gave her a bag of cookies. "Here, I thought you might want these for your long trip. I packed extra for you to be able to share."

"You're so sweet. I appreciate this." Erica headed to the door. "I just hope you're still talking to me next Monday when I come to collect her."

Angie made swishing motions with her hands. "Go, shoo. Before I change my mind."

Waving and laughing, Erica headed out the door. Angie made a plate filled with the sweeter treats she'd made for the occupation. She poured a cup of coffee, knowing her guest liked it black. Then she went to the guest room and knocked. "Mrs. Potter? Are you decent?"

She heard the chuckle and decided to take that as a good sign. She opened the door and held out the plate. "I know you said you weren't hungry, but I made several of Nona's favorites, so I thought I'd bring them to you, just in case."

"I might eat later." She waved to the little table by the window. "Just set it there. I'm going to read for a while."

Angie moved toward the table, setting down the plate and cup. "What are you reading?"

"Erica got these from the used book store. It's a mystery but it's set in the future. I figured if I'm not going to live to see it, I might as well imagine what it's going to be like." Mrs. Potter patted the book. "Besides, her husband is a lovely man and a true hottie."

"Mrs. Potter." Angie laughed. "I didn't think you knew the term."

"Dear, I'm old, I'm not dead." Mrs. Potter patted the bed beside her. "Come sit a minute. I want to apologize for inconveniencing you in this way."

"Having you stay with me is so not a problem. I love it when you visit. Besides, Erica needs a break now and then." Angie sat next to Mrs. Potter, noticing how tiny her hands were now, the skin tight on the bones. "We'll have fun. I was thinking we'd do something with chicken for dinner. Do you have any preferences? I know I've been dropping off food for a few months, but I never asked what you really enjoy."

"I don't eat much. I'm afraid my appetite has gone the way of my youth. Anything you make will be fine. Although I have to admit, I'm partial to your soups. Especially that one with pork and hominy. That was yummy." She sat her book down on the bed. "I hope you don't think I'm being mean to Erica. I just didn't like her going behind my back and setting this whole thing up. I could have stayed in my house across the street."

"And I would have been worried about you constantly." Angie saw the fire alight in her neighbor's eyes. "Not that anything would have happened, but I would have kicked myself for not insisting you come stay with me if it had. And River Vista has been a little less safe lately."

"I'm sure you're referring to the awful Mr. Moss's death." Mrs. Potter shook her head. "That was bound to happen. The man was a menace."

Knowing how Mrs. Potter felt about Gerald Moss, Angie left that inaccuracy aside. "Actually, there was a woman killed in town a few nights ago. She was stabbed behind the Red Eye."

"Barflies have a habit of getting squished by being in the wrong place at the wrong time." Mrs. Potter added a disgusted sniff to the end of her statement.

"Mrs. Potter. You know women are allowed in bars unaccompanied now. They have been for years. Barfly is a derogatory, sexist term." Angie decided she needed to go clean the kitchen before she said anything more and the woman wheeled her walker across the street to her home. "Anyway, I need to get some chores done. Let me know if you need anything."

"I'm perfectly capable of walking into the kitchen for a glass of water." The woman's tone was ice.

Great, Angie thought. *Now I've insulted her.* She walked out of the room, softly closing the door behind her. She'd apologize after lunch, even though she'd done nothing wrong. Better to say you were sorry than deal with the cold shoulder for a week.

Angie's phone buzzed. Glancing down, she recognized Estebe's number. "Hey, what's going on? Are you coming over?"

"I am sorry, but I am unable to visit today." Estebe's voice was clipped. "I have been called to attend a council meeting and I must be in Boise. I probably will be there most of the day."

"Is this about Javier? Is your community upset he was questioned?" Angie didn't know a lot about the Basque community, but she knew they were conservative in nature. Javier's questioning in a murder investigation probably had everyone on edge. Especially since they had the festival coming up.

"I'm afraid so. Javier had been called to replace our leader in a few years. He's a very social man." Estebe didn't even chuckle at the statement. "So when the community looked for new leadership, they chose someone who is good at talking rather than someone who is good at leading."

"You think they chose the wrong person." Angie summarized what wasn't being said.

"I've said too much. Javier is a good man. He would never kill anyone, especially someone who had been nice to him. Heather was very sweet." Estebe paused and Angie realized he was calling from his car, probably already driving into Boise. "You will still come to the breakfast? I want to show you a happier side of my culture. And you'll love the food."

"If it's still on, I'll be there." She paused. "Are you sure you don't want to talk?"

A horn blared in the background. "Maybe someday, but right now I have to concentrate on these crazy drivers. Why do people go so slow in the fast lane? Do they not understand the rules?"

Angie started to answer and realized she was talking to dead air. Estebe had hung up on her. He was convinced of his cousin's innocence, maybe she should be too. She decided to take a trip into town and see what Felicia knew about the murder. Besides, it would be a good excuse to get out of the house. She called out to the closed door. "Mrs. Potter? I'm heading into town. Do you need anything before I go?"

"I'm fine, thank you" was the short, clipped answer. Nona had said Mrs. Potter could hold a grudge better than most. Angie guessed she was going to find out exactly how long she would be in the doghouse.

"Okay then. I'm leaving Dom here. He can let himself out through the laundry room." Angie didn't know why she was explaining this, but she didn't want to get home and have Dom wandering out in someone's field because the woman had let him out the kitchen door and expected him to stay around. Dom liked to explore. That's why Angie had spent so much on the stupid fence. To keep him safe.

"We'll be fine."

Angie could hear muttering after that but wasn't sure if she wanted to know what Mrs. Potter was saying. She decided to ignore the fussing. "All right then. See you in a few."

As she drove into town, she calculated the hours until Erica's return. It was too long. When she reached the parking lot behind the County Seat, she looked up at the lighting and made a mental note to call an electrician. That could be the official reason she had to come into town. To set up an appointment. It was lame, but at least it was something.

She parked, but instead of going into the building that held her restaurant, she walked right through the alleyway, pausing at the already loose crime scene tape. She looked at the stain on the broken concrete. This must have been where they found Heather.

She was about to go into the bar through the back door when she saw something sparkling under a stack of old wooden crates. Bending down, she pulled out a broken chain with a silver logo on the bottom. She looked at the letters *PF.* She'd seen the logo before on the boxes she'd received Friday morning. And on the barn of Pamplona Farms. And on the chain that hung around Javier's neck.

Chapter 6

Instead of dialing 9-1-1, Angie hit another speed dial she had set on her phone. When Ian answered, she quickly apprised him of what she found. When he didn't say anything, she asked, "Did you hear what I said? Where are you anyway? Just come down here and you can deal with it. Sheriff Brown likes you."

"He doesn't not like you. Besides, I'm out at Moss Farms going over the books with Mildred. I'll call Allen and have him meet you. Just don't touch anything."

"I'm not stupid," Angie snapped back. Although she had already touched the necklace.

His chuckle made her even madder. "I won't point out the obvious, but you are behind the bar looking for clues. Don't they call that investigating?"

"I wasn't investigating. I thought I saw something over here when I parked, so I walked over." Even to her ears, Angie's excuse sounded lame. "Fine, I was snooping. It's not a crime."

"You have to tell that to Allen, not me. I'm going to call him now. Just be careful."

Angie looked around the narrow alley and decided to sit on the steps going into the back of the realty office. She didn't want to get run over by someone stumbling out of the Red Eye. It was early for anyone to be blind drunk, but anything was possible. She tried to imagine what had happened to Heather in the alley. She hadn't gotten far from the door before she was stabbed. And if she was walking toward the County Seat, she might have fallen facedown with her arm outstretched. Maybe she ripped the necklace off her killer?

A cold shiver ran down Angie's back. Finding the farm's logo on a broken necklace didn't bode well for Javier's innocence. However, even though it was clear Estebe didn't have much respect for his cousin, he didn't think he could have killed someone. Maybe that was blind faith, though. How many times did you look at someone and say, yep, that guy's a serial killer?

"Miss Turner. I can't say I'm surprised to find you here snooping around." Sheriff Brown had come up the alley from the other way, surprising her. "Do I want to know why you're here?"

"I was curious. I know, morbid, but look what I found." She stood from the cement steps and pointed toward the box.

"Hold up, let me get in there. You didn't touch anything, did you?" He narrowed his eyes at her.

She was tempted to tell him what she told Ian, but she knew she needed to be totally honest. "Okay, I pulled it out of the crack. When I saw what it was, I dropped it."

"I can't believe Clyde didn't see this last night. Of course, it was dark and late. But if this necklace had been a snake, it would have bit him. I'm going to have to send him back to the police academy for some refresher training on murder investigations. Although in his defense, he hasn't needed to have any skill in that area until the last few months." Sheriff Brown narrowed his eyes and focused on her. "You're not involved in this, are you?"

"Because I'm new in town? Seriously?"

"I wasn't thinking about that, but from what I've heard, you had met the prime suspect and his victim just this week." He took a bag out of his pocket and a pair of tweezers, and bending down with a grunt, leaned in to snag the necklace.

"Isn't it prejudicial to call her his victim when you don't know if he really killed her or not?"

Sheriff Brown straightened and then sealed the bag. He wrote on the outside of the tape, ignoring her question. Finally, he glanced around, trying to see if there was something else they'd missed last night. When he was done, he turned toward her. "Things aren't looking good for Mr. Easterly. Even without this new evidence, the only person with motive to get rid of that young lady was the man she had a fight with less than three hours before she winds up dead. I'm not a genius, but the guy has a flashing red arrow pointing to him."

Angie bit her lip, thinking of a new argument. Nothing came to her, so she decided to stall. "Then why didn't you arrest him Saturday when you interviewed him?"

Sheriff Brown took off his cowboy hat and ran a hand through his thinning hair. "You want the truth?"

When Angie nodded, he repeated the motion and put his hat back on. "It doesn't feel right." He held up a hand. "Don't get me wrong, I'm not usually a slave to my feelings. In fact, if you chatted with Maggie, she'd tell you I didn't have any feelings at all. All the evidence adds up, yet two plus two is equaling three, and it should be four. If you get my drift."

Somehow, she did understand his convoluted reasoning. "Then who killed her?"

Sheriff Brown put his hat back on and started walking away from her. "Beats the hell out of me."

She stood there in the alley for a few minutes, shocked that the sheriff had cursed but even more shocked that he didn't have a clue about who had killed Heather. Could it have been a random killing? Just someone with a new toy they wanted to play with? She watched the sheriff disappear and then decided to do what she'd come for. Go into the Red Eye and talk to the bartender.

She pushed open the red door that led to a dark hallway. The floor was sticky with spilt beer, or at least she hoped it was beer. The bathrooms were on each side of the narrow hallway, along with a pay phone. The phone hadn't been used for a while since the metal cord that was supposed to attach the receiver to the phone was missing. She kept walking toward a muted light and all of a sudden found herself in the large bar area. Pool tables and dartboards were set up in the area closest to the bathrooms. The bar was to her right and, in front of that, a large dance floor with what looked and smelled like sawdust. A tiny woman sat at the edge of the bar. Her hair was bottle red and she wore a shirt two sizes too small that dipped down in front to show off her cleavage. She was flipping through a copy of *People* magazine. The cover showed a candid shot of the most recent celebrity found coming out of a hidden love nest.

The woman must have heard her approach, but she didn't look up. "Sorry, we don't open for lunch on Mondays. Come back after five."

Angie spoke before she could stop herself. "It's five o'clock somewhere."

"Being a wise guy doesn't get you a drink."

Angie sat on the stool next to the woman. "I'm not here for a drink. Let me start again. I'm Angie Turner. I'm the owner of the County Seat down the block?"

Now the woman sat the magazine down. She looked Angie over, then nodded. "Barb Travis. This trash heap is mine. Your friend Felicia is a nice girl. She sure can put back the brew, though. I don't worry about her much since she only has to walk a few steps home." She blew out a breath. "Of course, that didn't help poor Heather."

"You knew Heather?"

Barb worried her bottom lip, scraping some of the screaming red lipstick onto her yellowed teeth. "Of course I knew Heather. The girl was sweet. Way too nice for that jerk of a boyfriend. I was alternately giving her tissues Friday night and then holding her back from rushing at him to stab him in the heart with a cocktail swizzle stick."

"Javier could be a jerk." Angie had only met the guy once, and she knew that was a true statement. "But you don't think he killed Heather, do you?"

"Honey, I've bartended here at Red Eye for thirty years. I guess I liked it so much, I bought the place." She took a sip of her coffee. "Want some?"

"No, I'm good." Angie didn't think she could stay seated if she drank more caffeine. "You didn't answer my question."

"I'm getting there. First, I'm going to tell you a story. There was a guy sitting right on that same barstool as you, oh, about ten years ago. It was a Saturday and he'd been here all day. Bad breakup with the love of his life—she'd caught him swimming in another pool and kicked him out. Which, according to him, made him realize he'd been a fool." Barb got up and walked around the counter, refilling her coffee cup. "You sure you don't want some?"

"Already over my daily limit." Angie wasn't sure what day, or even month, the too-dark brew had been made. It was probably just better to decline.

"Ha, if I limited myself on coffee, I'd be napping right now. Anyway, so this guy's sitting there, whining in his beer when a woman walks in the door, pulls a pistol, and shoots off six rounds at him." Barb walked back around and sat at the door.

"The wife or the girlfriend?"

A ghost of a smile creased Barb's darkly tanned face. "Wife. My bouncer took the gun from her, but the weird thing was, she missed hitting the loser every time. I didn't even think that was possible. Even a blind dog finds his dinner sometimes."

Angie's phone chirped. She looked down at the display and saw it was the house number. But she wanted to figure out this puzzle that Barb was setting up. "The moral of the story?"

"Love makes you do crazy things. It could have been Javier or someone else. But love is crazy." She nodded to the ringing phone. "You might want to answer that."

"It will just take a second." Angie picked up the phone. "What's going on?"

"Where do you keep the fire extinguisher?" Mrs. Potter sounded out of breath and her words squeaked out.

"Oh, my God, are you okay?" Angie stood and tucked her purse under her arm. She paused, trying to hear what was going on. "Mrs. Potter?"

"I can't find anything in this kitchen. Margaret had it so organized. What did you do to all her stuff?"

"What's on fire?" The phone clicked off and Angie tried to call back, but all she got was a busy signal. She turned to Barb. "Sorry, I've got to go. My house guest said something about a fire, now I can't reach her."

"Do you want me to call the fire department and have them meet you out there?" Barb headed toward her phone. "You live out at the old Turner farm, right?"

"I don't know if there is really anything wrong or not." Angie made a quick decision. "Call them. But let them know that it might be nothing."

"Better safe than sorry, that's what my grans always said." Barb waved her hands, shooing Angie out of the bar.

Once Angie hit the alley, she ran to her car, dropping the keys as she tried to unlock the door. "Please be all right." She said the mantra over and over during the drive home. Erica would kill her if she let something happen to Mrs. Potter on the first day she was responsible for her. It took her less than twenty minutes, and thankfully, Angie didn't hit any cows, horses, or even sheep on the way, although there was a squirrel that she wasn't quite sure she'd missed. All she could see was her house, Nona's house, going up in flames. "Please let them be okay," she whispered as a mantra as she drove.

She turned into the driveway, gravel flying behind her. It didn't look like the house was on fire. Maybe things weren't as dire as she'd thought. She flew out of the car and up the stairs onto the porch. Swinging the door open, she stopped short in the middle of the doorway.

Mrs. Potter sat at the table with Dom at her side. She'd been telling the dog something, and as Angie entered, they both turned to look at her.

"I didn't realize you were so close. I wouldn't have bothered calling you, but you didn't say when you'd be coming back." Mrs. Potter pushed a plate of cookies toward her. "Macaroon?"

"Where's the fire?" Angie sniffed the air. Nothing. Confusion muddled her adrenaline-full brain. "I don't understand. Why would you tell me there was a fire when there wasn't one?"

"I never said there was a fire. I merely asked you where you kept your fire extinguisher. If I'm going to feel comfortable living in this house for the next week, I need to know these things. My bedroom window doesn't open all the way either."

Angie wanted to scream. Instead, she sank into a chair, the air going out of her faster than she could take it in. Rubbing her forehead, she tried to bring her blood pressure down by slowing her breathing. When she looked up, they were still watching her. "Why did you hang up on me?"

"Oh, the phone receiver slipped out of my hand and into the sink. I'm not sure it works anymore. I had the sink full of soapy water to clean up around here." Mrs. Potter looked around the kitchen like she'd found the solution to cure cancer. "Don't you think a kitchen is at its best when it shines?"

The siren on the fire truck barreling into the driveway kept Angie from telling her house guest that her kitchen had been plenty clean when she'd left that morning. She jumped out of her chair and went to the door to look out. Two fire trucks and ten pickup trucks were surrounding the house. "I need to deal with this."

She walked out to where the men were standing, staring at the house, then the barn, then their phones. Man, she was never going to live this one down. "Sorry, guys. Misunderstanding. I have a houseguest and I didn't understand what she was saying."

"It's against the law to call in a hoax fire report. Someone could have been hurt getting here." A tall man wearing a ball cap that said Chief stepped toward her. She recognized him as Rob Harris, the guy who owned the winery. "Tell me again why you called in a fire when there clearly isn't one? You're not under duress, are you? Who else is in the house? Come on out, I know you're watching."

"No, I'm not under duress. Like I said, it was a misunderstanding. And technically, I didn't call in the report anyway, it was Barb." She blew out a long breath. "Look, Rob..."

He interrupted her apology. "It's Chief, not Rob." He leaned forward and whispered, "I'm on official River Vista Volunteer Fire Department business. I have to show my authority around the guys."

"Oh," Angie looked back at Mrs. Potter and Dom, who had exited the building. The woman had her hands in the air. "Put your hands down, Mrs. Potter. Everything's okay."

"Maybe she called in the hoax so we'd come save her from you." Rob eyed Angie suspiciously. "Are you holding this sweet old lady hostage?"

"No, but I'm beginning to think it's the other way around." Angie shook her head at his confused stare. "Never mind. Look, we're all okay. There's no fire. See?" She pointed to the house.

"I'm afraid I'm going to have to do a walk-through before I can send my guys home. This is definitely a suspicious situation." He leaned close again. "The Idaho Fire Union came out and did a Saturday training for all of us on what to look for in case of a terrorist attack. They even catered lunch. And it wasn't just sandwiches. Pizza, salad, and some sort of pasta. I tried to get them to hire the winery for the gig, but we got undercut."

"Fine, if you need to walk through, go ahead." She waved her arm out in welcome. "I just want to get this day over."

"Just to be clear, I have your official permission to enter the residence?" He smiled. "When there's not a visible active fire, I have to ask permission."

"And what if I don't give it to you?" Angie's frustration level was reaching a boiling point.

He glanced around at the men, who were all watching him now. "I guess we have to stay here until you do." He pulled a small, well-worn book out of his coat pocket. "I've never seen anything in the handbook about a homeowner being noncompliant."

"If I tell you that you can go in, you'll leave?" Angie shushed Dom, who was barking at one of the men who had walked over to pet him. He plopped on his butt and stared at her, certain she'd kept him from saving the day.

"Yes, ma'am." He winked at her. "Unless I find some freaky stuff in there. Then we might have to talk again."

"Just go." She walked over and sat in the porch bench next to Dom. "It's okay, boy, they don't mean us harm."

He growled lightly in his throat—apparently, he didn't agree with her assessment—but he let Rob and a second man walk past them without a problem.

"Terry and I will be right back out. As soon as we ascertain there is no fire." Rob held the screen door open for the man now known as Terry and disappeared into the house.

Mrs. Potter moved her walker and came to sit down by Angie. "I'm so sorry about all of this. I just don't understand why you would have thought there was a fire."

After Angie explained herself, again, Mrs. Potter nodded. Just to make sure she understood, Angie went on. "So, let's promise each other for the week, we won't say things that might be misunderstood. Does that sound like a plan?"

"I can go back and stay at my house." Mrs. Potter started to stand. "Just bring my stuff back and I'll be out of your hair."

Angie put a hand on her arm. "Don't be silly. I love having you here. I just want us to be more careful of the words we use."

"That's reasonable." Mrs. Potter's stomach grumbled. "What are you making for dinner? All this activity has me starving."

"I thought I'd make a tuna casserole. Will that work?" Angie stroked Dom's head as he laid it on her lap. The dog was growing fast. Last month he hadn't been tall enough to sit and lean on her. She didn't know what had possessed her to purchase a St. Bernard puppy instead of the smaller cocker spaniel she'd had in mind when she'd visited the local breeder, but Dom was hers and he was here to stay.

"That would be lovely." Mrs. Potter looked at her delicate silver watch. "*Jeopardy* comes on in ten minutes. Do you think they'll be done by then? I hate missing out on even a part of my shows. It's like walking into a party late. You've missed all the good gossip."

As if she'd called him, Rob came back onto the porch. He turned to Terry. "Tell the boys to go on home. There's no fire here. At least not today. Seriously, Angie, do you always leave your small appliances plugged in? That's the cause of most home fires."

"Give me a break. Really?" Angie had never heard that.

Rob nodded. "The guy from the state had a slide on it and everything. So go unplug all those coffeemakers and I'll see you at the winery soon. You need to come in on a Thursday. It's ladies' night and drinks are half off. I've got some friends who are dying to meet you."

"I'm seeing someone, thanks." Angie stood and helped Mrs. Potter up from the bench. "Time to start dinner."

"I know a brush-off when I hear it. Good night, Mrs. Potter. Nice to see you again." Rob stepped off the porch and waved back. Most of the pickup trucks had already left, but Terry sat in the other fire truck, waiting for Rob.

"One day done," Angie said to Dom when they were alone on the porch. "One disaster averted. I have a feeling it's going to be an interesting week."

Dom barked his reply. She didn't speak dog language, but the look on his face told her he totally agreed.

Chapter 7

Tuesday was typically her stay home and veg day, but since staying home meant talking to Mrs. Potter continuously, she decided to run into town for groceries she didn't need. What she really wanted to do was stop by the police station and talk to Sheriff Brown. If he didn't think Javier would have done this, she wanted to know who he thought might have.

She was already in the car when her phone rang. When she picked up, she recognized Estebe's voice almost immediately. "How are you? How's your cousin?"

"Javier is fine, although he's probably going to lose favor with the elders. He still insists that he didn't hurt that girl, but I'm afraid the chickens are coming home to roost with him. His inability to settle down or even have a decent relationship with a woman for longer than a few weeks hadn't gone unnoticed by the community."

"Just because he's a horndog doesn't mean he's unfit to hold an office." Although Angie had known of several past presidents who had believed that the rules didn't apply to them. What was the saying—Power corrupts, but absolute power corrupts absolutely?

"You don't have to defend my cousin. He is not a good man." Estebe blew out a sigh. "Anyway, I called to tell you that we don't need your help. Javier has an attorney, and she believes it's better to let the law investigate rather than..." He paused and Angie could almost hear the word choices that ran through this head. *Chef, amateur, woman,* whatever word he chose, he'd wind up annoying her.

"I realize I'm not a professional investigator, and I'd never do anything to mess with the investigation, but I think your cousin might need some help. You realize all Sheriff Brown has to prove is he might have killed Heather.

Tell me what happened." She pulled over and took out her notebook. When Estebe didn't respond, she tried another tactic. "Humor me."

"I don't want you getting yourself in trouble, but I guess I owe you the story. Javier did dance with another girl. He said he was getting tired of how clingy Heather was. I told him that was love and a relationship. Anyway, he and Heather got in a fight. He left, taking this new girl home, stayed the night at her house, and then went home Saturday morning to find the police at the farm."

"What's the girl's name? If that's true, he has an alibi."

"Now, that's the place where my cousin being a jerk comes in. He called her star girl. Apparently, she had several star tattoos on the inside of her forearm. He didn't get her name. In fact, it was a joke between them. The encounter would be more exciting if they were total strangers." He sighed, showing his disapproval with Javier. "See what I'm dealing with?"

"But he has to remember where she lived. At least the police could go talk to her."

Estebe sounded tired. "I don't know if they are even trying."

"Well, give me the address and I'll go talk to her." At least that would keep her from having to go back and watch soaps with Mrs. Potter. She wrote down the directions. "I'll call you as soon as I find this woman. He's going to be okay."

"Thank you."

After she hung up, she looked up the address on her phone to see where she would be going. The address was in Nampa, the next town over and in the opposite direction of River Vista, where she was heading. Instead of turning around, she continued her way into River Vista and parked in front of the County Seat.

She dialed Felicia's number. "Want to go on an adventure with me?"

"Sure, let me get my shoes on. When will you be here?"

"I'm out front." Angie leaned over so she could see the living room window in Felicia's apartment. She saw her friend looking down at her and waved. "I'll buy you lunch."

"Sold. I'll be down in a few."

Angie turned up the music as she waited. She'd only listened to half of Carrie Underwood's new duet with Keith Urban before the passenger side door opened. Turning down the tunes, she waited for Felicia to climb in. "That was fast."

"I'm hungry. I didn't eat breakfast." She buckled in. "Where are we going?"

Angie pulled the car back on the street and headed out of town. "Somewhere in Nampa."

"I haven't been to Nampa yet. What's there?" Felicia flipped open the vanity mirror and slipped on some lipstick that she didn't need. The girl was always beautiful.

"A one-night stand."

When Felicia turned, her mouth half fire engine red, and gaped at her, Angie laughed and told her the story. By the time she was done filling her in on Estebe's story, Felicia had finished putting on her lipstick and was staring at her. "Let me get this straight. We're going to find some woman who slept with Javier but didn't give him her name? Who does that these days? With all the crap going around, I usually want to see a blood test report before I even think of kissing someone."

"Well, I guess Javier thought he'd gotten lucky. Sex with no commitment. But now it means he has no alibi, or at least not one that can be confirmed." Angie turned onto the road that followed the railroad tracks into town. She and Nona had usually shopped in Nampa, so she was familiar with the area and the best way to get into town. "Google restaurants nearby and we'll see what we can find."

When they hit the city limits, Angie looked for landmarks that Javier had relayed to Estebe. There was a small college in town, and the apartment building he'd described sat between that and the park. "The good news is Javier's a snob about the gas he puts into that car of his. He only uses Chevron gas, and there's only one station on this side of town. And he said the woman's apartment building was next door."

Felicia looked up from her phone. "You're really good at this detail stuff."

"That's why I'm a great cook. I pay attention to the little things. And Estebe does too, so our information source is good." Angie pulled her SUV into the parking lot. "Second floor. Apartment 205. Apparently, they made out in the hallway for a while before going in."

"And what exactly are we going to do if she answers the door?"

She pursed her lips, thinking. Then it came to her. She'd use Javier's reputation against him. "You play the upset fiancée. She just met the guy last weekend, she doesn't know about Heather."

"I can do that, but my name's Liz. I always wanted to be called Liz or Beth." Felicia flipped her hair back off her shoulders. "Let's go see what Javier picked up this time."

The foyer had a wall of mailboxes on one side and a stairway on the other. A big sign had been hung on the elevator. Repairs in Progress. Angie pointed to it as they started up the stairs. "Looks like that sign has been up for a few years."

"It's a short building. I think too many people take the elevator when they could just as well take the stairs and get some exercise in their day."

Angie didn't respond. She liked using elevators. It got her where she needed to go faster. Besides, who wanted to hoof it up three or four flights of stairs? Well, besides her friend, Felicia, and fitness nuts like her.

They found 205 easily, but no one answered the door. When they knocked a third time, the door across the hall opened. A curly-headed kid of about seven stared at them. "She's gone to New York City for the summer."

Angie turned to eye the little girl. "You know who lives here?"

The girl sighed and put her hands on her hips, leaning on the doorway. "Of course I do. Just because I'm a kid doesn't mean I'm stupid. Carrie Sue lives there. But like I said, she's in New York City. She's going to bring me home a new outfit when she comes back in the fall that I can wear to school. No one but me will have a dress from New York City."

Angie glanced at Felicia, not sure how to proceed.

"When did Carrie Sue leave for New York?" Felicia took over the questioning.

"Right after school got out in May. Her dad's paying the rent so she doesn't get evicted. If you don't pay your rent, they boot you out on the street with all your stuff." The little girl shook her head. "It's sad."

"Is anyone staying here while she's gone?"

Before the little girl could answer, a woman with two grocery bags in hand came into the hallway. "Tasha, what are you doing outside the apartment? I told you to stay inside and not answer the door." She looked at Angie and Felicia. "I was only gone for less than thirty minutes, and she was watching a movie when I left."

"I'm not a baby." Tasha crossed her arms. "Besides, they didn't knock on our door, they want to see Carrie Sue."

"You take these bags to the kitchen and start putting things away." Then she turned back to Angie and Felicia. "Are you friends of Carrie Sue? She's on a summer semester out of town."

"New York City, we heard." Angie smiled, trying to relax the woman. "Actually, we were looking for whoever is renting her space while she's gone."

The woman looked blankly at the door. "No one's renting her space. The apartment has been empty since Carrie Sue left, mid-May. She'll be back late August if you want to speak to her. Or I have her dad's number in case of emergency. Is this an emergency?"

Angie shook her head. This alibi just went south fast. Besides, maybe she had the wrong apartment building or Javier had seen the number wrong. He had been drunk. "No, ma'am. Sorry for the bother."

"No trouble." The woman started to close her door.

"Wait, one more thing. Are there any other young single women who live on the floor?" Felicia asked.

"That's a random question, but no. The other two apartments are rented to retired couples. I think they've lived here since the place opened. Tasha gets on their nerves, so we tend to stay away from that side of the hall. Carrie Sue, on the other hand, loves my daughter."

They didn't talk until they got back into the car. Angie scanned the area. "This has to be the apartment building unless there's another Chevron station on this side of town I don't know about."

Felicia keyed information into her phone. "Nope. There are two in Nampa. This one, and one on Nampa-Caldwell Blvd. It looks like it's on the other side of town from this map."

"It's on the way to the mall." Angie started up the car. "I don't think I'm going to be much help to Javier. I wouldn't mind so much, but Estebe is really worried about him."

"Let's go eat lunch and brainstorm. Maybe we can figure out something." Felicia put a hand on her stomach, which growled as if on cue. "Did I mention I missed breakfast?"

"Tell me where we're going." Angie pulled the car out of the parking lot and followed Felicia's directions to a renovated building downtown. Around the restaurant were bars and small specialty shops selling tourist-type items. They parked in front and walked into the brightly lit café. As soon as they opened the door, the smell of baked bread, warm soups, and coffee hit them.

As they scooted into a booth, a waitress came to give them menus. She froze when she saw Felicia. "Wow, I can't believe you're here. Are you still looking for servers? I would love to work for you guys. I probably blew my interview. I'm not good at interviewing."

"Oh," Felicia's eyes dropped down to the name tag pinned crookedly on the woman's blue shirt, "Marie, so nice to see you again. Yes, unfortunately we are fully staffed right now, but I'll keep your résumé on file in case we increase our staff."

"You will?" Marie gave a little shriek, which had most of the dining room looking at her. "Oh, sorry, I'm just so excited. I so hope you give me a chance."

"It may be a while before we need additional staff." Felicia tried to backpedal.

Marie leaned closer. "That's all right. I just want to work at a real high-quality restaurant, you know. I started at IHOP a few years ago, then moved here. Now I'm ready for the next step in my career."

"Can we get some iced tea?" Angie broke into Marie's recitation of her résumé.

The woman flushed. "I am so sorry. You all are here to eat, not see me. I'll be right back with your drinks."

Felicia leaned back in the booth. "Thank you. Honestly, I barely remember interviewing her. I think she was so quiet, I didn't get much from the interview. And we had so many qualified candidates who had already worked at fine dining. I didn't even consider her." She straightened her knife and fork. "I feel bad for not recognizing her."

"You can't hire everyone."

"I know, but sometimes enthusiasm does make up for experience. I'm going to pull her résumé out of my file and make notes on it just in case we have a slot open." Felicia sat up and smiled at the waitress, who was power walking back to their table. "I don't think this is going to be a relaxing lunch, sorry."

"So not your fault." Angie glanced over the menu and quickly made a decision on one of the seasonal salads. The place had some food chops, that was certain. And it appeared to be busy with local customers. She wondered who the owner/chef was and if she knew them.

Marie set down their drinks with a little bowl of lemons and a holder filled with sugars and sweeteners. "I hope you didn't mean sweet tea. We don't have that. In North Carolina, where I'm from, that's all they serve if you say iced tea. You have to request unsweetened tea. I don't know why we don't have that here in Idaho."

"Must be a regional thing." Angie gave the woman her order and then, as Felicia gave hers, she pulled out her ringing phone. Raising her eyebrows, she answered the call. "Yes, Mrs. Potter?"

"Oh, I didn't expect you to answer the phone."

Angie groaned silently. "Then why did you call me?"

"I wanted to let you know that I'm eating the leftover tuna casserole for lunch and you shouldn't worry about feeding me. I'm perfectly fine on my own."

"Thank you for letting me know. I was worried." Angie hoped the sarcasm she felt didn't come across in her tone.

Felicia looked at her questioningly and Angie shrugged.

"No need to worry. We're just two roommates with separate lives. You're not responsible for my well-being. It's like I'm in college or like that *Three's Company* show, but without the kind of cute guy living with us too."

Angie stifled a laugh. "Now, that would be interesting. Look, I'll be home in a couple of hours and I'll make us a stir fry. How about that?"

"That would be lovely. Of course, I need some kind of meat."

"Make a decision on what you want and I'll make it." Angie shook her head. "Talk to you soon."

The phone clicked off. Angie looked at it to make sure she hadn't disconnected the call, but no, it had been Mrs. Potter. "I guess goodbye isn't in her vocabulary. Estebe does the same thing. When they're done talking, they hang up. No salutations at all."

"How's it going with your new guest?" Felicia dipped her head, but Angie caught the grin.

Angie slipped her phone back into her purse. "Don't ask. Half the time I feel guilty for not waiting on her hand and foot, and the rest of the time I want to kill her, so I find reasons to leave the house."

"Erica will be back when?"

"Monday, and I can't wait. I so hope she's having the time of her life because the next time she asks a favor, I'm going to be away for a month hiding from her."

Somehow they got through the meal without any additional conversation with Marie. She seemed to want to show her best side as a server. When they left, she came running from the back to say goodbye.

"Thank you so much for coming in today," Marie gushed as she walked them to the door.

When they got into the car, Angie glanced at Felicia. "I blame you for that."

"I can't help it if everyone wants to work for us." Felicia refreshed her lipstick in the vanity mirror as they drove away. "We're a hot commodity right now."

When her cell rang again, Angie answered it without looking. Mrs. Potter was going to drive her insane. "What's going on now?"

"Funny, that's exactly what I was going to ask you." A man's voice boomed in the car speakers.

"Sheriff Brown?" There was no way he'd found out about their visit to the apartment building so quickly. Besides, they hadn't even verified Javier's story.

"Can you come into the police station? I've been talking to Javier this morning, and there's a few things I'd like to make clear."

"On my way." Angie hung up feeling like she'd been sent to the principal's office.

Felicia grinned at her. "Uh-oh, you're in trouble."

Chapter 8

The officer on the desk glared at her. The guy hated her and she didn't even remember his name. She glanced at her watch. She'd been waiting for the sheriff for over twenty minutes. She'd ignored three calls from her home number and Mrs. Potter while she sat there. If the house was burning down, it was too late to get the fire department involved anyway since they had already cried wolf once. The sad part was she didn't know which was worse, sitting here on the plastic chairs waiting or going home and dealing with her temporary houseguest.

The sheriff's door opened and he stuck his head out. "Come on in, Angie."

She followed him into the large office, where he was already making her a cup of coffee. "Sorry about the wait. I've been on the line with Heather's parents. They're out of town, so they were making arrangements to fly home tomorrow. They're crushed."

"I can only imagine." She took the cup of coffee he handed her and sat in the visitor chair. When he didn't say anything more, she broke. "So why am I here?"

"Tell me about your trip this morning. And don't bother lying, I got a call from the Nampa police chief asking why someone from my staff was looking into Carrie Sue Franklin's visit to New York." He tapped his pen on the desk.

"Why do you think it was me?"

He raised his eyebrows.

"Okay, it was me, but I didn't say I was with the police." Angie thought about the conversation with the neighbor. She'd never even told the woman her name. "What gave me away?"

"Nothing except a suspicious witness. The woman you talked to? She's the police chief's daughter and she got to wondering about you. In true cop-family style, she watched out the window as you got into your SUV and drove off and copied down your plate."

"Honestly, I never said I was with the police." Angie sipped her coffee. "Besides, we ran into a dead end. Estebe said that Javier had told him that he'd taken a girl home and stayed with her all night."

"I know. I interviewed Javier. I also sent a couple of officers over to try to find the building, but they haven't been successful yet. How come you were able to find the needle in a haystack so quickly?" He stared at her.

"The gas station that's next to the apartment building. Javier only uses Chevron gas. There's only one Chevron on that side of town. And I knew the building from when I lived here before. A friend of mine lived in that same building when she went off to college. I helped her move in." She shrugged. "Small town, you know things."

"I keep forgetting that." He rolled his head from side to side, the fatigue showing on his face. "You think this Carrie Sue's apartment is where Javier spent the night?"

"I did, except this Carrie Sue has been out of state for a few months. She couldn't have been his one-night stand. I hate to say it, but maybe he was familiar with the area too. He could have met Carrie Sue before and didn't know she was gone." Angie worried her lip, thinking about the options.

"Except if he had known her and he knew we would go asking questions, she would have denied seeing him. No, there's something fishy going on. Someone had access to that apartment." He looked at her. "Anything else you've been working on? I'd hate to duplicate your efforts in the investigation."

"You're mad." Even Angie could hear the sarcasm in his tone. And typically, she was pretty clueless when it came to subtleties.

"Not mad. I just think you need to stay out of this. You're not trained. And if," he paused, making eye contact, "if he's being set up, someone is going to a lot of trouble to make it look like Javier killed Heather. I don't think you want him to notice that you don't believe that story."

She hadn't thought of that. And she'd dragged Felicia into the spotlight too.

"Good, it looks like that sank in." He stood up, glancing at the clock. "I'm heading home. You should go too. And please, stay out of trouble."

As she walked out to her car, she thought about the sheriff's warning. She hadn't even thought of the killer watching the case and her. A chill went down her spine. She thanked God that she wasn't going home to an empty house.

Man, she hadn't expected those words to ever come out of her mouth.

* * * *

Wednesday morning she'd woken up with a promise to herself that she wouldn't do any more investigating. Estebe and Javier needed to hire a private investigator rather than put her into harm's way. She felt good about her decision. She called Ian to talk while she got ready for the day. Wednesdays, she worked at the restaurant dealing with food orders, checking reservations, and paying bills. And for the first time in a long time, she was looking forward to the office work part of owning a business.

She popped out of the office to grab some coffee and ran into Felicia. She refilled her cup as they said their good mornings.

"Hey, I didn't think you'd be here today. Aren't you spending time with your new BFF?" Felicia took out a plate of zucchini bread and sat it on the table.

"I think Mrs. Potter can survive on her own for a while. Besides, she has Dom to keep her company. I'm afraid I'm losing my dog. Dom loves her." Angie broke off a piece of the still-warm bread. "This is good. Better than the stuff they make in the bakery. You should make Ian a loaf. He loves this stuff."

"I think he has a lot of people cooking for him. I saw Missy Stockwell heading up to his office with a box of cookies yesterday."

"The town sure has taken him under their wing." Angie wondered if Ian thought small-town America was all this way, opening their arms wide to visitors. She knew sometimes it just didn't happen that way. River Vista was different. And different in a good way. She always thought the town mirrored that old show Nona used to watch, where everyone knew everything and there was an Aunt Bee to take care of you.

"On the other hand, the town is ready to drive Javier to the police station themselves. No one at the bar understands why he's still walking free." Felicia cocked her head toward Angie. "Barb says you were in the Red Eye this week asking about Heather."

"Monday. That's where I got the lead on Javier's girlfriend. I thought I told you that."

Felicia shook her head. "Probably, but I thought you had talked to Kelly, the bartender. Barb's an interesting person. She knows more about the people in this valley than their relatives do. It's funny what someone will tell a bartender that they won't even tell their priest."

"What did Barb tell you about this woman? Did she know her?' Angie broke off a piece of the bread. This really wasn't investigating, so she wasn't quite breaking the promise she'd made to herself just that morning.

"I told her we tried to track her down, but the lead we had went nowhere. Funny thing is Barb has never seen the woman before, and she said she remembers everyone who came in when she was there. And she's always there."

Angie paused, holding the treat halfway to her mouth. "Interesting. So either the woman just happened to be in the Red Eye that night, or she came specifically for Javier."

"Why would someone try to break up Heather and Javier? It doesn't make sense."

She set the bread down. "Unless they didn't want Javier to have an alibi for Heather's death. It's a long shot, but work with me. Someone sends this girl into the bar to get Javier's attention. I take it she was beautiful."

"Blond, blue-eyed goddess from what Barb remembers. She thought it was funny the girl was so focused on Javier. Now, looking back, I wonder if your scenario doesn't fit. The funny thing is she never heard a name. She bought her first drink with cash, then she nursed that until Javier started buying. Right in front of Heather." Felicia looked at her watch. "He fell right into her plan. Sometimes men are too easy to manipulate. Anyway, since we don't have a staff meeting today, I made plans to meet Ted for lunch in Boise. Do you need me for anything else?"

"No, go ahead, have fun." Angie held up her hand when Felicia started to stand. "Wait, do I know Ted? I thought the guy you were dating was named Mike something."

"Mike was last week. I'm not serious about either of them. It's just a casual thing. I'm not sure I'm ready to settle down. Not like you. You hit it off with Ian and that's all there is. You're a serial monogamist." Felicia squeezed Angie's shoulder. "I know what you're going to say, be safe. But don't worry, it's just lunch."

Angie refilled her coffee cup and went back into her office. She and Felicia were different. That was probably why they'd become friends. As she worked on the accounting, she thought about Javier. Who was the mystery woman and what had been her motive?

The phone call she'd been expecting came around three. "Hello, Mrs. Potter. What's going on?"

"I was just wondering if you'd be home for dinner."

Angie shook her head. "Of course. Why wouldn't I be home for dinner?"

"You and your young man might have plans, especially since you can't go out on the weekends. Ian's a lovely man. You need to take care of that relationship. I hate to see you ruin it."

"Ian and I are fine, even if we can't go out on the weekend. Look, I'm just finishing up here, and I should be home in about an hour. If you're hungry, there's soup in the freezer."

"An hour? That fast? I'm not sure I can be finished in an hour." Panic echoed in her tone.

"Wait, what are you not going to be done with?" When she didn't get an answer, Angie looked at her phone. Mrs. Potter had hung up. She glanced at the spreadsheet she'd been updating. If she stopped now, she'd lose her place. Besides, she needed to get this done. Trying to not imagine what Mrs. Potter was doing at the house, Angie went back to her work, her mind continuing to drift off to the different possibilities. Maybe Mrs. Potter was just making her tea cozies for her table.

Unfortunately, she didn't think she'd be that lucky.

When she finally got home, she walked into a kitchen that had every kitchen item she owned out of the cabinets and the table. Dom slept in his bed. He opened one eye and beat his tail in welcome when she came through the door. Mrs. Potter was nowhere to be seen.

She carefully moved through the mess that was her kitchen and into the living room. Mrs. Potter sat in front of the television, remote in her hand, fast asleep. Angie took the remote out of her hand and turned off the game show that was blaring at almost full volume.

"Oh, dear, you're home." Mrs. Potter pulled herself upright in the chair. "I must have taken a nap. I had planned on getting everything put back before you got back."

Angie sat the remote on the side table. "What where you looking for?"

"I wasn't looking for anything. I just thought you hadn't had time to organize your cupboard space. I had to teach your grandmother the same thing when we first started keeping house. Your cups are too close to the stove and your pans too far away." Mrs. Potter stepped toward the kitchen. "You'll see. It will be so much more convenient this way."

"Instead of doing that, why don't we go down to the River House and get dinner. My treat." Erica had said the small upscale restaurant a few towns away was one of Mrs. Potter's favorites. "We'll ask for a table on the deck and watch the river."

"Oh, my, I'm not really dressed for dinner." She ran her hands down her polyester shirt and pants.

"You look great. Go freshen up and we'll leave in about fifteen minutes. I need to feed the animals real fast." Angie watched as Mrs. Potter headed to the guest bedroom and then sighed. She'd let Mrs. Potter rearrange her kitchen because it gave the woman something to do. Nothing she did had to stay that way after this week was over, she reminded herself. She headed out to the barn, not letting the mess in the kitchen waylay her.

Precious was lying in the straw, her food dish full and her water clean. When she saw Angie, she came running up to the gate to get petted. "So, is Mrs. Potter taking care of you too? How many times has she fed you today?"

The goat bleated, which Angie took as *don't mess up a good thing.* She scratched under Precious's chin and gave her a rub on her nose. "Don't get used to it. Your food fairy godmother is only here a few more days."

Mabel clucked as she walked out, a pile of dried corn already in her usual snacking spot. "Good night to you too, Mabel."

Angie went back into the house, checked on Dom's food and water in the mudroom (also full), then ran upstairs to put on makeup and pull her hair back. She changed her shirt, but decided to keep on the tan capris she'd put on that morning. Good enough, she thought as she looked into the mirror. Besides, it wasn't a date.

When they got to the restaurant, they were quickly shown to the last table on the deck. They ordered their dinner, and Mrs. Potter excused herself to the restroom. As Angie waited she leaned back and watched the river float by. Several people in kayaks played in the water below the bridge. They ran a few rapids and then paddled back to the bridge, where they did it all over again. Not quite whitewater rafting, but a good place to practice and play.

"They look like they're having fun." Javier stood at her table, watching her watch the boaters. "I've never kayaked before, have you?"

"No, I'm not so good at water sports. I used to run, but since I've been back, I've been too busy to even do that." She looked at him, noticing his sunken eyes and pale complexion. "How are you doing? I'm sorry for your loss."

He barked out a short laugh. "You are the first person to say that. I do grieve losing Heather. I might have been a horrible boyfriend, but I cared for the woman."

"I'm sure you did." She glanced around. "Are you here alone? Do you want to join Mrs. Potter and me? We've just ordered."

"Thanks, but I'm here with my uncle and my brother, Stephen." Javier pointed to an older man sitting at a table across the deck, watching them. A younger version of Javier stared back at them. He waved to his uncle, who turned back to his meal. "I'm afraid he's here to deliver the bad news that I can't be trusted to be promoted in the community if I can't stop sleeping with everyone in town. I think the fact I'm the lead suspect for Heather's death isn't helping either."

Angie didn't know what to say. Javier was being so up front with his weaknesses. "I'm sure that's not the case."

He smiled at her. "Now, even I could see the lie in your eyes. Seriously, I need someone to believe me. I didn't kill Heather. I was sleeping next to a hot blonde when she died."

"Who didn't give you her name."

Javier shrugged. "It was a game. It was a turn-on."

"And who doesn't live in the apartment you and she ended up in after the bar." Angie added the information she knew.

"Wait, what? You found her?" He slipped into the other chair. "Who is she?"

"That's the problem. I found the apartment you were in. Or at least, I'm pretty sure it was that apartment building." She waved down the excitement she saw in his face. "Hold on a minute. I only found the apartment. The woman who lives there is in New York for the summer."

He slumped back into the chair. "I know it makes me sound like a cad, but I was with another woman when my last love was killed in an alley. I swear."

"Now we just have to prove it. Tell me about your necklace." Angie stared at the same symbol she'd seen in the alley where Heather was killed. Only this one was shiny, whereas the other looked like it had been worn for years "Who else has one?"

"No one." Javier instinctually reached up to touch the circular logo. "I'm the only person that has this. I'm on my third one. But this one is silver, whereas the last two were cheaper. My jeweler in Boise made it. I actually own the brand too, if I ever go into ranching. Why do you ask? The sheriff asked about it too."

"Because one like it was found at the murder scene. Are you sure you didn't give it to Heather?"

"Why would I do that? I was breaking up with the girl. She was too clingy." Javier spat out the word like he'd just told her that Heather was a drug dealer or thief. He must have seen the look on Angie's face, because he started to backtrack. "I mean, she and I weren't going to work out. I cared for her, but I did not give her jewelry. I wouldn't do that unless I was thinking about committing to someone."

"How would it get there, then?"

Javier paused, thinking through the answer. "Heather must have taken it from my place the last time she stayed over. She was always getting into my things. That's one of the reasons we broke up. She was too nosy."

Angie wanted to tell him that his response sealed his title as the worse boyfriend ever, but she saw him glance up and a look of fear crossed his face. Then, it was gone and replaced with the calm, slightly calculating look he mostly wore.

She followed his gaze and Mrs. Potter stood at the table, staring pointedly at Javier.

"That's my seat, young man."

Javier popped up and pulled out the chair. "Just keeping it warm, ma'am."

She slipped into the chair and, without looking at him, said, "Thank you."

"Well, I better get back to my group. I'm sure he's ready to give me the bad news unless he has more to review on his list of disappointments I've caused in my lifetime." He nodded to Mrs. Potter and Angie. "Have a nice dinner, ladies."

As he walked away, Mrs. Potter took a sip of water, focusing her gaze on Angie. After touching a napkin to her lips, she cleared her throat. "That man is trouble. You should stay away from him."

"I'm not interested in dating Javier. Ian and I are doing fine." Angie started in on the salad the waitress had brought them as they settled in for dinner. "But I'm curious, what do you know about Javier?"

"Besides he's a cad? I've heard the women talk at church. More than one young, innocent thing has fallen for his charms only to have her heart broken sooner rather than later." She examined a crouton, then set it aside. "He's only interested in one thing. Sex. That poor girl must have gotten in his way to the next conquest."

Angie glanced over at the table where the older man was now shaking his finger at Javier. And the brother, he was grinning from ear to ear, watching the show. "No family love lost there."

"Between Javier and Stephen? Those boys have always been oil and water, or Cain and Abel, to use a biblical example, from the time Stephen was born and took the spotlight from his older brother." Mrs. Potter looked at Angie and laughed. "Dear, you don't get to be my age without hearing something about every person who lives or lived in River Vista. The Easterly family had a farm here in the valley years ago when Mr. Potter and I started our own place. The boys went to River Vista Elementary when I used to work in the office. They were always fighting."

Angie finished her salad as she listened to Mrs. Potter talk about her thoughts about the family. She hadn't expected to learn so much about Javier from her houseguest. Maybe she should talk to her more about the past. Sometimes, history gives perspective of what's going on now. But all she did know was she wanted to know more about Javier's brother Stephen. Could he have a reason to frame his brother?

By the time they were done with dinner, Mrs. Potter looked worn out, and Javier and his dinner guests were long gone. Driving home, Angie turned on the music at a low level, and before they got out of town and across the river, Mrs. Potter was snoring in the passenger seat. Angie smiled and focused on the road and Heather's death. Tomorrow she'd be busy in the kitchen running through the weekend's menu. She had Estebe coming in as well as Hope to give her some cooking time. Maybe she'd casually broach the subject of Stephen then.

As soon as they were home, she pulled out her calendar to check on her plans for tomorrow and remembered she had agreed to go to the volunteer breakfast for the festival. It was going to be a long day. Breakfast started at nine, and it was close to an hour drive to the site in old-town Boise. She was surprised that Estebe had agreed to come into work that afternoon, but maybe he'd just forgotten to tell her he couldn't come. She'd call in Matt for some hours if Estebe called off. Between him and Hope, they should be fine.

She knew the dry run wasn't really necessary, but she felt practice made perfect, and if there was going to be a problem with the menu, she'd rather find it before customers were waiting to eat.

Mrs. Potter had already gone to bed by the time Angie started turning lights off around the house. Having her around hadn't been that big a deal. Well, except for the fire thing. And the fact she'd destroyed the kitchen. Angie glanced around at the mess and just turned off the light. Dom looked at her as they made their way to the stairs. "It's just a week," she explained to the dog as they went to the bedroom. "Things will go back to normal around here as soon as Erica gets home."

Dom sank into his bed with a huff, apparently not agreeing with Angie's strategy of path of least resistance, but she was too tired to do anything else.

* * * *

Angie finally found a place to park two blocks away from the community center. If this was just the attendees for the volunteer breakfast, she'd hate to see how crowded it was going to be next weekend with the actual festival.

Matt called to her from across the street. She waited on the sidewalk for him to catch up. Jaywalking across the street, he grinned as he fell into step with Angie. "Hey, boss. I don't know if Estebe told you, but I'm your sous chef today. He said he'll be at work tomorrow, but he needed the day. Apparently, he's having family issues."

"I wondered if I needed to call you in." Angie shook her head. She should have realized that Estebe would have taken care of his replacement if he wasn't going to be able to show up. "I'm surprised he didn't call me, though."

"He said he did. Maybe it skipped his mind. I don't know about you, but if my cousin had killed someone, I'd be a mess." Matt held the door open for her.

She was going to ask him why he thought Javier had killed Heather, but the noise from the crowd of people made it impossible to talk. Matt took her arm and pointed toward the number 54 in the middle of a table near the back.

"I think we're over there." He took her hand and they weaved through the people standing, chatting, and in a few cases, hugging. The atmosphere was jovial, friendly, and, to Angie, felt like one big family.

The room quieted and everyone made their way to their assigned tables. Angie looked around to see what had clued the group into the program starting. At the front of the room, Javier's uncle stood behind a podium with Stephen by his side.

"Here we go," Matt whispered in her ear as they quickly found their seats. The anticipation in the room could be cut with a knife. The older man tapped on the microphone and started to speak.

Chapter 9

"Thank you all for coming this morning. Next week will be our twenty-fifth annual celebration. I'm Ander Diaz, but most of you call me Papa." Cheers came from the room as well as chants of "Papa" over and over. He waved the crowd down, and they quickly quieted. "I expect to have a big announcement at the end of the festival this year. I hope you will all support my decisions."

With that, he turned and walked away from the podium. Surprise covered the face of one woman, who apparently expected the talk to go longer. She was dressed in a bright red pantsuit, and she ran up to the empty microphone and pasted on a smile. Angie glanced at Matt, who seemed just as surprised as the rest of the people in the room.

"Well, now that Papa Diaz has given us his blessing for this lovely meal, I'd like to invite up Father Morin for the benediction before we eat. Oh, and the dancer troupe will be onstage as soon as we start serving, so enjoy your breakfast. And thank you all for your time and effort to make our festivals successful." She waved a man in a black suit with a white collar up to the podium and then stepped back.

"Clearly things aren't running as usual." Matt leaned toward her and whispered, "I think Papa typically takes a bit more time in the limelight."

Angie wondered if the meeting with Javier and Stephen last night had something to do with his clipped message. She looked around the table and realized she didn't know the people sitting with them.

Then Estebe sat next to her and smiled. "Good morning. I'm happy you made it."

"I'm so glad you invited us." Angie glanced around the room, decorated with flags and banners. "You guys go all out."

"Just wait until the dancers get onstage. You're going to love that." Estebe held a hand out to Matt. "Thank you for covering for me today." Matt shook his hand. "No problem, dude. I could use the extra hours." Estebe glanced at the other people at the table. "Hope and her family almost fill the chairs."

Angie glanced over and saw Hope waving at her from the other side of the table. She waved back and called over the din, "I didn't see you over there."

Hope stood and came around to Angie's side. "I think I was in the bathroom when you came in. Boy, that place is crowded. The dancers were all in there getting ready for their performance. I wish I had a hobby like that."

"When would you have time?" Matt shook his head. "If you're not working, you're in class. Hobbies are for people who aren't trying to build a career."

"I have hobbies," Angie stated. "I read and take care of my pets and garden. And I cook."

"You cook because it's your passion." Estebe said.

Hope hurried back to her seat as the servers set plates of sausages, eggs, and potato hash in front of them. A second server sat large glasses of juice in front of each place and then a woman filled their coffee cups and left two carafes on the table. "Enjoy," she called out before she left.

Angie put her napkin on her plate. "This is amazing. I don't know if I can eat all this."

"Make sure to save some room for dessert. It's a huckleberry cobbler." Estebe focused on his own plate. "Tell me if the sausage is too spicy. I made it yesterday."

Matt held up a slice. "Man, this is amazing. You're a sausage god."

"I'm pleased you like it." Estebe blushed at Matt's praise. The group ate with a few comments here and there, especially when the dancers came on the stage.

Angie felt a sensory overload with the smells, the tastes, and the colors flying by her. If this was just a prelude to the actual festival, she was going to drag Felicia down here at least one day while it was happening.

After the cobbler came, with vanilla ice cream on top that Estebe had failed to mention, Angie groaned. "I'm stuffed. But there's no way I'm letting this go to waste. It's so good."

"My mother's recipe." Estebe smiled. "I would share it with you, but she insists it has to stay in the family."

"Challenge accepted. I'll have to find some huckleberries and start experimenting. This would be a lovely dessert for the County Seat." Angie closed her mind and let the tastes explode in her mouth, trying to separate each flavor out to the ingredient.

"That's our boss, always looking for the next menu selection." Matt stood up. "I've got to go run some errands before work. I'll see you later."

"I need to get back to the kitchen as well." Estebe smiled at her. "They haven't adopted your 'I cook, you clean' motto yet. I'll see you on Friday."

Hope and her family left soon after, and Angie realized she was alone at the table. She was about to stand and leave when an older woman plopped down in the chair that Estebe had vacated.

"Are you having a good time?" the woman asked, pushing Estebe's dish away from her and toward the middle of the table.

"It was lovely. I was just about to head out, though. Work calls." Angie started to stand, but the woman put a hand on her arm.

"Sit, talk to me a while." She held Angie's gaze until she sank back into the chair. "That's better. Let me introduce myself. I'm Carlotta Mendoza."

"Nice to meet you. Angie…"

"Turner, I know. You're Estebe's boss at that new place in River Vista." Carlotta's eyes twinkled. "The boy talks about you all the time. I believe he has a crush on you."

"Oh, no, we're just friends." Angie didn't want any rumors to get started.

But it was like Carlotta didn't even hear her response. "And Javier, he seems to think you can get him out of this mess he's gotten into. Are you a private investigator as well as a chef?"

"No, just a chef, I'm afraid." Angie studied the woman's face carefully. She acted friendly, but something underneath gave Angie the chills. She was definitely not saying something that she wanted Angie to hear.

"A chef should stay in her own kitchen. It's a dangerous world out there. Just look at what happened to poor Heather." Carlotta's eyes narrowed.

Angie felt a stab of fear but didn't understand why this total stranger was making her feel that way. She gripped her chair, looking for a way out, but as she was planning, a young woman came up to the table.

"Mother, there you are. Stephen went to get the car. He sent me to come find you." She looked over at Angie. "Oh, you're Estebe's friend. He's told us all about you and that restaurant of yours. Stephen and I have reservations for mid-August after this whole festival is done. We'll be ready for some downtime. I'm Kendra."

Angie took the chance and stood, moving away from Carlotta, and held her hand out to greet Kendra. "Nice to meet you."

"Silly, we don't shake hands here, especially with close friends." Kendra pulled her into a hug. "So very nice to meet you. I'm looking forward to finding out all about you soon. We should do lunch."

"Kendra, let's go." Stephen stood by the door and waved her toward it. He looked calm, cool, and smug. Javier had already disappeared from the room.

"He's always so busy. Run, run, run." Kendra held a hand up to help her mother out of the chair and they started toward the door. Kendra called over her shoulder, "See you soon, Angie."

Carlotta didn't say anything, but she turned and stared at Angie as they left the room.

"That was weird." A young woman stood next to her, clearing plates off the table. "Mrs. Mendoza isn't friendly with most people, but she sure doesn't like you. What did you do, take one of the prizes she set up for her precious daughter?"

"I never met her before." Angie shook her head and headed back to her car. Her thoughts kept going back to the conversation with Carlotta. When she got back to River Vista, she headed straight for the County Seat. Time to cook. Cooking made sense.

Hope was sitting on the steps when she arrived. Angie quickly locked up the car and headed to the back door with her keys jangling in her hand. "Hey, why didn't you ring up Felicia's apartment and have her let you in?"

"That's all right. I haven't been here long, and it was too nice a day to wait in my car." Hope stood to let Angie pass by her.

Angie turned as she slipped the key into the lock. Hope was staring down the alley toward the Red Eye. When she caught Angie looking at her, she pointed. "That's where Heather died?"

"Yes." Angie put her purse on the floor to keep the door from closing all the way and then walked over to where Hope stood. "I'm sorry about your loss."

"It's not like we were real close." Hope sniffed as she wiped a stray tear off her cheek. "I don't know why it's affecting me so hard."

"Maybe because you relate to her and it scares you." Angie watched Hope's face, wondering if she'd been too direct for the young woman.

Hope shrugged. "Maybe. All she wanted was to be loved. Is that a crime?"

"No, no, it's not."

They stood there in silence, staring down the alleyway for a few minutes. Hope was the first to break the silence. "We came to cook. I guess we better get busy."

"I find cooking eases the questions in my head. It's pure. No one's going to get between you and the food." Angie followed her inside.

"You make cooking sound like a prayer."

Angie shrugged. "Maybe that's what it's made for. To bring peace to the hands that prepared the food and nourish the ones who eat the food."

"My grandfather used to say something like that before dinner prayers every Sunday." Hope smiled at the memory. "He's been gone three years, and I still see him at the head of the table. Good memories can help during times like this. I'm going to just think of the good times I had with Heather."

"Sounds like a plan." Angie flipped the lights on in the kitchen. "Now let's cook."

Matt soon joined them, and the three of them made the entire weekend menu. It helped Angie see where the roadblocks to quality service would show up and if the recipes were detailed enough for anyone to replicate. It was her version of a dress rehearsal. When they were done, Angie smiled at the spread sitting at the chef table. "Let's go check these amazeballs recipes and talk about what worked and what didn't. We need to know now, so we can get it fixed before time for service."

They were discussing the main course dishes when Felicia and Sheriff Brown walked into the kitchen.

"Uh-oh, the man is here." Mark held up his hands in fake surrender. "I give up. Don't shoot me."

"Matt, you don't need to be rude." Angie shook her head. "Sorry, Sheriff."

"I'm not being rude, that's my funny side." Matt took a bite of the chicken dish. "But I'm sorry too, it was probably in bad taste."

"You're lucky I'm too busy to run your name, young man." Sheriff Brown winked at her, then nodded toward Angie's office. "Can we talk in private?"

"Sure." Angie follow him into her office, then closed the door. "What's going on?"

"When was the last time you saw Javier?" He eased himself onto the couch in her office.

"I don't remember seeing him at the festival breakfast, but I saw him last night when I took Mrs. Potter to the restaurant in Murphy. He was there with his uncle and brother. Why?"

"Javier is missing."

Chapter 10

"What do you mean, *missing*?" Angie couldn't wrap herself around what the Sheriff was saying. She sank back down into her chair. "Like kidnapped?"

"Like he was supposed to attend a meeting this afternoon and he didn't show up. He's not at the farm. People haven't seen him since this morning." Sheriff Brown leaned his head back and sighed. "I'm hoping he's just hiding somewhere trying to get past this whole thing with Heather and the loss of status in his family."

"But he could have been kidnapped." Angie thought about their conversation. "He didn't seem really upset last night. Sad maybe, but not suicidal."

"Now, that's one alternative I don't want to leave this room. I'd rather you telling everyone he was kidnapped, although I think the chances of that are slim to none."

"Why don't you think he was kidnapped?"

"No ransom note. And Javier's family doesn't have money. Although it could be an old lover gone crazy." Sheriff Brown took out his pen and wrote some notes. "What time did you talk last night?"

"About six? Mrs. Potter likes to eat early, so we left the house a little after five, and with the drive, it would have been six before we were seated." Angie glanced at her phone. "Did you try Estebe? Maybe Javier's just over there sulking."

"I've tried everyone in that family." The sheriff lumbered out of the couch and onto his feet. "Well, I guess we'll talk later. Do me a favor and stay out of this investigation. There's something off about the whole thing."

"Why do you think I'm investigating?" Angie tried for a sweet and innocent look. From the laugh she got from the sheriff, she must have missed the mark.

"Seriously?"

She shrugged, not able to meet his steady gaze. "Let's just say I'll be careful."

"I guess I'll have to take that. For now." He tucked his notebook into the pocket on his shirt. "Call me if he shows up here."

Matt and Hope still sat at the table, although it looked a little off-kilter, like they'd just gotten back to their seats when Sheriff Brown opened the door. She couldn't blame them for eavesdropping. She would have done the same thing, but she would have been more careful about being discovered afterward. She shook her head and followed the sheriff out of the building toward the front where he'd parked his car.

She stood watching the empty street for several minutes after the police car pulled away from the curb. First Heather was stabbed in the alley on the same block as the County Seat. And now, Javier, the sheriff's best suspect, was missing. River Vista was turning out to have a darker side, more than the sleepy farming community portrayed.

"I didn't take you for a smoker." Barb Travis leaned against the brick wall of the building, watching her. She flicked the ashes of the long, thin cigarette she was smoking.

Angie moved down the stairs to stand near her. "I'm not."

"Don't know why anyone would hang out in this disgusting alley if they didn't need a drag." She nodded toward where Sheriff Brown's police car had been parked. "You got trouble in there?"

Angie followed her gaze and realized what Barb was asking. "No. He just came by to see if I'd heard from Javier." She narrowed her eyes at her. "He's not sitting, drinking in your bar, is he?"

Barb cracked a smile. "Not at the moment. You're telling me he's missing?"

"*Currently unaccounted for* is a more precise term. I guess he missed a meeting and his family is worried."

"If I was that guy, I'd get in my car and keep driving until I hit the border. He should be able to cross into Mexico before the APB hits." She took another drag off her cigarette. "I never knew what women saw in him. He was always too cocky for my taste. Anyway, I remembered something."

Angie was taken back at the quick change of topic. "About?"

"Heather. You ran off to play that prank on the firefighter guys, and after you left, I remembered something about that night."

"I didn't..." Angie sighed and let it go. "Sorry, what were you saying?"

"Heather had some guy chatting her up after Javier left." She crushed out her cigarette with her foot on the cracked asphalt. She turned to go.

"Wait, who? Did you tell Sheriff Brown this?" Angie stepped around Barb, blocking her movement. "What did he look like?"

"You know I probably had over a hundred people in there that night. And only two bartenders, three including me. You think I have time to check out every cowboy?"

"Felicia says you know everyone who comes in." This was almost as frustrating as talking to Mrs. Potter. Angie leaned against the building, trying to mirror Barb's stance. "What do you remember?"

"Your friend is sweet, but my memory isn't as good as it used to be. But, okay, so maybe I did check this one out a little more. Heather was a good kid. She didn't deserve a second jerk in her life." Barb pulled out another cigarette and lit it as she thought. "He was tall. Good looking and he knew it. Wasn't a real cowboy, just a wannabe from town."

"Why do you say that?"

Barb coughed and Angie wondered if the second cigarette was really a good idea. Not her life, she pushed the worry away with a quick closing of her eyes.

"His boots were brand new. Not an ounce of dirt or cow manure on the outside. You can't really work in a pair of boots without getting something on them."

Angie wished she had a piece of paper handy, but she knew if she stopped Barb's story to run and get one, Barb would be gone back to her bar and she might not be able to get her talking again. "Did you get hair color or eye color? What about a name?"

"I took a copy of the credit card he used to pay for his drinks. We do that on all tabs from non-regulars since a guy stiffed us for over five hundred dollars." She pulled a piece of paper out of her bra and handed it to Angie. "I'd rather give this to you than that old fart Brown. He's not real happy about having my business here in town."

"Most towns have a bar in them. He has to realize that, right?" Angie took the paper and unfolded it. "Jerry Reno, it sounds like a stage name."

"It does, doesn't it." Barb smiled and crushed out her half-smoked cigarette. "I've got to go back inside. It's inventory day. They don't like to move and open all the boxes if I'm not there to watch."

Angie watched her neighbor saunter down the alley. Even at her age, Barb still had moves that could make a man shiver. She definitely didn't like Sheriff Brown. Angie went back inside to finish the menu and send it to the printer. Tomorrow morning they'd have all new cream-colored menus on thick paper. She just hoped Estebe wouldn't go looking for his cousin, leaving her down a sous chef.

She was about to call the police station with Barb's information when her cell buzzed. It was her home number. Part of her didn't want to even think about answering the call, but she did.

"Hello, Mrs. Potter. What's going on?"

"Oh, Angie, I don't know how it happened, but you need to come home quickly." Mrs. Potter's voice wavered.

"I'm on my way. What happened? Is Dom all right? Mabel? What about Precious?" Angie rapid fired questions as she grabbed her purse and headed toward the back door and her car.

"It's all my fault. Please come and help."

At that the phone went dead. Angie considered calling Sheriff Brown and asking him to meet her at the house, but she figured having one false alarm in a week was probably her quota. She kept it close to the speed limit, but even with clear roads, it took more than twenty minutes to get home.

The house didn't look like it was on fire when she pulled into the driveway. As a precaution, she thought about where her fire extinguishers were in the kitchen. She burst through the door and took a step into the house, and water splashed on her sandals.

She looked down at the floor. "Water? Where's the water coming from?" She grabbed dish towels from the third drawer and threw them on the floor. "Mrs. Potter? Where are you?"

"I'm in the laundry room. I'm so sorry. I just wanted to help."

Angie made her way through the kitchen and into the mudroom. A stream of water was coming out of the water hookups for the washer. Mrs. Potter was fiddling with the controls. Angie reached over her, turned off both faucets, and the water stream stopped.

Mrs. Potter pushed her hair out of her eyes. "How did you get it stopped?"

"I turned off the supply. It looks like one of the hoses came loose. Were you doing laundry?" Angie grabbed a stack of towels she kept in the mudroom for Dom and started sopping up the water.

"I put Dom's bed in to wash. I was only trying to help. Then I must have fallen asleep when I was watching my show, and a large banging noise woke me."

Angie put the wet towels in the sink and grabbed a mop. It wasn't as bad as she'd thought when she'd walked in, as long as she could get the water up fast. She'd tiled both rooms when she'd remodeled, and the living room had a step up between it and the kitchen, so the water had stayed on the tile. Dom licked some of the water off the floor.

"Dom, go on outside." She opened the door for him and then closed off the doggie door. She didn't need him getting sick from laundry soap or bleach. River Vista's veterinarian had recently closed up shop—involuntarily. "Mrs. Potter. Go upstairs and get more towels out of my linen closet by the bathroom. We need to get this cleaned up, and it will be faster using towels than this mop."

An hour later, the house was dry again. Angie reconnected the hose and got Dom's bed to spin evenly by adding weight to the other side of the basket. Then she put the bed into the dryer and hoped it would be close to being dry before tomorrow. Dom liked taking his naps in the kitchen.

Glancing at the clock, Angie swore and went outside to feed Precious and Mabel. When the black-and-white hen gave her a disapproving stare, Angie laughed. "Sorry dinner's late, but we had a bit of a disaster in the house."

The hen turned her back on Angie and settled into a nest she'd built with straw on the floor. Precious, on the other hand, didn't care when or if she was fed as long as Angie spent some time with her before her meal. Angie stroked the goat's fine coat and felt her heart beat slow. "Just a few more days and we'll have our lives back."

Precious bleated and gently butted her head against Angie's in a sign of comfort. Angie gave the goat one more rub on the top of her head and stood. Tomorrow was going to be a busy day. The County Seat was booked solid this weekend. Angie just hoped she had her sous chef working beside her.

* * * *

As they prepped the kitchen on Friday afternoon, Estebe's absence cast a gloom over the room. Hope came over to where Angie was working on prepping the trout for tonight's dinners. "Thanks for calling me in early today. I really appreciate the hours."

"No problem. I'm glad you could step in. Estebe should be here before we open." At least she hoped he would. When he'd called, the family was still searching in vain for Javier, and Estebe had been charged with driving up to the family cabin in McCall to make sure he wasn't there. "Are you doing all right with the prep? Do you have any questions?"

"Nancy has been showing me the knife cuts, so I'm good. I just wanted to tell you how much I enjoy working here. I've been a dishwasher at places before, but that's all they let me do. And the cooks there wouldn't even talk to me about what they were making. It was like it was some big secret." She smiled. "My instructors are going to be amazed when classes start up next month. I think I've learned more the last couple of months than all last year in school."

"I'm just glad you're willing to jump in. We're a team and you're a big part of it." Angie glanced around the kitchen. "Looks like we're in a good place. You want to take a break and grab some iced tea with me?"

"Sure." Hope helped her store the trout in the walk-in and then went to the drink station to fill a pitcher with iced tea.

Nancy and Matt finished up their projects and joined them at the chef table. As Angie poured the tea, Nancy pulled out a pan of brownies she'd baked for service, dishing up the treat and then throwing some whipped cream on top. "Tell me if you think I should make ice cream instead."

The chocolate brownie was thick and delicious, and the cream cut the chocolate taste perfectly. Angie moaned a bit after the first bite. "I'm so glad I hired you. I'm good with desserts, but you're amazing."

"I'm thinking about making a raspberry syrup to go around the edge of the plate. Pamplona Farms dropped us a flat of berries on the house since they were a little late with our order this morning." Nancy focused on cutting another bite from her brownie. "I take it Javier's still missing?"

"I told her about what Sheriff Brown said yesterday." Matt jumped in. "Sorry, but we could hear everything. You probably need to soundproof your office."

Angie looked at her team and saw the worry in their faces. "Look, I know you are all concerned about Estebe, but there's nothing we can do to find Javier or figure out who killed Heather. We're chefs and we have a dining room filled with people to serve tonight."

Hope raised her hand. "Actually, I was going to ask you about something. I didn't realize I had any text messages until this morning and, well, I don't want to get into trouble."

"Wait. A text from who?"

"Heather. She must have texted from the bar. Actually, I have several from that night. She was so steamed. Three messages where she tells me over and over what a butt Javier is and what she's going to do to him and his house." Hope shrugged. "I'm sure she wouldn't have really burned the place down, but the girl was mad."

"Would have served him right." Nancy broke into the conversation. "I swear, horndogs like that seem to get away with being a jerk, and the girls are the ones that have to repair their broken hearts."

Matt put his hand over his own heart. "I can testify there are plenty of women out there who are good at breaking hearts too."

"You're both right." Angie held up her hands, blocking off the argument. "When it comes to love, everyone's vulnerable."

"That's why this is so sad. Her last text that night was about this new guy. She said he was perfect and she was going to show Javier that someone loved her." Hope pulled her phone out of her pocket and scrolled to the picture. "He was a cutie."

Angie took the phone and glanced at the guy. This must have been the man Barb had seen talking to Heather that night. She gave the phone back to Hope. "Can you send me that picture? And I think you should go see Sheriff Brown and tell him about the texts. Maybe you could run by the police station before service starts?"

Hope's eyes widened. She took the phone back and quickly sent Angie the picture. "Do you think it's important? Could he have killed her?"

"Probably not, but I'm sure Sheriff Brown would like to talk to him about that night." She glanced at the clock—almost four. "Why don't you go over to the police station now and see if he's in. That way it's done before service because until Estebe shows up, we might be having you on the line instead of washing dishes."

"Really?" Hope stood up and giggled. "Then I hope he's delayed on the road. I'd love to work the line for at least a little while. I'll be right back."

Nancy stared at Angie. She waited for Hope to leave the kitchen, then said, "You realize once you let her on the line, she's going to be hard to get back doing dishes."

"Yeah, I know. But I have a feeling she's ready for the next step. I guess I better ask Felicia to hire us a new dishwasher to start up next month." Angie pressed her lips together. "Unless the school won't let her."

"They want their students working. It makes it easier for them to teach someone who's motivated by a salary." Nancy stood. "I'm grabbing a smoke and then I'll be back. Thanks for being a good boss, Angie. It's a pleasure working in your kitchen."

Matt followed Nancy out the back door, reminding Angie of Dom and his insistence on being wherever she was. If Angie was right, Matt had it bad for his coworker.

Alone in the kitchen, Angie studied the picture Hope had sent her. Could this be the face of a killer? The guy looked like he spent his mornings playing polo and his evenings drinking gin and tonics. Not the typical patron of the Red Eye. No wonder Barb had been suspicious and Heather in over her head.

Felicia sat next to her and poured herself a glass of tea. While she dished up a brownie, she glanced down at the picture. "You thinking about getting tickets? I'd love to go with you."

Angie frowned. "Tickets? For what?"

"For *Our Town*. I know it's an old play, but Boise's not going to be getting *Hamilton* any time soon." She piled on the whipped cream, took a bite, and groaned. "I am so glad Nancy works here. Although she makes me go to the gym every weekday since I can't resist her desserts. I'd rather run them off than deny myself."

"What are you talking about?" Angie shook her head when Felicia held out a fork filled with the chocolate delight. "No, before you went all gooey eyed about the brownie. Why do you think I'm looking at going to a play?"

Stuffing the bite into her mouth, she tapped on the picture showing on Angie's phone. "Him," she said between swallows. "That's the guy playing the lead. I saw it in today's paper. It's front page on the entertainment section. I guess locally, he's kind of a big deal."

"He's an actor." Angie tried to remember the name Barb had given her. "Jerry Reno? That's the guy's name."

Felicia shook her head. "I'm certain it was Thomas something. Hold on, I have the paper in the front."

Angie waited, her stomach rolling. She pushed away the brownie. No way would she be able to eat. Not if she'd already found out who Heather had spent her last hours with. She was so glad she'd stayed behind when Hope went to talk to Sheriff Brown, but now she thought she should call with the new information at least.

"Here. His name is Thomas Post." Felicia pointed to the picture of the smiling Thomas-slash-Jerry with a caption under his photo. "He's a big shot in the local theater community and even owns the place downtown where they have a dinner theater five times a year."

"Thomas Post used a Jerry Reno credit card last Friday night at the Red Eye." She glanced at her friend. "Have you seen him in there?"

"No, and I would have remembered. The guys who frequent the Red Eye are nice, but not amazingly handsome like this guy. Even if he was with someone, I would have noticed him." Felicia grinned. "I have an eye for handsome men. What can I say, it's a weakness."

"I'm running over to the police station." Angie picked up the paper. "I'll be back in time to start service."

"What did you find?" Felicia called after her. "Tell me."

She couldn't stop to chat; she just needed Sheriff Brown to have this piece of the puzzle as soon as possible. Once Heather's killer was found, she'd get her sous chef back and not have to worry about him. At least that was the plan.

Chapter 11

"You can't have my phone. What am I supposed to do without it? It has all my contacts." Hope banged her fist on the counter in front of the police receptionist. "This is just bureaucratic nonsense. Give it back and I'll forward you the texts."

"Miss, I'm sorry, but that would break chain of evidence. We appreciate your cooperation, and as soon as the investigation is over, your property will be returned." He handed her a receipt. "Just come back with that in about sixty days…"

"Sixty days? Are you nuts?" Hope turned and saw Angie standing behind her. She'd come into the small lobby about five minutes earlier, but both Hope and the police officer had been too busy to notice. "Angie, you have to tell them. I can't be without my phone that long. I'll go nuts. And I can't afford to buy a new one."

Angie put her hand on Hope's shoulder. "We'll get you a second phone for as long as you need it. This was my fault. I sent you down here to talk to Sheriff Brown." She focused on the officer. "Where is the sheriff?"

"He's already gone home for the night. It's his anniversary, so he left on time for once." The man crossed his arms. "I'm not calling him in for a few texts. He can see this first thing in the morning."

"Well, when he does, give him this too." Angie handed him the newspaper along with the copy of the credit card that Barb had given her. "Your man in that picture was going by an assumed name and probably knows more than any of us about what happened to Heather. But I'm sure the sheriff won't be upset if he decides to bolt overnight."

The officer sighed and picked up the phone. "His wife is going to kill him and probably me for making this call. I'm still not giving back the phone. You both can leave the station, and thank you for your cooperation."

When they got outside, Angie realized Hope was crying. "It's okay, it's only a phone. I'll pay for a second line to your account and you should be able to transfer all your contacts over."

"You don't have to pay for it. I'll find a way." Hope sniffed as they walked up the street back toward the County Seat.

Angie shook her head. "No, I'm the one who sent you down to talk to Sheriff Brown. Go down and get a new phone and I'll pay the cost. Just bring me the receipt."

Hope paused as she opened the door to the restaurant. "I could probably do without a phone until they return it."

"And how am I supposed to get a hold of you if I need you to work another shift?" Angie shook her head. "That just won't do. We have customers to think about."

"I'll make it as cheap as possible." Hope hugged Angie tight. "Thank you so much."

"Get the phone you need. I don't want you to not be able to be online twenty-four-seven." Angie stopped at the hostess station where Felicia was standing, watching them. "Go ask Nancy what she needs help with. I need to talk to Felicia."

"Sure thing, boss."

As Hope disappeared into the kitchen, Felicia leaned on the wooden podium. "Do I want to know what we just bought her?"

"Just a phone. That uptight receptionist took hers into evidence and wouldn't give it back. She needs something so we can get a hold of her." Angie squirmed a little under Felicia's unwavering gaze. "I probably should have asked you first."

"No need. We both have a little bit of a slush fund when it comes to employee benefits. I would say this situation fits." Felicia held out the reservation list. "I wanted you to see this."

Angie glanced at the paper. Every slot was filled, with a list of names and numbers at the bottom. "We're fully booked? After only a month in business?"

"Well, yes, I thought you knew that." She pointed a pen at a name at the end of the page. "I wanted you to see *this*."

Angie read the name. "Ander Diaz? Papa Diaz is coming here to eat tonight?"

"A party of one. Which is weird. From what I've heard about the old man, he typically has an entourage of people with him." Felicia shrugged when Angie gave her a pointed look. "What, you're the only one who can poke their nose into other people's business?"

She ignored the barb. "Maybe he's coming to see how Estebe is doing?" The door opened behind her. "Who knows, but for now, it's showtime." Felicia put on a wide smile and greeted the new arrivals. "Good evening. Do you have a reservation?"

Angie quickly walked away and said a silent prayer, hoping that Estebe would be in the kitchen when she opened the door. Maybe if she wished hard enough, he'd appear. She let out a disappointed sigh when the sous chef wasn't behind the large cookstove. "First guests are in the house. Are we ready for service?"

A trio of "Yes, chef" filled the kitchen, making Angie smile. Especially when she saw the grin on Hope's face. They could get by for a few hours without Estebe, but with the place fully booked, sooner or later the inexperience of the girl would start to show.

Angie had just expedited another eight-top when the back door flew open. Estebe hurried through the door, pulling on his chef coat as he walked. She glanced at the clock. Just a little after seven. "Thanks for gracing us with your presence."

"I told Felicia I was going to be late. Is that not enough?" He took his normal spot on the cook line and glanced at Nancy, who stepped aside. "What are you working on?"

Nancy ran him through the dishes in progress as a new ticket spat out from the automated ordering system.

"Two-top, strawberry salad and a bowl of Famous Idaho Soup." Angie read off the appetizers and got a solid "Yes, chef" in return. She turned to Estebe and lowered her voice. "Everything all right? Did you find him?"

The grief in his eyes when he looked at her answered both questions. Estebe was most definitely *not* all right, and Javier hadn't been found. "It's hard on the family. His mother is emotional." He cleared his throat. "But I am here to work, not talk about my troubles. Thank you for your concern."

"Just let me know if you need anything. I know you're off next week, but if you need to have tomorrow too..."

Before she could finish the question, he shook his head. "No. I will be at work tomorrow and on time. I apologize for my tardiness today. Now I must focus on these entrées."

Angie knew she'd been shut down. He didn't want to talk about what was going on, so she'd honor that. Besides, she had enough people who did want to talk to her about Javier and Heather. Estebe was a grieving family member, not a source. She needed to help Sheriff Brown find Heather's killer so Javier would come home and just be a thorn in Estebe's side again. Now it looked like his cousin was carving a hole in his heart.

The service was flowing nicely even with Hope popping back and forth from the dishwashing station as Estebe called her to watch him cook a steak or the trout. She kept a notebook in her pocket and wrote down everything he said. Angie had seen her studying the notebook before, but she'd thought it was for school, not learning the restaurant's recipes.

Angie's cell phone buzzed, and when she looked at the display, she saw Ian's number. A smile curved her lips as she stepped away from the expediting station and took the call.

"Hey, stranger. What are you doing?"

He chuckled. "Actually, I'm picking up my date for dinner."

"Excuse me?" Angie's eyebrows rose even though she knew he couldn't see her expression.

"I'm taking Mrs. Potter out to grab a bite, so you don't have to worry about her. We have plans for tomorrow night too."

"Thank God. I was afraid she'd try to cook and burn the house down. And this time, the fire department wouldn't come." Angie straightened a stack of menus sitting on the chef table. "That was thoughtful. Thank you."

"I am a very thoughtful man. Besides, Rob told me about the false alarm fire run. He was all excited since they beat their earlier record of getting out to the house by three minutes. I guess your grandmother had them on speed dial for her last caretaker. The woman couldn't cook a piece of toast without burning it."

At the mention of Nona's caretaker, Angie felt her heart twinge. "I should have been there for her."

"You were busy building a life. She knew that." Ian's tone softened. "I shouldn't have brought it up. I called you to make you happy, not sad."

"You didn't make me sad. Okay, maybe just a little. It's been a stressful week. I don't know how Erica does it." Angie watched the dance of servers and chefs in the kitchen as she talked. This was what she'd always wanted, and Nona had supported her dreams. "It's just regrets that won't ever go away. I know she loved me. That's not the issue. You never think they are going to leave as soon as they do."

"Do you need me to come give you a hug?" Ian offered.

"Go have dinner. You're doing something better than giving me a hug. You're taking care of Mrs. Potter." She paused a minute. "I really am grateful you jumped in on this. You're pretty special."

"And don't you forget it. Oh, by the way, I've already fed the zoo, so don't let Dom guilt you into another dinner when you get home."

"Thanks." A server was standing at the expediting section looking at the plates that had come up from the cook line. "I've got to get going. We still on for Tuesday?"

"I'll be there bright and early to pick you up for breakfast. Take care." She hung up the phone and then hurried to the station. "What table?" The server jumped back, surprised at Angie's appearance. Apparently, she hadn't seen her standing to the side. She lowered her voice as she glanced at Estebe on the other side of the kitchen. "Fourteen. It's Papa Diaz. And he's asked to speak with you."

"Was something wrong with his appetizer?" Angie found the ticket and handed the server the plate.

"No, ma'am. He ate all of it and said it was wonderful. Then he asked for you specifically." She placed the plate on a tray and held it over her shoulder. "Should I tell him you're busy?"

"No, I'll follow you out. Easier to deal with things now than let them pile up." Besides, Angie was curious why the Basque community patriarch was asking for her and not Estebe. She paused at the kitchen door. "Going to do the dog-and-pony meet and greet. Be back in a few minutes. Estebe, can you expedite for me?"

She saw him nod, then heard the response. "Yes, chef." She knew it was more out of habit or respect for the kitchen, but she appreciated his willingness to help build a well-running team.

She waited for the server to finish dropping off the food, then stood next to Papa's table. "Mr. Diaz, I'm so honored you chose to dine with us tonight. Is everything satisfactory? Iris said you wanted to speak with me."

He waved his fork at her. "Sit down. You've probably been standing all day."

She pulled out the chair and sat across from him. From across the room, she saw the question on Felicia's face, but she ignored it, focusing instead on Ander Diaz. The man filled out his suit with a few extra pounds. His large face was ruddy and his jowls hung down almost to his neck. A shock of white hair topped his head, but his deep blue eyes were sharp. "Thank you. What can I do for you?"

"Straight to the point. I like that in a woman. My wife is the direct sort as well. She doesn't let me get away with much." He took a sip of wine, watching her.

"I hope you bring her next time you come to the County Seat. Was she busy tonight?" Angie figured she knew the answer. Tonight was business, not pleasure. She just didn't know what kind of business this powerful man could have with her.

"I will bring her the next time." A small smile curved his lips. "You are sharp too. So I guess I'll stop trying to figure you out and just ask what I want to know."

She made a point of looking at her watch. "I think that would be best for both of us since I still have a full dining room to feed."

He sat back, wiping his mouth with a white cloth napkin. "I want to know what you've found out about that unfortunate girl's death."

Shock hit Angie full force. How had he even known she'd been looking into Heather's death? "I think you have me confused, I'm a chef, not a police officer."

He laughed then, full and loud, but the sound was not unkind. "Oh, my dear, you are far more than a chef. I know you're investigating because I have ears and eyes everywhere. And before you wonder, Estebe didn't tell me." He took another sip of his wine. "Although he does harbor kind feelings for you. I'm sure he thinks you can do anything."

"Estebe is a good chef and a valuable asset to our team." Angie narrowed her eyes. "Why do you want to know about Heather's death? Do you think Javier could have anything to do with it?"

"Now, see, that's why you have the reputation you do. You're direct and don't worry about anyone's feelings." He held up a hand as Angie started to respond. "Don't take that as a negative. It makes you good at this. To answer your question, no, I don't think Javier could have done this. But unfortunately, there's the matter of the missing knife."

"What missing knife?" Angie leaned forward, lowering her voice.

The smile widened. "Oh, so the sheriff doesn't share everything with you. I wondered."

"He doesn't share anything. What missing knife?"

In answer, Ander pulled out his phone. He scrolled through some pictures and then handed the phone to Angie. "That is rumored to be the knife of my great-grandfather, the first Basque sheepherder in the Treasure Valley. He is said to have had it made in France and only used it during Festival to prepare the meat for the meal. Of course, now we don't use a ceremonial knife in our kitchens. We are bound by health department standards. My great-grandfather would have used that knife for everything, including killing rattlesnakes that got near the sheep."

Angie stared at the stained blade and ivory shaft. A delicate carving of a house was at the bottom of the knife. "When did it go missing?"

"Now, that I'm not sure of. I store the knife in my home, waiting for Festival time, and then display it as part of a collection in the community center. When I went to get it on Saturday, it was gone."

"And Sheriff Brown thinks it's the murder weapon?" Angie handed him back his phone.

Anders put it away in his coat pocket and sipped more wine. "That's what he's telling me. But I don't know how he found out the knife was missing."

"Sounds like someone is feeding him information." Angie looked up into Ander's calculating gaze. "Wait, you thought it was me? I didn't even know about the knife."

"I wasn't sure how much of our culture Estebe had shared with you. He can be very prideful of our culture and traditions." Ander shook his head. "But I see you are different than what I thought you might be. You are strong and a good friend to our Estebe. I hope you will become my friend as well."

He picked up his fork and began eating. Angie knew she'd been dismissed. She stood and touched the table. "Enjoy your meal."

Then she hurried back to the kitchen, ignoring Felicia as she passed into the kitchen. She stepped up to the expediting station next to Estebe and took a ticket off the machine. "Where are we?"

Estebe stepped aside and updated her on the tickets. For the rest of the night, the kitchen team worked on completing service. At the end of the night, Estebe waited for everyone to leave and then walked over to Angie with a beer in one hand and a bottle of water in the other. "Which one?"

Angie grabbed the water and used a towel to wipe the sweat off her brow. She cracked the bottle open, then drank half of it while Estebe replaced the beer and got his own water. He sat down across from her, studying her face. "You look concerned. Is the kitchen staff not living up to your expectations? I could do a training and try to make them faster."

"No." She shook her head at his devastated look. "It's not the kitchen team. We're doing awesome. I'm just tired. Besides, I should be asking how you are. You have had quite a week."

"Javier has made his family's life hard. I am trying to help out. That's all." He folded his hands on the table in front of her. "Iris told me you were talking to Papa Diaz. Can you tell me what he wanted?"

"Nothing really. He's under the impression that I'm investigating Heather's murder with the full force and confidence of the police department behind me." She laughed. "I think he was a little disappointed to find out I'm only a chef."

"You are not only a chef. You are a smart, capable woman who likes to solve puzzles. Why wouldn't you be curious about Javier's involvement in poor Heather's death? He was not as nice to her as he should have been." Now he uncapped his water bottle and took a sip. "Javier has always been a problem. He does what he wants. I'm afraid for the first time in his life, he doesn't know how to charm his way out of this."

"I don't think he killed Heather."

Estebe stood and drained the water bottle in three gulps. When he was finished, he spoke. "Sometimes it doesn't matter what the truth is, all that matters is what the police can prove."

Chapter 12

"Your young man is quite the storyteller." Mrs. Potter sat at the kitchen table Saturday morning sipping her coffee. "He has done so many interesting things."

Angie sat a mushroom-and-swiss omelet in front of her houseguest. "Tell me about them. Ian and I don't talk about the past much." In fact, they didn't talk much at all, at least not the last few weeks. Either he was swamped with work, or she was. Owning your own business was supposed to give you freedom, but really, all it did was make you work even harder.

She listened as Mrs. Potter gave her a blow by blow of the entire evening. As she was finishing, her phone buzzed with a text. She read it with a laugh. "Speak of the devil. He said to tell you he'd be by at six to pick you up for dinner."

"I don't know if I should go out with him again. I mean, the boy may get ideas." Mrs. Potter cackled with glee. "Gotcha. You should have seen your face."

Angie's phone rang and she picked it up, thinking it was Ian. "Why are you calling me?"

"Because I wanted to talk to my grandmother?" Erica's voice held a touch of humor and a touch of annoyance. "Is she around?"

"Oh, Erica, I thought you were…never mind. Of course she's here. Every morning she's tied to the kitchen chair. I move her at noon to the living room so she can watch her shows," Angie teased. "It's harder to tie her up in there, so Sheriff Brown loaned me his handcuffs. Nothing ever bad happens in River Vista, right?"

"You're a funny girl. Can I talk to her?" Erica didn't seem amused at Angie's try at humor, but maybe the last few days had made her kind of edgy.

"Hold on." Angie handed the phone to Mrs. Potter. "Don't tell her I beat you every night directly at six p.m."

"I definitely won't tell her that, but I may mention the gruel for breakfast." Mrs. Potter grinned, getting in on the action.

"Don't forget lunch and dinner. Gruel is a good alternative for all meals." Angie went to sit down on the couch with Dom, leaving Mrs. Potter to have some privacy. Dom looked up at her with soulful eyes. "Hey, buddy, tonight is a work day. I told you to get ready for these."

He whined softly and laid his head down in her lap, apparently understanding that she was going to be gone from him for a while.

"No worries. Sunday I'll take you on a walk down at the park." The river canyon park was more aptly described as hiking, not walking, but Dom loved the area. He was always finding new and exciting things, like lizards and someone's shoe. Now, how that person got off the trail with only one sneaker, Angie couldn't imagine. The day they'd found that, she'd sat it near the edge of the trail, hoping someone would come back to retrieve it. Someone had, as the shoe was gone on their next visit.

She turned on the television, quickly turning down the volume. She scrolled through the channels looking for something to distract her as she waited for Mrs. Potter to be done with her phone so she could head into town and the restaurant.

"Local man still missing. Police are asking for anyone with information to call the River Vista Police Station. Lines will be open twenty-four hours until Javier Easterly is found." The newscaster focused on the camera, his look serious. "In related news, the death of Heather McCurdy remains unsolved. According to River Vista's Sheriff Brown, they are looking into any and all leads."

"What a sad story." The female newscaster tsked. "I'm sure the man is just beside himself with grief."

"You would think, Joan, you would think." The newscaster stared directly into the camera, then flashed a smile. "Turning to local sports…"

Angie turned off the television. Where had Javier gone? Was he hiding because he killed Heather? Or was he hiding from the people who did? Either way, Estebe and Javier's family got the worst of it. He was probably in some luxury suite, drinking himself blind to deal with the grief. Although he really hadn't seemed too broken up at the knowledge of Heather's death. He reacted more like a child who'd been told the toy they'd tossed away had been put into the trash. What toy, his eyes had seemed to say the first time they'd met. Which Heather?

Mrs. Potter used her walker to enter the room, holding out Angie's phone. "She wants to talk to you."

Angie took the phone. "Hey, Erica, are you having fun?"

"It's so beautiful here. I needed the head space. I won't sugarcoat the bad news. I guess there's a storm coming in so we might be leaving early or late, depending on the airline. So I could be home early tomorrow or not until Monday afternoon."

Angie didn't respond. She'd been planning on Erica to come Monday morning so she could do the handoff. She tried to make her response convincing. "I guess we'll see you when you get here."

Erica laughed. "You almost sounded like you meant it. Has she been awful to you?"

"No, really, we've been having a great time." Angie smiled at Mrs. Potter. "And she's standing right next to you. We'll talk when I get home. Thank you again for this week. You're the best."

After she'd ended the call, Angie went back to the kitchen and finished her breakfast. It was still a little early to go into town, but Mrs. Potter didn't know that. Angie grabbed her tote and headed out the door after giving Dom a rub behind the ears. "I'll see you tomorrow."

"Have a good day at work." Mrs. Potter grinned. "I haven't said that in years since Mr. Potter retired. How strange it feels."

As Angie drove into town, she felt just a bit guilty leaving Mrs. Potter on her own. Of course, Erica went to school every day, so the woman was used to being by herself. Besides, she loved her game shows, and Angie knew the first would start in a few minutes. Angie was an introvert, and having someone in her house all the time, well, it had been harder than she'd expected. She made herself a large coffee when she got into the kitchen, then headed into her office. By the time Erica got back, Angie should have all the bookkeeping, payroll, ordering and inventory completed. She might even have time to start planning next month's menu.

Two hours later, Felicia stuck her head in the office. "I should have known you were here hiding from Mrs. Potter. What did she do now? You've had fire, flood—wait, isn't the next plague some sort of insects?"

"I actually think it's frogs, but no matter, she didn't do anything. I'm just not used to having someone in my house." Angie sighed. "What are you doing today?"

"I just got back from a massage. You should try it sometime. I'm going to be all relaxed and you're going to have your shoulders up around your ears tonight. What did Papa Diaz want last night?" Felicia sank into a chair.

"That was weird. He wanted to know what I knew about Heather and Javier. And, get this, he wanted to know if I knew where Javier would be. Like we're best friends or something." Angie laid her head on her desk. "I should have never started looking into this. Now everyone thinks I'm some sort of Miss Marple or something."

"You are pretty good at this. Did you ever find that woman Javier slept with? Maybe he went back to her place."

Angie shook her head. "Except she didn't really live there. Although I didn't try to reach out to the woman who did rent the apartment. Maybe she gave one of her friends a key."

"For random hookups? Eewwwww." Felicia shuddered. "I never got why people just want the one-night stand. I want a real relationship. One that I can count on, not just random sex with a stranger."

"And yet you've dated a ton of people since you moved here." Angie lifted her head off the desk.

"Dated, not slept with. I'm a very traditional type of girl." Felicia grinned and flipped back her hair. "I've got to go get the dining room set up. One of my waitstaff is going to be late, so I told her I'd cover the setup time."

Angie flipped through her notebook and found the name of the woman who rented the apartment. Then she called the apartment manager and told him she needed her cell number because of a change in her school schedule for next semester. Angie held her breath, but the guy bought the story and gave her Carrie Sue's cell.

She had just enough time to call and leave a quick message asking Carrie Sue to call her back about the apartment before Estebe came into her office.

"I am disturbing you. I will come back later." He turned and started to leave.

Angie set down the phone. "No, come on in. I was just finishing a call. What's going on?" She pointed to the chair Felicia had just vacated. "How are you doing?"

"I am better today. I spent the morning calling Javier's old girlfriends to see if they had heard from him."

Angie waited for Estebe to go on. After a pause, he continued.

"As you can guess, it was a long list. But no one has heard from my cousin since he dumped them. A few of them gave me a message to tell him if I ever found him."

"Do I want to know?" Angie sat on the corner of her desk.

Estebe shrugged. "I won't use the exact words, but some version of 'I hope he rots in hell.' I don't think Javier is well liked among his exes."

Angie stifled a chuckle. "Well, maybe not well liked, but typically he knew how to end a relationship. He didn't need to murder someone to get them to go away."

"That is true." Estebe stood. "I wanted to tell you I am here to work prep. I need to get my mind off my problems and onto cooking."

Angie stood. "I understand. Cooking has always helped me through the bad times." As she watched him leave, she thought about the nights she'd cooked until the morning light had peeked through the window. Nona had been in and out of the hospital but kept telling her she was fine and not to worry. And then there had been Todd. He'd been secretive and absent. Angie hadn't really noticed until she'd needed him. Then his absence had been like a knife to her heart. When she'd found out he was sleeping with one of el pescado's servers, she kicked him out of the house and out of the business. Felicia had stood behind her and Todd hadn't argued. Of course, he still got paid his third of the profits for not working, so why would he have a problem?

She sank back into her chair and tried to push the past away with the work in front of her. She didn't have to worry about Ian in the same ways she'd worried about Todd. The guy was stable and their relationship too new to break apart. She picked up her phone. When he answered, she swiveled her chair away from the desk so she was facing the window and her view of the park. "What are you doing for lunch?"

"Is this an offer?" He responded quickly. "Although I do have to tell you I have a girlfriend who may not be happy with me taking off with some stranger."

"Ha ha." Angie glanced at the clock. "Come by around one and I'll let you taste-test tonight's menu."

There was no answer.

"Hello? Are you still there?" Angie glanced at her display to see if she'd lost the call.

He chuckled. "I'm here, I was just thinking about my dinner date."

"With Mrs. Potter? I'm sure she'll be fine on her own for lunch. Please don't go out to get her. I'm hiding here at the restaurant to try to stay away from her." Angie leaned on the brick wall, watching a mother push her young son on the swings at the park.

"The week is almost over."

"Thank goodness. I'm not sure how Erica does it. I guess that's probably why Nona hired someone to come stay with her rather than call me. I don't have a lot of patience."

"It's different when it's your flesh and blood." He paused, then added, "Your grandmother was probably trying to be as independent as possible."

"You're right." Angie stopped watching the mother and son and went back to her desk. "So will you come at one?"

"I'll be there with bells on. I've been missing you. I hope we can get out for a long dinner and drive as soon as Erica gets back into town."

Angie liked the sound of that. Time with Ian where she didn't have to think or keep up a conversation. "I suppose we should wait until Erica comes by and actually picks up Mrs. Potter."

"You're always the thoughtful one. I'll see you in a couple of hours."

After she'd hung up, Angie felt better. Stronger. Holding on to other people's pain was a habit she needed to break. Javier would show up. Estebe would be fine. And Sheriff Brown would find out who killed Heather. Her job was to feed the people who were planning on showing up tonight at the County Seat. And be a good friend to Felicia. And a girlfriend to Ian. She grinned as she focused back on the accounting. Girlfriend. It did have nice ring to it.

By the time Ian arrived, Angie had already run through all the dishes for the evening. It was starting to feel like old hat. She loved the fact that the menu changed based on what she could find at the farmers market or what her suppliers brought in. She took a bite of the spicy salsa Hope had made out of the box of produce they'd gotten from Pamplona Farms Friday morning. The driver had been less than talkative, probably being questioned by all of his customers about Javier and his connection to Heather. Turning to Estebe, she asked, "Who do you think will take over running the farm until Javier returns?"

Instead of answering, he nodded toward the kitchen door and then left the prep station and went into the walk-in. Angie turned and followed his gaze. Ian stood at the edge of the kitchen, watching her.

"Hey." She glanced at the clock, not realizing what time it was. "You're right on time."

Ian glanced around the room, his gaze lingering on the walk-in refrigerator where Estebe had just vanished. "I can come back another time."

"No, this is good. I just need a few minutes to make up one more entrée." She pointed to the table. "Take a seat. Hope, can you get Ian a drink and then give him a plate of your chips and salsa?"

Hope came around the stoves with her appetizer. "I was just plating up a sample." She held it up for Angie to inspect. "Does it look okay?"

"It looks wonderful." Angie took the plate and set it in front of Ian. "Now, what can Hope get you to drink? Beer? I don't think Jeorge is here yet to make a margarita."

"How about a Coke and a glass of water. I have a feeling I might need two drinks, from the smell of this salsa."

Hope nodded, then ran to the drinks station to get Ian's order. He dropped his voice. "Are you going to be joining me?"

"As soon as I get this last entrée done." She squeezed his shoulder. "I'm so glad you could come today and see the magic behind the County Seat."

"I wouldn't have missed this for the world." He leaned back for Hope to set the drinks down. "Thank you."

"No problem." Hope glanced at Angie. "Okay if I make up another batch of salsa? I have one last box of tomatoes and peppers still in the walk-in."

"Great idea." Angie smiled at Ian. "I'll be right back with our lunches."

She gathered up the plating experiments she'd been doing with the last few dishes she'd cooked and brought them over to the table. When she finally sat down after refilling her glass of iced tea, the butcher block table was covered with plates. Ian hadn't touched anything except the chips and salsa. "Go ahead, eat. I'd like to know what you think of the dishes."

"I think I'm not going to have to eat tonight when I go get Mrs. Potter. Even between the two of us, we can't finish all of this." He waved his hand across the table. "Maybe you should invite the rest of the crew to join us."

"Nah, they'll make their own lunch. Besides, I invited you to a meal. What's been going on?" She brought a plate with crispy trout and roasted fingerling potatoes toward her and took a bite. The sauce Estebe had made was heavenly, light and lemony. She closed her eyes as she enjoyed the first bite.

Ian started on the chicken and dumplings. The filling homemade noodles were her Nona's recipe, and Angie loved seeing him enjoy the dish. "I think I'm going to have to kill Mildred. I swear, that woman demands the world, then doesn't understand the cost in time or outlay. She's got big plans for Moss Farm and the goat dairy."

Angie leaned closer, wondering what the woman was planning on changing on the piece of property Angie considered almost heaven, when a scream came from the prep station. She rushed over to see Hope staring into a box.

"What's wrong? Did you cut yourself?" Angie tried to see the young woman's hands, but they were behind the table. She moved over to get a better angle and sighed quickly when she didn't see any blood or missing body parts.

Hope didn't answer, just stared and pointed at the box. It had to be a snake or a spider. Creatures were always hitching a ride from the farm to the city in the produce boxes. Angie bit her lip to keep from grinning. Then she looked down into the box. A chill ran down her spine and she looked up into Estebe's eyes. He'd seen it too. Ian stepped toward the prep table, cell phone in hand. "Do you need me to call an ambulance? Is anyone hurt?"

"Call Sheriff Brown." Angie could barely utter the words. After pledging to stay out of the investigation, she'd been railroaded back into Heather's death with lightning speed. And an item in the bottom of a tomato box. "Tell him we might have found the murder weapon."

"It's the Diaz family knife." Estebe meet Angie's eyes. "It shouldn't have been on Javier's farm, and it shouldn't be here. This does not look good for my cousin."

Chapter 13

Felicia pulled her aside. "I need you in the dining room. We have a problem."

Dinner service had started almost on time with Sheriff Brown and his guys taking the box filled with the knife and a few tomatoes from the kitchen a little over an hour ago. Finally, Angie was able to get the shocked crew steady enough to start cooking. "What is it this time? Did someone fall over dead in their soup bowl? Because if it's not at that level of problem, I don't want to be disturbed."

"Don't be such a diva. You need to nip this in the bud, now." Felicia took the whisk out of Angie's hand and gave it to Estebe. "Cover for your boss for a minute, will you?"

"Yes, ma'am." Estebe took the utensil and then turned away, apparently hoping to miss the fire that Angie knew was coming out of her eyes as she glared at him.

As they left the kitchen, she grumbled, "Yes, ma'am? What, do you have my kitchen staff afraid of you too?"

Felicia laughed, a sweet sound that mimicked birds chirping. "But of course. Since I'm the nice one, they know when I'm demanding, they better listen."

"So being nice means you could be a royal…" Angie didn't finish the sentence as they'd stopped in front of a table. An older woman sat alone with a bowl of Nona's chicken and dumplings in front of her. Felicia nodded toward her, giving Angie some secret sign that she couldn't read at all.

"Mrs. Eisenhower, this is our chef, Angie Turner." Felicia turned toward Angie. "Mrs. Eisenhower has a problem with her meal."

"I don't have a problem with it, I just want to know how you got my recipe." The woman's eyes flashed and Angie could feel the anger flowing off her in waves. "I come to this overpriced diner because all the women in my church group are raving about the food, and find you're serving my chicken and dumplings?"

"I'm sure a lot of dishes are similar, Mrs. Eisenhower." Felicia lowered her voice in an attempt to get the woman to calm down or at least quiet down a bit.

"It's not similar, it's exact." She pointed a finger at Angie. "Did you steal my cookbook? I haven't even let the church group put this into their annual cookbook."

"Ma'am, I'm sure this is a misunderstanding. This was my Nona's recipe. Maybe you knew her, Margaret Turner?" Angie hoped by throwing out her grandmother's name, the woman would calm down. Instead, it had the opposite effect.

"Margaret Turner? I should have known." Mrs. Eisenhower stood and threw her napkin on the table. "I never did trust her. Don't expect me to pay for my own food."

Angie and Felicia stood by the table as Mrs. Eisenhower marched out of the restaurant, her white purse tucked under her arm and her polyester pantsuit making noise as her thighs rubbed together. Diners at nearby tables watched the show, then returned to their meals, apparently bored by the outburst.

"I can't believe she thought Nona stole her recipe. I found it in her journal just last week." Angie looked at the door. "Do you think I should go out and apologize?"

Felicia grabbed her by the arm and pulled her out of the dining room and into the servers area. "What are you thinking?"

"Well, if the recipes are close…"

"The woman is insane. She ate all but a few bites of the dish, then threw a fit when the server tried to hand her a bill. It's a scam. She just didn't want to pay for her supper." Felicia shook her head. "I should have realized that before I let her yell at you. We just haven't had any complaints since we opened, I thought you'd want to deal with the first one."

Angie poured herself a glass of Coke. "Seriously, all I want is for this day to be over. I like being a chef. Just a chef. And I don't want to deal with murder weapons in the pantry or screaming lunatics in the dining room." She drank the soda, then filled the glass again. "Is that too much to hope for?"

Felicia gave her a hug. "Sorry, I didn't realize you were this stressed. You know the sheriff doesn't think you had anything to do with the murder, right?"

"You mean, not like last time?" She gave her friend a hard stare. "I move back to town and there are two murders in less than three months? Why wouldn't he look my way? Or yours?"

"Because we're nice, upstanding members of the River Vista community. Besides, he loves your bread."

Angie narrowed her eyes. "Wait, has he even been in the restaurant?"

Felicia squirmed. "I guess I've been taking him over a lunch a few days a week."

"Don't let his wife find out. I think she likes being in charge of his eating habits." Angie finished off the rest of the drink. "I've got to get back in there. Anything else you want to tell me?"

"You look amazing?" Felicia grinned. "Do you want me to come over tomorrow morning for breakfast so you don't have to entertain Mrs. Potter alone?"

Relief filled Angie. She'd been dreading spending the entire day with the woman. And then she felt guilty. "Would you? That would be awesome."

Felicia checked her hair in the mirror above the ice machine. "No problem. What are friends for?" She glanced toward the door. "New customers, I need to play hostess."

Angie watched her friend cheerfully greet the young couple that had walked into the restaurant. She blinked when she saw who it was. Stephen and Kendra stood chatting with Felicia. She tucked into the kitchen before they could see her staring.

After washing her hands, she stood by Estebe and took over stirring the gravy. He glanced her way. "Everything all right?"

No, everything was not all right, she thought, but she didn't want to alarm him. Besides, Stephen had a right to eat wherever he wanted. And he probably wanted to support Estebe in his new job. "Fine, just fine. A woman just accused me of stealing her recipe for the chicken and dumplings."

"That is impossible. I saw you adjusting as you were cooking it yesterday. This recipe came from your heart and mind, not by being copied." He shook his head, his tone taking on a sadness. "Sometimes, people just don't think about how their words will affect another person. It's all me, me, me. Like Javier. He always put himself first above all else. He would have made a terrible leader for our community."

"What do you think about Stephen?"

Estebe paused, plated an order, and then wiped an imaginary spot from the edge of the plate. "Stephen is young and sometimes impulsive, but he will be a better choice than Javier ever was. And I believe his Kendra has settled him."

"So you like them?" Angie didn't know how far she could push the questions before he got suspicious, but she was going to try before she blurted out that the couple was in the dining room.

A smile curve Estebe's lips. "I do like them. I think they make a nice couple. Did you meet them at the breakfast?"

"I met Kendra and her mother there." Angie decided not mentioning where she had met Stephen was a better choice.

"Her mother is…" Estebe handed a plate to the server who was waiting at the pass. "Table fourteen."

"Her mother is what?"

He glanced around the kitchen, but it appeared everyone else was busy and not listening. "Her mother is crazy."

"That seems to be going around." Angie waved away the confused look and took over the expediting. "Let's just work and be happy. We have the best job in the world. Besides, happy cooks make happy food."

"There is no proof of that." Estebe handed her a plate. "I've known chefs who were miserable who put out amazing food."

Angie shrugged. "My kitchen, my rules."

"Did you hear your chef?" Estebe called out to the rest of the team. "It's a 'don't worry, be happy' day."

Hope grinned as she ran another load of dishes into the stainless-steel washer. "I totally agree. No wonder I love working here."

Angie smiled at the young woman who just hours before had been shaken by her discovery. The fact the knife probably was the murder weapon hadn't occurred to her until Sheriff Brown had sat her down for a quick interview. Then the implications were clear, even to their naïve Hope.

"I've got someone who wants to talk to you." Felicia stood next to her. The volume of the music in the kitchen had made it easy for her to come in without Angie noticing.

"Me or…" She jerked her head toward Estebe.

Felicia narrowed her eyes. "I thought you saw them come in. When I turned around, you'd disappeared."

"I had to get back into the kitchen." Angie knew it was a lame excuse, but right now, it was the best she had. "Busy night."

"Whatever. Anyway, they want to see you. They think you played some magic with their reservation and moved it up to tonight." Now Felicia was watching her.

"I don't mess with your reservation process. I don't think I'd know how now that you went to the online booking." Angie felt bewildered and broadsided. If she hadn't changed their reservation… Both she and Felicia stared at Estebe.

He sat a plate on the warming table and frowned. "What?"

"Did you pull some strings to get Stephen and Kendra a table tonight?"

"Pull strings? With who? You two are the only ones I know who deal with reservations." He glanced toward the door. "I suppose I should go say good evening. Stephen is family."

"Hold on a moment, let me talk to them first." Angie took Felicia's arm and led her out of the kitchen. She paused before they entered the dining room. "Who got them a reservation?"

"I don't know, but I'm going to be looking into it right after service tonight." Felicia glanced at the table where Stephen held Kendra's hand. "It's weird, right?"

"Most definitely." Angie couldn't think of any other excuse to delay the conversation so she weaved her way through the candlelit tables, smiling and greeting people who had become regulars in the short time the County Seat had been opened. Finally, she arrived tableside, and both Stephen and Kendra looked up and smiled at her. "Are you enjoying your visit so far?"

Kendra held up the corn bread Angie had placed on every table when the guests arrived. "I love corn bread, but this is heavenly. You are such an amazing chef. Estebe raves about you all the time."

"He does?" Stephen and Angie said in unison, then he laughed.

"I didn't realize you and Estebe talked all that often, love." He reached her hand to his lips and kissed it.

"Just recently, since I've been helping out with the festival. I've probably seen him every day. The man's a hard worker." She smiled up at Angie. "You must be happy to have him on staff."

"Estebe's an amazing chef. I'm sure he could do anything he put his mind to." Seeing the discomfort in Stephen's eyes, she smiled at Kendra. "So what did you want to talk to me about? It can't be just your love of corn bread."

"Almost." Kendra smiled, and Angie knew why Stephen had fallen for the attractive blonde. She almost lit up the room when she smiled. She'd noticed she was pretty at the breakfast, but now she just radiated beauty. "We wanted to thank you for rearranging our dinner reservation."

"I'm not quite sure what you mean." Angie stepped out of the way of a server with a pot of coffee heading to a table and not watching where he was going.

"When I called to get a reservation, you were booked more than three weeks out. Then this morning, I got a call from someone saying you'd had a cancelation and did I want to come in tonight." She squeezed Stephen's hand. "Since we had to be at a bed-and-breakfast down the street anyway, this worked out perfect."

"Oh, why are you staying at a B-and-B?" Angie wasn't sure what the story was, but she knew she had to keep Kendra talking to try to find out.

"My mother had to have the house fumigated. She found a roach." Kendra shivered. "So she paid for me and Stephen to have a little staycation, here in town."

"Don't get all creeped out. I sincerely doubt she actually found a roach. Idaho isn't known for roaches. That's more a warmer climate bug." Stephen took a sip of his wine. "But I'm not complaining. Kendra and I have been talking about doing a getaway to relax before the wedding, but with everything that's going on, it's hard to get away."

Kendra giggled. "Eighteen months and I'll be Mrs. Stephen Easterly. Isn't that insane? And there's so much to do before that. I don't think I have enough time."

"Well, there's no way I'm letting you push out the date." Stephen shook his head. "Being engaged for two years is way too long. I can't believe we let your mother talk us into this."

"Mother's very traditional," Kendra explained.

"Well, congratulations. And thanks for stopping into the County Seat." She glanced toward the kitchen. "I guess I better check on your dinners."

"Tell Estebe hi from us. He doesn't have to come out and slow down the kitchen." Stephen took out his phone and started going through texts. Angie had been dismissed.

The man clearly thought he was someone important. How Estebe had grown up fairly normal with family like that, she didn't understand. But she hoped repeating Stephen's directive wouldn't hurt his feelings. She'd seen the flash of jealousy when Kendra had mentioned Estebe. Even though it had been innocent, Angie thought he didn't like to share her with anyone. Including her mother.

She hadn't needed to worry, Estebe just brushed off the slight with one comment. "Stephen is very protective of the time he gets with Kendra. I can understand his reluctance to share the company of such a beautiful woman, inside and out."

They got back to work and Angie was just feeling the magic of the flow when Felicia came back into the kitchen.

"No. Whatever it is, the answer is no. Unless the building is on fire, I'm not going back into that dining room tonight." Angie didn't let her talk, just handed a plate to the server waiting on her other side.

"You're going to want to see this. It's sweet." Felicia took her arm. "I'm stealing her one last time. We'll be right back."

This time Estebe didn't even respond, just nodded and moved in front of the cook line, taking over expediting. The team was actually working as a solid unit.

"Next weekend, you're going to have to leave me be since Estebe won't be here to step in like he has tonight." Angie followed Felicia into the dining room. She scanned the room, seeing people eating, servers floating between the tables, and Jeorge, the bartender, chatting up a red head sitting at his bar. Nothing out of the ordinary. "What is it now?"

Felicia pointed to a table near the door. There Ian sat with Mrs. Potter, who saw Angie and waved her over. "He brought her here."

"He's such a sap." Angie shook her head as she headed toward the table. When Ian stood and greeted her with a kiss on the cheek, she slapped his arm. "You could have told me you were eating dinner here and turned me down for lunch."

"And miss seeing you in your natural element?" He moved a section of hair away from her face and tucked it behind her ear. "Mrs. Potter and I are having a lovely time."

"It is such a beautiful place." Mrs. Potter reached her hand up and waited for Angie to lean closer before kissing her on the cheek. "Margaret would have been so proud of you. It's a joy to eat here."

Angie stepped back as the server brought out their dishes. Mrs. Potter had ordered the chicken and dumplings. She used her spoon to move around the flat dumpling noodles and examined the dish. "If I didn't know better, I would have said your Nona made this. She loved taking this to the church potlucks. It reheats really well."

Ian had chosen the pot roast, which she knew was too heavy for summer, but she loved making the tender meat and red wine sauce. "We won't keep you from your work. I told Felicia that we'd talk later, but the girl has a mind of her own."

"She does at that." Angie turned toward the kitchen, then paused and turned back. "Thanks for bringing Mrs. Potter here, Ian."

"Best place in town to eat. And I didn't really feel like hitting the drive-in again." He touched her upper arm. "It's my pleasure."

She turned toward Mrs. Potter. "I feel like I've been a bad hostess for your stay."

"Nonsense. You have a job, you need to do it. Erica doesn't hover around me twenty-four-seven." An old-fashioned phone rang from Mrs. Potter's purse. "I think that's her. She should be getting on the plane first thing in the morning."

Angie said a quick goodbye and left Mrs. Potter to get an update from her granddaughter. As she passed by Felicia, who stood in the server area, watching her, she paused. "Thanks for making me come out."

"You shouldn't have missed it." She met Angie's gaze. "He's a keeper. You know that, right?"

"I don't know what you're talking about." Angie hurried into the kitchen so she didn't have to think about Ian and his status as a keeper in her life. Because when she did, her stomach twisted, and she didn't need any digestive issues. Not tonight.

Chapter 14

"Come have a drink with me." Felicia kicked off her shoes and put her feet up on the chair across from her.

"I have to drive home, and as tired as I am, if I have even one drink, I'll be sleeping on your couch. Mrs. Potter needs me at the house, just in case." Angie scrubbed her face with her hands. "Besides, I smell like I've been cooking for hours. I need a shower before I see real people."

"Oh, I signed us up to work the mission kitchen next month. It's a Wednesday, so I thought we'd bring the whole team and give them a full-service dinner." Felicia put her head on the table and kept talking. "They invite all the local restaurants to volunteer, but I guess it's hard to get them to agree."

"Who have you been talking to?" Angie sipped on a bottle of water. She wanted coffee but thought the caffeine might make her too jittery to sleep when she got home.

"This guy, Taylor. He's super cute and he works at the mission. He makes virtually nothing, but he says he doesn't need the money. Trust fund baby, I suspect."

"Are you dating him?" Now Angie was curious. She hadn't heard anything about a Taylor in the months since they'd moved from California.

Felicia sat up and glanced at Angie. "Maybe."

"Way to commit." She stood and stretched. "And I don't need a lecture about black pots and pans. I'm heading home. I'll see you tomorrow for breakfast?"

"Sounds like heaven. Since I don't have a wingman for tonight, I'm heading upstairs to a long, hot bath." She glanced out toward the street. "I know Heather's death had nothing to do with me, but ever since she was killed, I'm having trouble walking around alone at night. I keep hearing sounds, but when I turn around, no one's there. Probably just my imagination, right?"

"Do me a favor, don't use the alley as a shortcut until Sheriff Brown finds this guy." Angie stifled a yawn. "You want me to stay a while? Or drop you somewhere?"

"No." Felicia rolled her shoulders. "I think once I get out of the bath I'm going to have to pour myself into bed. My muscles are all tight. Good thing I have a massage scheduled on Monday."

"We'll have fun tomorrow celebrating Mrs. Potter's last day at Casa Turner. I'm looking forward to getting my house back. It's like living with a house mom again." Angie glanced around the dining room as she grabbed her tote. "It's turning out to be pretty special, isn't it?"

"I think so. And our guests leave happy. I've been giving them all survey cards with their bill, and the comments for the most part have been amazing. We have some server issues, but I'll deal with those in our next staff meeting."

"Bring them tomorrow and we can skim them for possible marketing quotes." Angie gave her friend a quick hug. "I've got to go or I will be sleeping on your couch."

Felicia followed her to the back door and stood in the light of the kitchen while Angie unlocked and started her car. As she pulled out of the lot, she waved at Felicia and waited for her to shut the door after her. She hated that her friend was feeling unsafe in the apartment. Maybe Angie should invite her to move into the farmhouse. They might be out in the boondocks, but she had Dom for protection.

She turned the music up loud and slowly drove out of town, speeding up as soon as she saw the city limits sign. All she wanted tonight was a hot shower and maybe a cup of cocoa.

When she got to the house, she was surprised to see all the lights on and Ian's car still in the driveway. Entering the kitchen, she saw Ian sitting at the table, drinking tea. "Good evening. Was your evening uneventful?"

"Not really." She started the hot chocolate as she told him about the complainer as well as Stephen and Kendra coming in. "I think there's a leak in our computer system, or they just lucked out by talking to someone who found a random empty reservation."

"But she said someone called her? Wouldn't that have been Felicia?" He added more sugar to his cup and stirred the tea.

"She says she didn't call anyone. See, it's weird." She sat down at the table and sipped on the hot chocolate. "Anyway, we'll figure it out. Why are you still here? You and Mrs. Potter have a game of Monopoly going?"

"I'm better at card games. They might be called different names here in the States, but I can do a smart game of Go Fish." He shook his head. "No, I stayed until she calmed down. I swear after Erica called, she was inconsolable. She thinks the girl is looking around for a home to place her in. She says the Mexico trip is all a scam."

"Erica wouldn't do that." Angie sighed as she lifted her cup and took a sip. "But I can see how it's tempting. The woman is a handful. She's either washing things that don't need washed or rearranging my kitchen."

"I'm sure she's only trying to be helpful." He scratched Dom behind the ear as the dog planted himself on the floor between him and Angie. "Anyway, since you're home to oversee, I'll be heading back to town. She went to bed about an hour ago, but I just didn't feel right leaving her alone. And I fed Precious and Mabel before we went to dinner. So your chores are done."

"I appreciate it." She smiled. "Keep taking care of me and I'll have to start paying you for your time."

"No need. The pleasure of your company is more than payment enough." He stood and gave her a kiss. "Can we change breakfast to dinner on Tuesday? I've got some things I need to handle with the board."

"Definitely." She watched as he dumped out his teacup, ran water through it, and then gently placed it in the dishwasher. "I'll be glad when life slows down a bit."

"Me too. But I'm not counting on it for a long time."

Angie stood at the back door and watched him leave. Then she locked the door and started walking through the house, checking other doors and turning off lights. The television was on but the sound muted. A news story from earlier questioned when the Treasure Valley was going to get rain. The local anchorwoman had been on the same news channel since Angie was in high school. Her blond hair was showing signs of gray and she had laugh lines now, but her smile was the same, warm and welcoming. Things didn't change quickly around here. And that was one reason she was glad to be back.

* * * *

"She's still not awake?" Angie looked up as Felicia came back into the kitchen. Angie had been up since seven. Felicia had arrived just before eight. And Mrs. Potter was still locked in her room.

Felicia shrugged. "I knocked and told her breakfast was ready. She said she was getting dressed."

"I wonder what she's getting ready for? We're not really the dress for breakfast crowd." Angie poured huckleberry syrup over a waffle and added a dollop of whipped cream. "Bacon?"

"Yes, please." Felicia refilled the coffee cups and poured three glasses of orange juice. "So do you know what Erica really said?"

"No, and I've tried to call her three times. Mrs. Potter has me worried." Angie sat a plate in front of Felicia, then glanced down the hallway to check for Mrs. Potter. "I hate to eat before she comes to the table, but I'm starving."

"Make her a plate and put it in the oven. I'm starving too. I'm always this way after a service." Felicia chatted on about the number of covers they did last night. Then she paused and grabbed her purse. After digging around for a few minutes, she pulled out an envelope that she handed Angie. "I forgot you wanted to see these."

Angie dumped the survey cards on the table in front of her and started going through them. The ones with just ratings she put into two piles. Good and not so good. The good pile was way larger than the other one. She also had a pile of cards where people had added comments. Those she studied more carefully.

"You shouldn't work at the table."

Mrs. Potter's voice behind her made Angie jump. She quickly stood up, grabbed the breakfast plate out of the oven, and sat it on the table. "Can I pour you some coffee?"

Mrs. Potter moved around her and sat with her purse on her lap. She was dressed in a cotton shirtdress that looked like she'd purchased it in the seventies. "Coffee would be nice, but we don't have a lot of time. Sunday school starts at nine."

Angie poured the coffee, then sank into her chair. Hopefully, she asked. "Is Delores coming to get you?"

"Delores isn't able to drive until she gets that gout settled down in her right foot." Mrs. Potter sipped her orange juice. "I'm sure Erica told you I teach the retired women's class every Sunday."

Angie searched her memory about the conversation she'd had when Erica had asked her big favor. No, nothing was mentioned about having to escort the woman to church services. "Not that I can recall, but I can run you into town and then come get you when you're ready. No worries." "I'm afraid I might be a bit under the weather. It would be more helpful if you'd just stay. There's a young adult group that both of you girls would enjoy. Plenty of single men in that class every Sunday, just waiting to have the Lord match them up with their soul mate." She cut into her waffle. "Of course, you two need to change clothes. You can't really be thinking of going to church in shorts, are you?"

"Actually, I'm heading into Boise this morning right after breakfast." Felicia didn't look up at Angie, not even when she felt the sharp kick under the table. "You and Angie go and say a prayer for me."

"It doesn't quite work that way, dear. You are in charge of your own salvation." Mrs. Potter took a bite of the waffle.

If only that was true. Angie closed her eyes and then focused on her food. Even though she didn't feel hungry anymore, she knew after the three hours she'd be stuck in church, she'd be starving. So she kept eating. "Too bad you're not going to be able to go with us, Felicia."

"Yeah, I'm all broken up about it." Felicia polished off her breakfast, then took her plate to the sink and mirrored the actions that Ian had done just a few hours ago. "Guess I better head out. I'm meeting up with the man who is sponsoring our Rescue Mission night. Time to finalize dates. At least I'm doing the Lord's work, feeding the poor."

"That's very nice of you." Mrs. Potter beamed at her. "I'm sure I'll see you next week, then?"

Angie snorted. Both women turned and looked at her. "Sorry, allergies." Mrs. Potter hurried them all out of the house and into their cars. Angie barely had time to pour a cup of coffee into a travel mug for the drive before she was shooed out of the kitchen. She wished she'd put on different sandals as she remembered the ones she'd grabbed when she was sent upstairs to change pinched her feet. At least the dress fit and, from what she could tell, didn't have a huckleberry syrup stain from the uncleaned breakfast table. If she was lucky, Mrs. Potter would have mercy on her and not make her go to the drive-in for lunch after services broke up.

Driving into town, the car had been quiet. Finally, Angie turned down the music and asked the question she'd been wanting to ask since last night. "What did Erica say when she called you?"

Mrs. Potter pulled a tissue out of her patent leather purse and snapped it shut. "She said she had missed their transport into town and she might not make her flight."

Angie waited for the rest of the story. When it didn't come, she glanced quickly over to the woman next to her. "That's all? She missed her transport from the resort into town? You don't even know if she is going to miss her plane or if she'll be home as planned tomorrow at noon."

"If you want to continue the charade, fine. You're right. Erica might still be home on Monday at noon." Mrs. Potter dabbed the tissue at dry eyes. "But we both know the real story."

"What real story?" She turned left on the road into town and slowed down.

Mrs. Potter didn't say anything until Angie had parked at the church. Then she turned toward her as she was unbuckling her seat belt. "My granddaughter is looking for a home for me where I won't be so much trouble to her."

Angie reached for Mrs. Potter's hand. "You know that's not true."

The woman paused in her flight to get out of the car. She held her Bible in one hand, like it was a shield against her body. "No, Angie. I know it is true."

As she slammed the door and carefully walked across the paved lot into church, Angie watched her. She greeted people as she walked, finally settling with a group of women who seemed to be about her age. Angie recognized the taller woman in the group. Mrs. Eisenhower, the woman who had called her a copycat and accused her of stealing her recipe. The day just kept getting better.

Angie closed her eyes and wondered how long she could stay out here in the car without someone coming to get her.

A knock on the window told her it wouldn't be that long.

She opened her eyes and stared at Ian.

He opened the door for her and held out a hand. "Come inside. The air-conditioning is on and I think you'll like my class."

"Get out. You teach a Sunday school class?" She snuck a quick glance at him as they walked into the church. He didn't look like he was teasing.

"You look like I just admitted I was a petty thief or bank robber." He held the door open. "I enjoy the class. We're researching Acts right now, mostly focusing on history and trying to nail down some of the actual places the stories took place."

"I thought the Bible was full of morality tales, not history." She followed him down the stairs into the basement where he opened the door to a room set up with a round table and ten chairs. A coffeepot sat on a table under the window, and there was a plate of cookies next to it.

"Not always." He nodded to the coffee. "May I pour you a cup? I guess it's early in our relationship to start talking about beliefs, but you were the one sitting all forlorn in the parking lot."

"I wasn't alone." She took the cup he offered and sat in one of the chairs. "Mrs. Potter kind of pushed me into bringing her and staying. She said she might need a ride home sooner rather than later."

"You fell for that?" He sat next to her. "The woman is as strong as an ox, and her memory is better than mine."

"Yeah, I realized once I got here that I'd been played." Angie sipped her coffee.

A striking blonde in a summer dress strolled into the room. "Oh, Ian, I brought you your favorite cookie." She held out a plate with what looked like store-bought chocolate chip. She frowned when she saw the other cookies on the table. "I guess I'm too late."

"Katherine, this is Angie, my girlfriend." Ian took the plate of cookies and set it on the sideboard. "Angie, Katherine is one of my students."

Angie wondered if Ian even knew that the woman wanted to be more than just a Sunday school student, but she decided to take the high road. She stood and held out a hand. "Katherine, so nice to meet you."

"I didn't realize Ian had a girlfriend." The woman narrowed her eyes and studied Angie. "Are you the one who opened that restaurant down the street?"

"Guilty as charged. The County Seat is mine. Well, mine and my best friend's brainchild. Have you been in yet?"

"No, I've been a little busy."

People started coming in and Ian greeted them all. Finally, the chairs were all filled and each person had a Bible open in front of them. Since Ian had brought several, he opened one to the page they were discussing and put it in front of Angie.

Angie tried to pay attention, but something about Katherine kept bothering her. She knew she hadn't met her before, but something about the woman seemed familiar. Like she knew of her without knowing her. She pulled out a notebook and started making notes about her appearance. Maybe Felicia had talked about her.

Ian nodded supportively, and Angie felt a twinge of guilt since he must have assumed she was taking notes about the class. Honestly, she wasn't quite sure she knew what they were talking about. She hadn't been in this church since she'd left Nona's for college. Yes, she'd been raised in the religion, but she didn't think of herself as religious.

When the class was over, they closed up the room, turned off the coffeepot, and threw away the empty plates that had held the cookies. Store bought or not, the group devoured both sets as they talked. They went upstairs and Katherine was talking to a man. She grabbed his arm and laughed, flirting hard. And it was with that gesture that Angie realized why Katherine looked familiar. She looked just like the description Barb had given to her of the woman who had been Javier's one-night stand. She had a sprinkle of star tattoos on her forearm, just like Javier had told Estebe. If Angie was right, she was the only person who could prove to the sheriff that Javier hadn't been in that alley killing Heather.

Chapter 15

"What do you know about Katherine?" Angie leaned close so she could lower her voice. She kept her eyes on the woman just in case.

Ian looked at her in surprise. "Don't tell me you're jealous. I never dated her."

"No, I'm not jealous. I think she might be the woman who was with Javier the night Heather was killed." She pulled Ian into a corner where they could watch Katherine and the man. Thinking fast, she pulled her cell phone out of her purse and snapped a picture. Even if Javier couldn't identify her, maybe someone else could. Like Barb. "What's her last name?"

"Let me think. We don't use last names a lot, but if I recall, she works at a marketing firm in Boise. She offered to do a free campaign for the River Vista Farmers Market next year." He pulled out his wallet. "Hold on, I've got her card."

Angie grabbed it out of his hand and stared. "Katherine Elliot?"

"Why do you think that's the girl with Javier? I don't think I've ever heard her mention him or anyone she dated, for that matter." He frowned. "Which seems a little odd, now that I think about it. We have several single members of the class, and they're always talking about a date or, more likely, a disappointment."

"Maybe she didn't want you to get the wrong idea. She was clearly hot for teacher." Angie tucked her phone and the business card into her purse. "Anyway, I'll go show the picture to Barb tomorrow and see if she's our girl. Then I'll let your friend Allen talk to her. I don't think she likes me much."

As Angie said that, Katherine looked over their way and threw dagger eyes at her. Angie moved closer to Ian and waved. Katherine turned quickly on her heel and disappeared into the chapel area.

"Now, that wasn't very friendly of her." Angie glanced up at Ian, who had a grin on his face.

"I could say the same for you. You knew what kind of a response you'd get." Ian kissed the top of her head. "I have to say, I kind of like this clingy Angie."

They started to walk into the chapel with the rest of the congregation. "Don't get used to it, pal, I'm playing a part."

"As being my girlfriend or just being clingy?" He motioned her into a pew where Mrs. Potter already sat. He put his hand over his heart. "Wait, don't answer that. I don't think my heart could take the letdown if you answered wrong."

"Funny boy. I'll be good." She patted his leg. "At least until we're out of here. I don't want to get struck by lightning or anything."

As the preacher gave his sermon, Angie thought about Javier and his lady friend. Had it just been a coincidence that he'd gone home with a woman who clearly wanted to keep her privacy? To the point she used a friend's condo? Angie could see the advantages. The guy couldn't stalk her afterward. It was only sex. Probably being open about her sexual habits in a small town like River Vista didn't earn a girl any brownie points, especially since she was in a high-profile field like marketing.

On the other hand, if she'd been there to set up the fight between Heather and Javier, she was one cool cucumber. Either way, it was up to Sheriff Brown to find out the real story. She was just the one with the information.

After the service, Ian walked them to Angie's car. "You seemed intent on Pastor Tom's sermon."

"What?" Angie paused as she unlocked her car with the remote. "Yeah, he was interesting."

"I always enjoy the story about the sheep and the shepherd, don't you?" Angie nodded. "Yeah, that's one of my favorites."

"Too bad he was talking about being fishers of men, then." He poked her. "You weren't even listening, were you?"

"Guilty. I was thinking about Javier and why someone would kill Heather." She shrugged. "I guess the quiet helped me to focus."

He kissed her gently. "My mind tends to wander a bit while Pastor Tom is rambling most Sundays. I'm glad I got to share this with you today."

Mrs. Potter spoke as soon as they were alone in the car and Ian was back at his wagon. "You need to make that permanent. Men like him don't come around often in life."

"Ian is amazing. But we've only just started to date." Angie turned up the radio. "Are you starving or should we drive out to the river and sit a bit before we go home and eat?"

"The river would be nice. It's not too hot yet." Mrs. Potter unclipped and clipped her purse. "You don't believe Erica is going to put me in a home, do you?"

"I don't. Erica loves you and she enjoys spending time with you. Besides, you're doing her a favor since she's so busy with school. If she had to find a place to stay, she'd probably have to get a job. You're helping her get a degree."

Mrs. Potter stared out the window. "I hadn't thought about that. I guess I was just too busy with my pity party to look at the reality of the situation."

"Erica's off having fun in Mexico. She'll be back soon." Actually, Angie had been thinking the same thing, wondering when her life could go back to normal. She really was going to be struck by lightning, she felt guilty being so selfish. "Besides, it gives us a chance to get to know each other again. I may not be like my Nona, but I'd like for you to consider me a friend."

"You are a wonderful woman and your grandmother was always so proud of you." She stared out the window. "I told her to call you home. When she got bad, I told her you'd want to be here, but she was a stubborn old coot. I guess we all feel like we're invincible."

Angie felt the jab to the gut as she thought about her own guilt in not recognizing the signs of her grandmother's aging. "I should have realized and come home on my own."

"She would have had a fit, put on a show for you, and then sent you back to your life. Margaret wasn't one to mess with." Mrs. Potter smiled and patted Angie's arm. "There's no use taking on blame for something you didn't do. We all have enough crosses to bear of our own making. Did you enjoy Ian's class? He's been a joy to have in the church family. He's always so giving."

"I've noticed that." Angie pulled the car into the parking lot closer to the river than the canyon hills. Here the walking paths were flat and peppered with lots of places to sit and watch the river flow by. "He seems to be everyone's favorite person."

"If you are thinking he's involved with any of those women at the church, you're wrong." Mrs. Potter unhooked her seat belt. "In fact, I don't know of anyone he's dated since he moved here, until you."

"I really wasn't looking for information." Angie climbed out of the car and met Mrs. Potter on the sidewalk. "I do have some questions about one of the women there. Katherine Elliot? Do you know her?"

Mrs. Potter made a face. "Only by reputation. The girl's too busy with her career to do anything but make an appearance now and then at Sunday services. I think the only reason she comes now is to appease her folks. The girl was wild when she was in high school, and I doubt that has changed much."

The River Vista community had a long memory. No matter what type of adult you were, your crazy high school days always came back to haunt you. They'd only walked a few feet when Mrs. Potter motioned to the next bench.

"Let's sit a bit and talk." She sat and patted the bench. "Now, you're not concerned about her and Ian, are you? I told you that he wasn't dating before you. I don't think he's the type to try to keep two home fires burning."

"No. It's not about Ian. I just thought I'd met her before, but I guess not." Angie leaned against the back of the bench and gazed out to the river. Watching the water relaxed her and helped her to think.

"Of course you've met her before. You went to school with her. But her name was different. She went by Katie back then. Katie Huff."

"What?" Angie remembered Katie Huff. Queen of the mean girls, she'd never had a kind word to say, especially not to Angie, who was quiet and a bit of a loner. High school was hard enough without the pain of losing your parents the summer before. "Katie Huff was captain of the cheerleader squad. I heard she married the quarterback. Ken…"

Before Angie could remember the guy's last name, Mrs. Potter nodded. "Ken Elliot. He was killed a few years later. His motorcycle hit a parked truck one night when he was coming home from Boise. You were probably in California by then."

"Wow. That must have been hard to be a widow so young." Now, instead of remembering how much she'd hated the girl, she felt sorry for the woman.

"It didn't seem to set her back much." Mrs. Potter patted Angie's hand. "Of course, that was catty and a totally un-Christian thing to say, so if you quote me, I'll have to disavow I ever said that."

Angie laughed and Mrs. Potter joined in. For a few more minutes, they were just friends sitting and chatting. Finally, Angie looked at her watch. "Ready to head back?"

"I guess." Mrs. Potter put her face up to the sun, drinking in the heat on her face. "My doctor tells me that sunshine isn't good for me without pouring on sunscreen, but I love the feel of it on my face. And at my age, I don't really care. I've earned my time in the sun."

Angie stood and held out her hand. "What do you think of fried chicken for Sunday dinner? Nona and I usually made a huge Sunday dinner, then warmed up leftovers for supper."

"Sounds good to me. I'd love to make a potato salad if you don't mind. I haven't cooked for a few weeks, and I'm feeling an itch to get back into the kitchen."

The two of them headed back to the car and back to the house to cook and enjoy a meal.

* * * *

Monday morning, Angie had already fed Precious, Mabel, and Dom and was working on transcribing recipes from Nona's diary before Mrs. Potter emerged from her bedroom. Angie started to stand, but Mrs. Potter waved her back down. "I can get my own coffee, dear."

She poured a cup of coffee, then grabbed the pill box Erica had filled and left with Angie before she'd left. She shook out the last set of morning pills, shoved them in her mouth, then sipped the coffee to wash them down.

"How did you sleep?"

"Fine. I'm getting used to that guest bedroom of yours. Erica better hurry back or I might not want to leave." She held up her pill box. "Can you take me over to the house today and help me refill the box for a few days? I think I know all the pills, but they make the lettering on those bottles so tiny, I can't make out the directions."

"Sure, we can go over right after breakfast." Angie stood and went to refill her own cup. "Although, you know, if we do, Erica will be able to make her flight and be home later today."

"I'd like that. I'm missing the girl." Mrs. Potter reached for a journal Angie had already finished. "What are you doing with your grandmother's journals?"

"I've been transcribing the recipes. I'm thinking of compiling them into a cookbook. Maybe I'll do one with recipes I grew up with, then one for recipes I develop for the County Seat. I could sell them out of the dining room."

"That would be a lovely tribute. Your grandmother helped me with several of the recipes I just couldn't make work. You cook a lot like she did." Mrs. Potter stood. "Do you mind if I make toast? I'm not very hungry this morning."

"I could whip up some eggs or a waffle?" Angie studied the woman in front of her. Did she look paler than normal?

"No, toast is fine. Sometimes my meds mess with my stomach. So I have to eat something, even if, like today, I'm not hungry. You make whatever you want for yourself. I'm good with toast."

"If you're sure?" Angie stood and opened the fridge. If she'd been here alone she would have a piece of that leftover chicken and a sliced tomato for breakfast. She pulled out the chicken. "Last chance."

"I'll have some for lunch. I'm sure you're going to head into work sometime today."

Angie cringed. She really didn't have to go in, but she wanted to talk to Barb over at the Red Eye about Katherine. "If you're okay with me leaving, I do have a couple of errands to run."

"I'm not a child. You don't have to babysit me." As she talked, smoke came from the toaster.

Angie stepped around her, pulled out the burned bread, and put in fresh, changing the setting from frozen item to bread. "I know I don't have to babysit, but I don't want you to be lonely."

"I never can figure out that darn toaster. The first one Mr. Potter bought me had one setting. If it wasn't dark enough, you pushed down the plunger again. This one you have to have an engineering degree to operate." She sank into a chair. "Despite what just happened, I will be fine in your house alone for a few hours this afternoon."

* * * *

Angie thought about the changes that Mrs. Potter had seen in her lifetime. Nona had told her that she'd gotten her first microwave in the eighties. Now Angie couldn't see working in a kitchen without one. She hoped Mrs. Potter would be fine, but if something happened, Angie understood. The world was changing too fast for her, and Angie needed to be more patient with her and her actions.

She parked the car in front of the Red Eye. The street was almost empty. Monday afternoons were always pretty quiet in River Vista. She pushed open the heavy wooden door and, like on her last visit, the darkness of the place enveloped her as she walking into a cloud smelling of old, spilt beer and cigarette smoke. Angie blinked her eyes and finally focused on Barb sitting at the bar, reading a newspaper.

She walked up and sat next to her. "How do you read in this light?"

"Years of experience." She sat the paper down. "Besides, the news is always the same, more roads, more schools, more taxes. I don't know why I even buy the stupid thing anymore."

Angie hadn't read a paper in years. Not since she'd left Nona's. "You may want to upgrade and read the news on your phone."

"Honey, my phone is hanging up there on the wall. I don't have one of those computers you young people are so fond of carrying everywhere. If someone needs to talk to me, they know where to find me." She got up and refilled her coffee.

She held out a cup, but Angie shook her head. "I'm good."

"So why are you here? I'm sure it's not to have a beer at one thirty on a Monday." She came around and sat next to her. "Not that I don't welcome the company. I'll get a few people in around five and a few tonight, but Mondays are usually pretty slow. People working off the Sunday guilts."

Angie pulled out her phone. "I wanted to show you something."

Barb waited as Angie found the photo, then she took the phone from her. Squinting, she sighed and reached for a pair of reading glasses. "I can't see anything without these damn things. Sucks getting older. I had perfect eyesight for years. Now I need these just to write out my checks."

The glasses had fake rhinestones on the side. But the circular frames almost looked cute on Barb's face. "They don't look that bad."

"I bought them at the Walmart over in Meridian. I don't expect them to be high fashion." She peered at the picture. "Well, I'll be."

Angie felt the excitement building. "You recognize her?"

"Definitely. That's the girl that was all over Javier that night. The one that made Heather so mad." She peered closer. "Wait, is that the Methodist church foyer? You found this girl in a church?"

Angie smiled and nodded.

Barb whistled, "So star girl is a believer. Do you know her name?"

"Katherine Elliott. She lives in Boise, but her folks live here in town. She went by Katie Huff in high school."

"Wait, that's Katie Huff? She used to sneak in here when I wasn't bartending. She had a really good fake ID. Finally, I took her picture and put it behind the bar. I heard after that she started driving into Meridian for her fun." Barb shook her head and put away the glasses. "I guess people don't really change."

After saying her goodbyes, Angie sat in the car and emailed the picture and what she'd found out to Sheriff Brown. She could have gone in the office and showed him, but she didn't want him doing something like lecturing her on staying out of the investigation. Or worse, taking her phone.

As she finished, a knock sounded on her window. For the second time in two days, she turned to look into Ian's eyes.

"You need to come speak with Allen." He opened the door and reached for her hand. "He got a call from Mexico."

Chapter 16

Ian hadn't said anything else but when she asked him what was going on, he shook his head, urging her to walk faster. "I don't know. I was visiting Allen when the call came in. He wrote a note asking me to go find you. I stepped outside to call you but saw your car."

"Erica has to be okay. Mrs. Potter needs her." Angie pushed away the fear. It could be anything. Like a lost passport. Or a misunderstanding from a language discrepancy.

When they got into Sheriff Brown's office, he was off the phone and writing down something. He looked up as the door opened. "Well, that was fast."

"She was just down the street." Ian gently moved Angie into a chair and then sat next to her.

"Did something happen to Erica?" Angie blurted out the words, hoping to get the bad news quickly. Ripping the Band-Aid off quickly was the only way she dealt with bad news.

"They don't know. They found her passport in the possession of a street thief. They were calling to see if she was actually still in Mexico. Do you have her itinerary?"

"Of course." Angie scrolled through her email, looking for one from Erica. "She just called Mrs. Potter Saturday. She was alive on Saturday."

"And no one's saying she's dead today, just that she doesn't have her passport in her possession," Sheriff Brown said quietly. "Don't jump to conclusions when we don't know what's going on yet."

"She was supposed to come home today, but she missed her transport from the resort. Maybe we should just try to call her." Angie's fingers were shaking so hard it was difficult to type in Sheriff Brown's email.

Ian took the phone from her. "Let me help."

He finished keying in the email address, then hit send. "What should we do?"

"We can't tell Mrs. Potter. Not until we know something definite." Angie's eyes went wild. "She'll be devastated."

"Then I suggest you pull yourself together before you go home. You look like someone just died." Sheriff Brown glanced at his computer screen and found her second email. He opened it, then forwarded it to an address he carefully typed into the address field from a written note from his book. After he sent the email, he turned and studied Angie. "Sorry if that came out a little harsh. Seriously, all we know right now is some lowlife has her passport. Or had. According to the guy who called me, the man isn't violent, he's a collector. I'm sure now that we have Erica's itinerary, we'll find her safe and sound and get her home."

"You're just saying that to get me to calm down." Angie tried to take in a breath but she felt like someone was squeezing her lungs. She closed her eyes and started counting to five. One, two, three, four, five, repeating the mantra. Finally the tightness eased and she could breathe. When she opened her eyes, both Sheriff Brown and Ian were watching her closely. "Okay, sorry, I was getting a little panicked there. But Erica's important to Mrs. Potter. She's so young."

"Don't get started again. We don't know what's going on. As soon as I do, I'll call you. Just try not to worry Mrs. Potter. I've reached out to the girl's parents and let them know what's going on. They asked me not to involve their mother until we have to. They are driving up from California, just in case." He smiled. "Having her itinerary is going to help, I promise you."

"Thanks." Now that reinforcements were on the way, Angie didn't feel so alone. She started to stand but then dropped back down. "Did you see my other email?"

"I've been a little busy here." He scrolled down and clicked to open it. He read it and then turned to her. "You think this has something to do with Javier's disappearance or Heather's death?"

"I don't know. One or both?" All of a sudden Angie felt too tired. Like the weight of the world was on her and her alone. "I guess I figured you'd want to talk to the woman who was Javier's alibi for Heather's death."

"And you know for certain this is her?"

Angie nodded. "I recognized her from the description Javier gave me of the sprinkle of star tattoos on her arm, but then, I took the picture to Barb and she confirmed it."

"I'll check it out. I just wish that boy would come out of hiding. He's making things worse." Sheriff Brown ran a hand through his thinning hair.

"If you don't need Angie, I think I'm going to take her for a quick lunch." Ian stood and held out a hand for her to take. "I'll have my phone on me in case you hear something."

As they walked out, Angie stumbled, feeling the shock of the day wearing down on her. "I'm not really hungry."

"Then it will be a cheap date. All the better for my pocketbook. Some of us don't have the advantage of running one of the premier restaurants in the Treasure Valley." He took her arm and led her to her car, easing her into the passenger seat. "May I have your keys?"

She dug into her tote and gave them to him. "Just to let you know, the car's close to empty. If you drive it, you have to fill it."

"See? Now you're feeling better." He started up the car and glanced at the gauges. "You like to live on the edge, don't you? First stop, the gas station on the corner."

After they filled the tank, he drove into Meridian and grabbed takeout chicken. As they pulled away, she reached into the bag for a biscuit. They were best when they were hot. She didn't even care that she'd just had better fried chicken at home yesterday. "You are a big spender. Where are we going now? Back to your place?"

"Someplace better." He turned up the music and drove back toward River Vista, except when he got to the turnoff, he kept going straight. Finally there was a sign, pointing to the left. He turned onto the dirt road and took the car up to a parking lot. "We're here."

"We're in the middle of nothing. Where's here?" Angie tried to see a landmark that would explain why they'd stopped.

"Grab the food." He opened the door. "I'll bring the drinks."

Shaking her head, she checked her phone. No service. She stuffed the phone in her pocket and followed him. "Do you even get cell service out here? Because I don't. We told Sheriff Brown to call us with any updates."

"Stop worrying. It's been less than thirty minutes. Things move a little slower in the southern hemisphere." He set the drinks down on a picnic table in front of a large stone with a plaque attached to the side. Checking his phone, he nodded. "Besides, I guess my service provider is better than yours."

Knowing that at least he could be reached, Angie relaxed a little. She started to unpack the food, but he waved her away. "Let me take that. Go read the plaque."

She stepped toward the rock and started reading. "Oh, this is Initial Point? I've never been here."

"I figured that when you thought I was bringing you out here to kill you and dump the body." He came up behind her and gave her the glass of tea she'd ordered at the drive-in. "I found this place a few months ago. I try to visit all the historic places in the area, but this one is special."

"It's the start of the entire valley. The point where the government took their first survey in Idaho to start measuring and breaking out the area." As a kid, that hadn't meant much to her. Just a rock in the middle of the desert. But now, looking around, she could see the history of the place. "Want to climb to the top?"

A small staircase took them up even farther, and from that vantage point she could see miles of empty land. Ian put his arms around her. "I like knowing where things began. Did you know this used to be an active volcano many years ago?"

"I think I remember that from fourth grade." Seeing Ian's confused look, she laughed. "We do Idaho history in fourth grade here. Then we learn about the rest of the world as we grow."

"That must be the reason I get along with the 4-H kids so well. We both are just starting out exploring our world." He leaned against the pipe fence that surrounded the platform. "You are very lucky to have grown up in such a place."

"I would have disagreed with you when I was in high school. Moving here from Colorado seemed like stepping back in time."

"Sometimes that's not a bad idea." He put his arm around her. "Let's go eat before the chicken gets cold."

They started down, and something flashed by the corner of the stairs. Angie leaned over the railings. There was something down there, but it was up against the rock foundation. "Hold on, I think someone dropped something."

"Be careful. It's probably a broken bottle. I understand this is quite the make-out spot when the sun goes down." He followed her down the stairs.

Casting a glance at him over her shoulder, she laughed. "So that's why you brought me out here? To make out?"

"What am I, a teenage boy? If I wanted to make out with you I'd invite you upstairs to my apartment to see my etchings." He joined her as she crouched by the wall.

Looking up, she tried to gauge where she'd been when she saw the flash. "One of us should have stayed where I was. It would have made this easier."

"No worries, I have a photographic memory." He counted up the stairs and then pointed.

Angie's gaze followed his arm, and when he pointed to the ground, she leaned forward. She picked up a stick and moved what looked like a rock out of the way. Turned over, the rock showed its true nature as a beat-up wallet, and the flash had been from the screen of a cell phone. "Well, I'll be."

"You were right. Someone did drop something. I bet the wallet has an unused condom in it and this poor chap didn't get lucky that night." Ian reached to grab the wallet.

Angie stopped his hand. She didn't know why, but something felt off. "Go get one of the plastic bags from lunch and put it over your hand before you touch that."

Ian rocked back on his heels. "Why?"

Angie pointed to the inscription on the leather. "Because that's the logo for Pamplona Farms. I think that wallet belongs to Javier."

Ian went back to the table and found not one but two plastic bags. Then he carefully flipped open the wallet. An Idaho driver's license was in the window pocket. Javier Easterly smiled back up at them. Ian quickly closed the leather and bagged it and the phone in the two bags. "I'm going to call Allen."

Angie walked back to the table and sat down while Ian spoke with Allen. Her stomach was growling, but she didn't want to unpack anything if they were just going to be heading back into town. Ian joined her at the table and handed her a plate. "We're staying?"

"Allen's on his way out here with the crime scene boys. I doubt if they'll mind if we eat lunch while we wait for him to arrive." He dished up mashed potatoes on both plates and then poured the gravy. Holding the bucket of chicken open, he smiled. "White or dark meat?"

"White, of course, it's the best." She took an oversized breast piece and put it on her plate.

Ian grinned and took out two drumsticks and a thigh. "Best answer ever. We won't have any disagreements over who eats what."

"You seem to be planning our future one decision at a time." Angie bit into the chicken, and crumbs from the coating fell onto her plate.

"I like to imagine where we might be in ten or fifty years. I'm a bit of a planner, if you haven't noticed." He cleaned the drumstick in one bite. "Besides, you should see your face when I talk about our future. You get all freaked out."

"That's not funny." She slapped him lightly on the arm. "I'm trying to be serious here."

He rubbed the spot where she'd hit him. "So am I, my dear, so am I."

They had finished their lunch and returned the empty containers to the back of Angie's SUV by the time Sheriff Brown and his deputies showed up. He got out of his car and walked over to the picnic table where Angie and Ian were sitting. "What did you dig up now? You know I have a life that doesn't involve following you two around every minute of every day."

"The evidence is over there." Ian pointed to the edge of the table. "We didn't touch either one of them. You should be thanking Angie, she found the stuff."

"Found it or planted it? It's quite coincidental that you two just happen to be out here today."

Ian's voice got low and dangerous. "It was my idea to come out here, not Angie's. Do you suspect me of having something to do with Javier's disappearance?"

"Of course not. You're twisting my words." Sheriff Brown took off his hat and ran his hand through his hair. "Miss Turner, I'm sorry for any misunderstanding between us. I know you had nothing to do with this, but you do seem to show up at the exact right or wrong time lately."

"Tell me about it. All I want is a successful business, a happy neighbor, and good friends." Angie checked her watch. "Speaking of Mrs. Potter, I should be getting back to the house. I suppose it's too much to ask if you've heard anything about Erica?"

"Sorry, not yet. I'll check my email as soon as I'm back in the office." He slapped a hand on Ian's back, but even Angie could see that bygones weren't bygones yet. "I'll talk to you tomorrow."

"Let's go, Angie. I'll drive you back to town. I'm sorry our date wasn't as relaxing as I'd hoped." He took her arm and led her to the passenger side, then with one last glance at Sheriff Brown, he got in the driver's side and started the engine.

"You shouldn't be mad at him. He was just doing his job." Angie spoke quietly.

Ian put the car in reverse and backed out into the desert, then turned around to get back on the dirt road. "No, he wasn't just doing his job. He's been concerned about us dating. Like I need someone to give me permission. This was just a continuation of that argument."

"Wait, he thinks you're too good for me?" Angie looked in the rearview mirror and saw Sheriff Brown talking to his men. "I should go back and kick him in the shins."

A smile curved on Ian's lips. "It's not that. He just thinks I should be more settled before I date anyone. I don't think he wants me stuck in River Vista, like he feels."

"He realizes you're an adult, right?" Angie shook her head. She thought of her conversation with Mrs. Potter about Nona not wanting Angie to come home for her final days. "Sometimes the people we love have weird expectations of us. I guess we've never talked about the long term, but it's early in this thing, right?"

"So early you cringe a bit when I introduce you as my girlfriend." He laughed as he caught her gaze. "Like now. Don't worry, I'm not ready for the whole lifetime commitment thing. I hope we're moving there, but we have time."

The rest of the drive into town was quiet. Between finding Javier's phone and wallet and thinking about what that might mean to Estebe's cousin, the possibility of Erica being missing, and the conversation she'd just had with Ian, Angie had a lot going on in her head. She needed some quiet to think, and she knew just the place to get it.

As soon as she got home, she loaded up Dom. Mrs. Potter was busy watching her shows, so she didn't even get up when Angie popped her head in to tell her she was taking Dom for a hike. She packed water bottles, dog treats, and a few granola bars into the backpack she kept hanging on a hook by the back door, just for this type of outing.

Back in the car, she breathed a sigh of relief. Mrs. Potter hadn't sensed a problem. If she could just get her game face on before she went back home, maybe Mrs. Potter wouldn't even have to know something was up with Erica. The girl could be at the airport waiting for her plane right now. Angie threw good vibes in the air, hoping that was exactly what was happening.

All she needed to do right now was hike. She parked in the canyon lot and got Dom out and on his leash. Checking the time, she put an alarm on her watch to alert her when an hour had passed. Then she'd make her way back to the car and head home to make dinner. Cooking would help ease this upheaval too. Right now, she wanted to not think. Maybe that way, she'd be able to unconsciously sort through all the things that had happened and figure out what had been bothering her since they'd found Javier's wallet.

She was at the top of the trail when she realized what she'd missed. What the sheriff had also missed. Angie hurried down to the car where she could get cell reception and put a call in to the police station.

Chapter 17

At home, Angie ran upstairs to take a shower before starting dinner. Sheriff Brown hadn't been overjoyed to hear from her but had grudgingly agreed to check out her theory. There was no way Javier's wallet and phone had fallen up against the stone foundation. If he'd dropped them, the items would have fallen a good foot away from the foundation. The top of the viewing platform had been expanded to allow for more visitors to the site. No, if Javier had placed those items there, he'd done it from the ground.

Letting the hot water flow over her, she thought it was more likely that whoever had Javier had hidden those items, thinking no one would notice them at the remote site or, if they did, they'd take the money and credit cards and probably sell the phone. To Angie, it was clear. Javier wasn't just missing or hiding out until this whole thing blew over, he'd been kidnapped. And that was where Sheriff Brown had disagreed with her conclusion.

At least he'd agreed to check out Javier's phone once they'd gotten it charged. Angie was sure that one of those calls had been from the kidnapper. And maybe that was the same person who had murdered Heather. The original plan of framing Javier for Heather's murder hadn't been enough. Javier being perceived as running off would seal his fate. At least, that was what was supposed to happen. As soon as Sheriff Brown had found Katherine, the frame-up had been busted.

Or maybe that was just wishful thinking. The logic made sense to Angie, but she didn't have to convince a jury. She dried off and then went downstairs to play dumb with Mrs. Potter.

Luckily Mrs. Potter was in her room on the phone. Angie mimed eating and Mrs. Potter nodded. They were getting pretty good at this sign language,

just like an old couple. Angie would miss her when Erica returned. She
didn't even let the alternative fill her mind.

She'd just finished cooking the pork chops and was ready to start plating
when Mrs. Potter came into the kitchen. Her face beamed, and the smile
that curved her lips could have been a mile wide.

"Sorry about that. My son and daughter-in-law are coming into town
tomorrow and wanted to make sure they could stay at the house. I guess
we won't have to wait for Erica to get home for you to get rid of me." Mrs.
Potter took down two glasses. "Iced tea?"

"That would be perfect."

As she poured the tea, Mrs. Potter kept up the happy chattering. "I bet
they're here to see Erica. They were so worried about her trip to Mexico. I
thought her father was going to try to forbid her to go. And you know how
well that works for children. I think your father tried that one summer,
forbidding you to go with your friends to the swimming hole down by
the creek."

Angie smiled. "I got on my bike and left when he went into the house.
Boy, I was in trouble for that one. They didn't think to look at the creek
for hours."

"I think your grandmother told them to let you have your head a little.
They were always so worried about you and what might happen." Mrs.
Potter sat and put a napkin over her lap. "We never worry about the right
things and then they smack us square in the face."

Angie knew she was talking about how Angie's parents were killed, but
a chill ran down her spine as she thought about Erica. *Be safe,* she thought,
trying to push the image across the wavelengths to Erica, no matter where
she was. "I'm glad your family is coming in to be with you."

Something must have shown through her tone or choice of words as
Mrs. Potter's head came up sharply. "What do you mean?"

Angie shook her head and tried to deflect the emotion. "Nothing, I'm
just glad they're coming. I've been thinking a lot about what you said about
Nona not asking me to come. I feel sad that she didn't trust me enough to
let me make my own decision."

Mrs. Potter tapped Angie's hand. "No use crying over spilt milk—or
bourbon, as my grandmother used to say."

* * * *

After a fitful night of sleep, Angie came downstairs to find Mrs. Potter
in the kitchen drinking coffee. "I hope you don't mind, I'm doing a load of

laundry before I pack the rest of my clothes. No need to haul dirty clothes home when no one's going to be there until after four today anyway."

"I don't mind at all." Angie poured her own cup, sipping the black gold like it was an elixir.

"You don't look well. Maybe you're doing too much." Mrs. Potter started to rise. "I could make breakfast."

"No, I'm fine. I just didn't sleep very well last night. What about loaded scrambled eggs over country potato hash for breakfast?"

Mrs. Potter sank back into her chair. "I was going to hard boil eggs with toast. You win."

"After breakfast, though, I need to run into town for some groceries. Do you mind?"

Mrs. Potter opened the paper that the carrier had started delivering to Angie's place last week when he was told about the temporary move. "I'll be fine. Sometimes I think you worry as much as Erica."

"Can I bring something back for you? Maybe fresh milk and bread since you'll be having visitors?"

"That's a lovely offer." She grabbed a piece of paper from the middle of the table. "I'll make you a short list. And I've got cash in my purse."

"I'm going to feed Precious and Mabel, then I'll be back in to start breakfast." Angie filled her cup again and headed outside to the barn. As usual, her hen was out in the yard, hanging around the water faucet. Angie refilled Mabel's water dish, then threw out corn for her. As Angie entered the barn, Precious ran to the gate and bleated. Angie gave the goat a rub on the top of her head, and then filled her feed dish.

Glancing out the barn window to make sure Mrs. Potter hadn't followed her, she dialed Sheriff Brown's cell. What did that say about her that she knew his cell by heart? Getting voice mail, she left a quick message. "Have you heard anything about Erica? Call me."

Tucking her phone back into her pants, she headed inside to cook and make small talk about anything but Mrs. Potter's granddaughter. Later that morning, she was almost done with the shopping. Mrs. Potter's few items had turned out to be a half page of things, but Angie didn't mind. It gave her time to think through what had happened the last week. As she turned the corner, she ran into another cart. "Sorry, wasn't paying attention."

Katherine Elliot smirked at her. "I thought I recognized you. Miss Grace from high school. I can tell you haven't changed any."

"And apparently, neither have you." Angie went to go around the cart and Katherine blocked her.

"So what's it to you if I slept with Javier? From what I heard at church, you already have two men on the line. Why do you want a third?"

"I don't have two men on the line. I'm dating one." She stared at Katherine. "Just one, Ian McNeal. Who told you I was dating someone else?"

"It's a small town. You can't go running around with Estebe and think that people aren't going to notice." Katherine smiled, and Angie was reminded of how mean she'd been as a teenager. "Although I wouldn't mind going a round or two with Estebe if he's as good as his cousin was. Maybe you could introduce me once you're done with him?"

"Again, I'm not dating him." *And two, I wouldn't introduce you to a stray dog on the street.* She said this last part silently because she really didn't want to get in a fight with Katie Huff from high school, even if she was all grown up in this shallow woman's body. "So you took Javier to that empty apartment."

"Friend of mine's place. I'm watering her plants."

Angie didn't think Katherine had any friends, but she let that one go. "I guess Sheriff Brown talked to you."

"Allen and I go way back. He's such a sweetheart." She glanced at her watch. "Oops, I've got to go. It's been great catching up with you, but I have a pedicure in ten minutes. Don't want to be too late, they might try to give away my slot."

Angie watched as Katherine rammed her cart into Angie's, then pushed through to the dairy section. When she reached the edge of the aisle she turned back. "I can't say it was nice to see you again. I'd like to hope our paths won't cross for another ten years."

And then she was gone, and Angie was left with all the things she wanted to say. Like how much of a jerk Katie, no, Katherine was and how she'd grown up just fine even though Katie and her gang had tormented her for years. She took a deep breath. This was the downside of living in a small town. Everyone knew your history and your dirty laundry. But if Missy Stockwell didn't stop telling people that Angie was two-timing Ian with Estebe, well, she would have to do something about it.

Angie was still fuming as she loaded the bags of groceries in her car. Even the checker's sunny banter hadn't gotten her out of the bad mood. As soon as she started the car, her phone rang. "What?"

"Wow, did you wake up on the wrong side of the bed or what?" Felicia sounded almost gleeful.

"Sorry. I just had a run-in with my high school nemesis. I really would have loved it if the girl had gained a few pounds and wore sweats to the store, but no, she looks like she's had work done on the top part of her and she was dressed in what I'm pretty sure was Marc Jacobs. Who wears designer clothes to grocery shop?" Angie started the car to turn on the air conditioner, but didn't pull out of her parking spot.

"Hmm, I think she might have some image issues if she's that dressed up before ten and not at the day job. Unless she's a salesperson. Maybe that's why she was so dressed up?"

Angie could hear Felicia's pondering about the reason Katherine looked like a big boss in some corporate office, but really, Angie didn't care. She blew out a breath. Staying away from the girl had worked as a teenager; she'd just have to implement that strategy now as well. Which would get her out of attending Ian's Sunday school class. She really liked sleeping in on Sunday since closing the restaurant on Saturday night took every ounce of energy she had. "Anyway, why did you call? I've got groceries in the car, so I need to get going."

"You won't believe who I met last night."

Now Angie did pull out of the parking spot. "Okay, you can tell me while I'm driving home."

"Actually, I think you'll want to hear this directly from me. Besides, I videotaped our conversation. You need to see this."

"You what? Isn't that illegal?" Angie turned the car right out of the parking lot and drove past the road that would have taken her home. Maybe this investigation thing was getting too dicey. If Felicia got arrested for taping a conversation, she'd never forgive herself for starting her down this path.

"Not when the other person knows about it." She sighed, and Angie knew she was testing Felicia's patience. "Just come by my apartment. I'll leave the back door unlocked for you."

Angie started to answer but realized Felicia had already hung up on her. This was serious. One, her friend was frustrated with her over a minuscule comment and two, she never just hung up. She glanced in the rearview mirror at the bags of food. The only good thing was she didn't have any ice cream in the bags and she'd repacked the frozen and refrigerated items together in a cooler bag she kept in the back of the SUV for bigger trips to the warehouse store in Boise.

She parked the car, hitting the fob to remote lock it, and jogged up the few stairs to the back door. As promised, it was unlocked, but as soon as she went inside, she locked it again. With a murder just down the alleyway, Angie wanted to make sure that her friend was safe in the building.

Felicia was waiting for her at the top of the stairs. "This will only take a few minutes, I promise."

Angie followed her into the apartment and Felicia waved her to the couch. "I'm sorry I'm a grump. That girl always knew just how to push my buttons."

"Don't let her in your head. You're a strong, capable woman. Don't let the past overwhelm that." Felicia fiddled with her phone and then pushed a button on the screen. "Watch this."

"Hi, Felicia's friend! I'm Thomas Post, and I understand you've seen one of my productions as Jerry Reno. Or at least you've been looking for my alter ego." He grinned at someone off screen.

"Is this for real?" Angie lifted her gaze to meet Felicia's.

She nodded. "It's real all right. Keep watching. What he says next is crazy but makes a weird sort of sense."

Turning back to the video, Angie focused on Thomas's message.

"Anyway, I'm sorry to hear about Heather. She was a sweet girl. Easy to get to know, but man, was she hung up on that Javier guy. I guess the person who hired me to seduce her wanted her to know there were other fish in the sea." He shrugged and glanced at what Angie assumed was Felicia holding the camera.

"Go on," the unseen Felicia, who must have been positioned in front of the guy, prodded.

"Okay, sorry, I'll try to make this short. I've had a couple of beers so I'm a little buzzed. Anyway, my agent got a call about this gig and gave me a picture of Heather. She told me where to find her and to flirt with her. I didn't have to actually do anything, let's get that straight. I don't have sex for money, unless someone's paying big film money. Then I would." He giggled.

"Actors," Angie muttered.

"All I was supposed to do was make her think there was a chance between us. And it was easy since that jerk had taken off with some blonde moments before. I saw my chance, jumped in, and we had a great time. I had to leave at midnight since I had an open casting the next morning, but we exchanged numbers—well, I gave her Jerry's fake number. And then I left."

"And she was still in the bar then?"

"Yep. Alive and well. You can ask anyone at the bar. Well, maybe the bartender. By that time, people were getting a little sloppy." He grinned. "And the next morning, I nailed the audition. I'm heading up to Vancouver in the morning to shoot a pilot. It's just a made-for-television thing, but you gotta start somewhere Wish me luck."

The video ended and Angie handed the phone back to Felicia. "Jerry Reno was hired to flirt with Heather?"

"And get this, his agent got the booking from an online request. He was paid standard actor fees and the funds were dropped off in cash at his agent's office. The secretary thought it was a video packet when it showed up on her desk. She claims she went to the bathroom and it was there when she came back."

"And no one thought this was weird?" Angie shook her head. "Why would someone hire a guy to be nice to Heather?"

"Actually, the way the instructions were written, he was supposed to get between her and Javier, one way or the other. Since he'd already taken off with Katherine, all Thomas had to be was a shoulder to cry on." Felicia glanced at her phone and tossed it gently on the coffee table. "He was at the Foothills Bar last night when I met a friend for drinks. He says if he gets this television thing, he's dumping the local show, by the way. I know you were dying to know that piece of industry gossip."

"How long did you have to be nice to him in order to get that statement?" Angie could see her friend had been annoyed with the guy.

"Too long. My friend took off after the first round of drinks. Man, that guy likes to talk about himself." She adjusted a pillow on the chair where she sat. "I don't get it. What's the point?"

"To help Heather realize she deserved better than Javier?" All of a sudden, Angie knew who might have hired Thomas. "That sounds like something a friend would do."

"Definitely. I'd do something that stupid if I thought you weren't thinking straight." Felicia narrowed her eyes. "Wait, you know who it was that hired him?"

Angie nodded. "I do, and so do you. I just don't know why."

Chapter 18

Angie tried to call Hope on the way home, but she only got voice mail. "Call me when you get this. I need to talk to you."

She hoped the sternness in her voice would get the young woman to call, sooner rather than later. Sheriff Brown had been looking at Thomas Post as a possible suspect when really, all he was doing was giving Heather some time and a boost in her self-esteem. "At least she died happy," Angie said as she pulled into the driveway.

An unknown car sat near the door, and as she got out of her car, a woman came out of the house with a box. "You must be Angie. So good to meet you. I can't believe I've never really talked to you in all the years Donald and I have been married."

"What's going on?" The woman clearly knew who Angie was, but Angie didn't have a clue.

"Oh, we're just moving Harriet back across the street. We have at least five hours before Erica's plane lands, so we might as well put the time to good use rather than sitting at the airport fretting." The woman put the box into the trunk. "You don't remember me, do you? I'm Robin, Donald's wife? Erica's mother?"

Memories flooded back to Angie as she stared at the woman. "I didn't recognize you. What has it been? Five, maybe ten years?"

"I don't think I've seen you since you went off to college. Your Nona was always bragging about how well you were doing in California. And now you have your own place here in town." Robin reached out and pulled Angie into a hug. "Thank you so much for taking care of Harriet. I was so worried that she'd be beside herself when she found out about Erica. And then to find out she didn't know, that was such a blessing."

"You didn't tell her, did you?" Angie's eyes widened. Mrs. Potter was going to be really, really mad at her if they'd told her everything.

Robin glanced at the door. "We didn't mean to, but Donald was so upset, and when he got the call from Sheriff Brown, well, he just broke down in front of her. So we had to explain."

"I would have thought that you would have respected me enough not to hide something like this from me, Angela Turner." Mrs. Potter stood at the kitchen door staring at her. "I'm truly disappointed in you."

"Mrs. Potter, we didn't know what was going on, and I didn't want to worry you." Angie took a couple of steps toward her, but Mrs. Potter's icy stare stopped her from climbing the steps to the porch.

"I'm neither an invalid nor a child." She moved toward the car. "You should have let me deal with my feelings on my own. Thank you for the place to stay. I'll be going home now."

Angie could hear the goodbye in her words. She didn't know if her neighbor would ever forgive her. She watched as Robin helped Mrs. Potter into their car.

Robin paused before she got into the front seat and looked up apologetically. "I'm sure Erica will be glad to see you when we get her home. Her flight is coming in around seven tonight. I know you must have been worried about her. I'd explain, but Mother seems to be in a hurry."

"Thanks for letting me know that Erica's okay and coming home." Angie stood on the porch as the car made the short trip across the street. Mrs. Potter didn't look back; instead, she marched right into the house as soon as the car stopped. Dom whined deep in his throat. "I know, boy. I messed up on this one."

She stepped off the stairs and went to the barn to feed Precious and Mabel. After the chores were done, she sank down on her knees next to the goat's pen and petted her. Dom lay down next to her and put his head in her lap. This was her family. A dog that full grown would be as big as a barrel, a goat that loved eating her way through random items that wound up in her pen, and a hen named Mabel who judged every move Angie made.

Her phone rang. She answered without looking at the screen. "Yep?"

"Angie? Are you okay?" Hope's voice echoed in the big, empty barn.

She stood and brushed the straw off her butt. "I'm fine. You just caught me in the middle of a pity party. I'm glad you called back. Why don't you meet me for dinner tonight? I need to talk to you."

"Sure, but we could just do it now." Hope's voice quavered.

"No, let's talk at dinner." Angie started walking toward the house. "What about seven at the Farmer's Pig in Meridian? I've always wanted to try that place out."

"One of the culinary students in my pastry class last semester is interning there. I'd love to go." Hope paused for a beat, and Angie wondered if they'd gotten disconnected. "Are you sure you're okay, though?"

"Fit as a fiddle." Angie threw one last glace at Mrs. Potter's house across the road as she went inside to shower and get ready.

* * * *

Angie sat on a bench in front of the restaurant waiting for Hope to arrive. She was ten minutes early, and the smells coming from the restaurant behind her were making her mouth water. The place was known for its barbecue and down-home Southern cooking, right in the banana belt of Idaho.

Hope walked down the sidewalk toward her. She was dressed in a floral sundress with her hair pulled back into a ponytail. She looked younger than her years, but Angie saw the concern in her eyes as she greeted her. Angie knew, without a doubt, that Hope thought she was here to be fired.

Angie gave her a quick hug to try to ease her fears. The way Hope had stiffened up, Angie thought she might have just made it worse. "Let's go eat. I'm starving."

The hostess quickly seated them, and they had dinner rolls and butter in front of them in what seemed like seconds. Angie glanced around. "Felicia should come here. Their service is amazing."

Water glasses were set and filled and a server in a white button-down shirt and black pants handed them two menus. "Our specials today are the rib eye steak—Idaho grown beef—and a loaded Idaho spud to go with it. Of course, you can substitute any of our other sides. And we have a trout from the Marsing farm, pan fried with freshly cut French fries. Take your time and let me know if you have questions. Can I get you something to drink besides water?"

Angie ordered a glass of wine, but when she looked at Hope, the girl shook her head. "Iced tea, please."

When the server left the table, Angie focused on her menu. "Do you drink, Hope?"

"Not a lot. We sometimes have wine with dinner at home, but I've got a lot to do tonight after dinner. I picked up my books and syllabus from school today. I need to get a head start on the homework if I'm going to be able to keep up."

"If work gets too much..." Angie started, but Hope shook her head. She swallowed hard. "I'm learning so much working with you and Estebe, not to mention Nancy and Matt. I don't want to lose that or fall behind in my classes."

"But if you need time to study, I'll understand." Angie smiled. "You'll keep your job, you just let me know what hours you can work and we'll make it happen."

"You didn't call me to fire me?" Hope's face brightened. "I was afraid when I got your call..."

"Let's order first and then I need to ask you something. And you have to be honest with me." Angie tapped the table. "I'm buying you dinner, so you're in my debt."

Hope laughed. "That line hasn't worked on me since I was in high school. But I'll answer your questions honestly." She held up a hand in a Scout salute. "I swear."

They chatted about the way the dining room was set up until the waiter came to take their order, then Angie took a deep breath.

"I know this is a hard time for you, since you and Heather were friends." Angie noticed the surprise in Hope's eyes. This was not what she'd been expecting to talk about.

"Yes. She'll be missed." Hope picked up her water and took a drink. "It's nice of you to think about me, but really, it's Heather's family who are really suffering."

"I bet. Anyway, I just wanted to know why you hired Thomas Post to hit on your friend."

Hope choked on the bite of bread she'd just taken. She took a while to answer as she took another sip of water and then wiped her mouth on the napkin. "I'm not sure I understand."

"It's simple, Hope. Why did you hire an actor to make your friend feel special?" Angie watched the emotion flow through Hope's face.

"She deserved more than that jerk would ever give her. But she was stubborn and maybe a little low on confidence. I decided to show her that other men would want her too." She sighed, leaning back in her chair. "Stupid, right? Wait, don't answer that. Anyway, how did you find out?"

Angie tore off a piece of roll and buttered it. "Felicia meets the most interesting people."

"Small towns, you can't keep a secret to save your life." Hope smiled. "He did a great job. She texted me that night and said she'd found someone new. She sounded happy. Well, you know about that, since the cops took my phone and all."

"That's nice. But how did you pull this all together? I mean, you're busy with work and school. Where did you find the time to set this up?"

"I had some help. Kendra's mom, Carlotta Mendoza, and I were talking after church one day. She said what a lovely girl Heather was and that she knew we were friends."

"Did that strike you as odd at all?"

Hope shook her head. "Not at all. She was saying that Javier could be a little bit of a jerk and I told her in no uncertain terms the guy was a huge jerk, not just a little bit. Then we got to talking. She said Heather deserved better and wasn't it a shame that someone didn't just show her what a gem she was."

"And then when you agreed, she told you she knew this guy," Angie guessed.

Hope nodded. "Exactly. She said he was an actor who was always looking for side jobs. She said we could trust him to be charming and make her see there were more fish in the sea." Her eyes widened. "He didn't kill Heather, did he? Did I send a murderer to date my friend?"

"No. Most definitely no. From what I've heard, when he left her at the bar, she was alive." Angie mused as she moved the food on her plate from one side to another. "I just don't get why Carlotta would want to help out Heather. She barely knew her, right? I mean, Javier goes through a lot of girls, why Heather?"

"Maybe she was getting tired of seeing him mess with the women's heads. If I had to go to family events with him, I'd be a little annoyed too."

"Maybe." Angie decided to push the questions aside and focus on getting to know Hope better. "We've talked enough about sad things. Let's change the subject. Tell me about your school. Any favorite classes or instructors?"

By the time they finished dinner, Angie felt like she knew her youngest team member a little more. The girl was honest, loyal, intelligent, and had a wicked sense of humor. Driving home, she made a decision to schedule one-on-ones with the rest of the team. Even Estebe, even though as soon as she set up a dinner to talk, Missy Stockwell would see them and run and tell Ian and the rest of the world Angie Turner was a cheater. And Mrs. Potter would chime in and call her a liar as well.

She wanted to fall into bed and sleep for days, but instead, she took care of Precious and Mabel, checked Dom's water and food, then dragged her tired body upstairs. Dom followed and soon both of them were asleep.

* * * *

When Angie woke Wednesday morning, she wanted to go right back to sleep. But the baby monitor told her that Precious was up and talking to Mabel about breakfast. Angie could probably not use the monitor anymore, but it was kind of cute waking up to the sound of a goat bleating for her breakfast. In San Francisco her secondary alarm clock was the traffic noise on the street below. As the day progressed, it got louder and louder, until finally, in the deep of the night, it quieted again. Her life here was so much simpler.

As she walked out to the barn, she glanced over at the Potter house. She could see people milling about the kitchen, up and making breakfast for the family. Having Erica home and safe was the best news of the week, even if Mrs. Potter was furious at Angie for not spilling the beans. She did her morning chores and then walked to the irrigation ditch behind the barn and let loose the water dam she'd set yesterday morning. Her neighbor would get water a few hours sooner than scheduled, but Angie's back pasture was soaked. Precious was a lucky goat because she had the entire pasture to herself. If the grass got longer, Angie might have to get a second goat to keep it down, but she didn't think so.

Walking back to the house, she saw Erica coming toward her. "Hey, girl, look at that tan."

Erica grinned. "I know, right? It was a perfect vacation right up to the time I missed my transport and someone stole my passport."

"So you did have fun?" Angie sighed. "I'd love to spend a week on a beach somewhere. I guess I'll either have to shorten my hours or just let the team run the County Seat without me."

"I'm sure you hire good people. You should take a vacation. Maybe Ian would like to go along." A wicked smile curved Erica's lips.

Angie shrugged, embarrassed by the suggestions. "Maybe. We haven't been dating that long. I hate for him to get the full weight of a week of being with me so soon."

"Whatever, that guy adores you." She glanced back at the house. "Mom told me that Granny went off on you. Sorry about that."

"I should have told her when Sheriff Brown told me about your passport."

"No. You did the right thing. Mom and Dad were already on their way. It was their job to tell her, not yours. You shouldn't have had to do that." Erica looked back at her house. "I think she's afraid of being alone."

"Actually, she's afraid of you putting her into a home." Angie nodded at Erica's shocked expression. "She told me that when you were delayed."

"There's no way we'd ever allow that to happen. At least until she really needs that level of care. My mom and dad are talking to her about maybe giving up the house when I graduate and moving her in with them. They have a great ranch with a separate apartment just waiting for her to say yes. But she hasn't wanted to leave home." Erica leaned against the porch railing. "I know it's hard on her to accept any limitations, including the fact she can't be alone at the house for long periods of time. I really appreciate everything you did while I was away."

They said their goodbyes and Angie wondered if Mrs. Potter would ever forgive her. She decided to stay away for a while and let the family talk out these hard options. She glanced at the house across the street. Not having Mrs. Potter live there would be a change for Angie as well. Typically, when houses of that age sold, a farm nearby would grab the property, tear down the house, and turn it into farmland. She'd had an offer from the neighboring farm for her house when Nona died. But she'd turned it down. There'd be no reason for Mrs. Potter's heirs to keep the old farmhouse in the family. Sooner or later, the house would be gone.

Feeling nostalgic, Angie pulled out her grandmother's journal and started flipping through it to try to find a recipe to make that would lift her spirits. She didn't have to be at the restaurant until that afternoon. As she started the dough for Nona's donuts, she turned on the music and tried to lose herself in the comfort of her kitchen and the actions of cooking.

A knock sounded on her door as she pulled the last batch of donuts out of the oil. She turned off the fryer and quickly sprinkled a cinnamon and sugar mixture on top of them before they cooled. She hoped it was one of the Potters so she could hand off a pile of these donuts before she tried to eat the entire batch. "Hold on, I'll be right there."

When she opened the door, her smile dropped. Instead of Erica, Robin, or even Mrs. Potter, Sheriff Brown stood on her porch. He tipped his hat and smiled. "Good day."

"Can I help you?" She couldn't help it, she was still steamed about his insinuation that she had something to do with Heather's death just because he didn't like her dating Ian. She leaned against the door, purposely not inviting him inside.

"May I come in, Angie? I think we need to talk." He took off his sunglasses and put them in his shirt pocket.

"I don't think we need to talk about anything." Angie didn't move.

"Look, I need to clear the air. I'll admit I was wrong about the whole thing out at Initial Point. I'm feeling frustrated, and now I have a missing person to deal with too. I shouldn't have taken it out on you."

"Fine, I accept your apology. Now can I get back to cooking?"

He sniffed the air. "You're making homemade donuts? Your grandmother used to bring a batch by the station every month or so saying she'd made too many."

His implication was clear; the cop wanted a donut. "Fine, come in and have one. But I'm still mad at you."

"Apologizing wasn't the only thing I came to talk about." He sat at the table and took the coffee she handed him as well as a plate of the donuts. He took a bite, sat back, and groaned. "I miss your grandmother. But these are almost better than hers were."

"Thank you." Angie grabbed her own coffee and a plate and sat across from him. "What did you need to talk about?"

"I want to know everything you've found out about this Thomas Post and why he was hitting on Heather the night of her death." He didn't look up as he continued. "And anything else you've found out while you've been nosing around my investigation."

Chapter 19

"I wasn't sure I had anything to tell." Angie took a bite of the donut, and the crunch of cinnamon sugar made her calm down a little.

He polished off the three donuts and then stood to get more. He glanced at her. "Do you mind? I haven't had breakfast yet."

"Go ahead." She watched as he piled three more donuts onto his plate. He must have really loved Nona's treats. If she ever got to where she liked him again, she might just have to make him a batch every now and then. She walked him through the video that Felicia had from Thomas Post, aka Jerry Reno. Then she told him about her conversation with Hope last night. "And don't be thinking she did anything but try to get her friend away from a bad relationship."

He nodded. "That matches what I've heard too. The guy was gone before Heather was killed, and from what his roommate said yesterday, Thomas was already home at the time of Heather's death."

"Who does that leave as a suspect? Heather didn't just stick that knife in herself. And we both know Javier didn't kill her since he was with Katie." Angie tore off a piece of her last donut and put it in her mouth to mask the bad taste just saying the woman's name left in her mouth.

"Katherine now. She goes by Katherine." He chuckled. "She was a troublemaker in high school. I can see why you don't like her."

"Everyone thought she was perfect." Angie shook her head. "High school drama isn't what the problem is today, though."

"You're right, it's not." He sipped his coffee. "What really bothers me is I can't figure out why someone went to so much trouble making it look like Javier. The only person who stands to gain if he's dead or incarcerated is his brother, Stephen. But on the night in question, he and his fiancée were having dinner in Sun Valley after watching an ice show. A gift from the bride-to-be's mother."

Angie ran her finger through the cinnamon sugar on her plate. "Wait, what did you say?"

"Stephen and Kendra were in Sun Valley?" He narrowed his eyes.

"No, about it being a gift from her mom. Seems like Carlotta is in a lot of people's business lately. She's the one who talked Hope into hiring Thomas." Angie sipped her coffee. "And she made a point of coming to talk to me at the volunteer breakfast."

"Just because a woman likes to stick her nose where it doesn't belong doesn't mean she's up to something." He looked pointedly at her. "I've already apologized for my thinking about you, now you want me to interview a woman because she sent her daughter on a holiday?"

Angie worried her bottom lip. "Okay, maybe it's reaching. But she's really nosy."

Sheriff Brown chuckled as he stood and put his cup and plate into the sink. "I'm not the one who's going to tell her that, either."

"Fine, but where is Javier?" She followed him to the door.

Sheriff Brown put on his hat and sunglasses. He looked like a bug staring at her. "That is the question, isn't it? Thank you for the donuts and coffee."

She watched as he climbed into his squad car and pulled out of the driveway. Erica was outside and gave the sheriff a quick wave, then glanced over to Angie's house. Angie closed the door.

* * * *

Angie looked forward to family meal Wednesdays. She liked listening to the chatter around the table as the servers and kitchen staff talked and bonded. Today she was going to make Nona's donuts for dessert, maybe with a drizzle of dark chocolate over the top and a bit of vanilla bean ice cream for the side. She loved taking simple desserts like donut holes and elevating them. She could try the dish out on the team and see what they thought.

Driving into town, she decided to stop at the market to grab the ingredients. She hadn't had time to add them to this week's grocery order. She grabbed a cart and almost ran into Kendra Mendoza, who was coming out of the store. "Hey, Kendra, what are you doing in town?"

"Mom's being generous. We're still at the bed-and-breakfast." Kendra flipped back her hair. "Don't get me wrong, I love being pampered, but

I really want to get back to my room and start planning my wardrobe for the cruise she wants to send us on next week."

"That's a lot of traveling." Angie leaned on her cart.

"I know, right? I swear, she has to have a boyfriend and doesn't want me to find out." Kendra's lips curved into a wicked smile. "I'd love it if she found someone. She's been alone since my dad died."

"That must be hard." Angie tried another tactic. "So why do you think she's being weird?"

Kendra looked around to make sure no one was listening. "Just between us, I went home yesterday to see if she was home, and she'd bolted the door from the inside. I knocked, but she didn't answer, and I know she was there. Her car was in the garage. And you know what was worse?"

Angie leaned forward, entranced by Kendra's story. "No, what?"

"She has the basement windows blacked out. I couldn't tell if it was paint or just paper, but who does that?" She swallowed hard. "You don't think she's into that kinky stuff, like in that book everyone was reading?"

The thought of Carlotta Mendoza even being with a man was more than Angie could stomach. "I'm sure that's not it. Maybe she's making you a wedding gift?"

Kendra nodded. "You could be right. Mom's not all that crafty, but she thinks she is. Maybe she didn't get the house fumigated. I bet she's started making something and it's turning out hideous and she doesn't want me to see until she can get it fixed. I sure hope she doesn't expect me to actually like it."

Angie didn't like the woman at all. Spoilt and ungrateful. "It's the thought that counts."

"Yeah, right." Kendra laughed like Angie had been teasing. Her phone buzzed. "Oops, I've got to go. Stephen and I are going to look at convertibles. I keep telling him it's stupid to have one here. We only have three months where you could even take it out of the garage. Nice to see you again."

Angie pushed her cart farther into the store. Kendra was exhausting, but at least she'd told her some more facts about Carlotta. Although she didn't think that Sheriff Brown would do anything if she told him that Carlotta was sending her daughter on a cruise. She finished shopping, hoping she'd get to the restaurant without meeting anyone else. She was done adulting and talking to people.

She turned the corner of the aisle and groaned. Mrs. Eisenhower was in front of the spices, and Angie needed vanilla bean and cinnamon. She took a deep breath and pushed the cart closer. "Happy Wednesday."

Mrs. Eisenhower glanced up and her face drained of color. "What are you doing here?"

"Same thing as you, shopping." Angie scanned the shelves hoping to find what she needed quickly and get away from the woman.

"I thought you bought your supplies from some business." Mrs. Eisenhower positioned herself behind her cart, like she expected Angie to strike out at any time.

"Actually, I buy my ingredients in a lot of different ways." She sighed and turned back toward Mrs. Eisenhower. She would try one more time to try to convince her she didn't steal her recipe. Angie wasn't hoping for much. She knew they'd never be best friends, but she didn't want to have to be actively avoiding the woman for the rest of her life. "Look, about the recipe—"

Mrs. Eisenhower turned red and interrupted her. "I'm so sorry. I didn't realize I'd actually gotten that recipe from your grandmother. When Missy told me that you were making dishes from the women's auxiliary church cookbook and calling them your own. I got mad."

"Missy Stockwell told you I was stealing recipes?" Angie couldn't believe it. She didn't know what she'd done to make her a mortal enemy, but it had to stop. "I have used several of my Nona's recipes at the County Seat. Of course, my staff and I play with them a bit to get them perfect, but I don't steal anyone's recipe."

"I realize that. I went home and talked to my husband, and he reminded me that Margaret gave me that recipe. He said I should have called you that night, but I didn't know what to say. And here you are, diving right in with an apology that I should have been giving rather than you." Mrs. Eisenhower patted her arm. "From now on, I've given up listening to gossip. You're a very sweet girl and I know you aren't trying to break Ian's heart. At least not on purpose."

Angie's lips twitched, but she was able to keep the grin away. "Ian and I are fine."

"I saw you at church with him. You two make an adorable couple." Mrs. Eisenhower continued to chat until she caught Angie glancing at her watch. "Oh, my, first I insult you and now I'm keeping you from work. Again, please accept my apology. I'm so glad we got this worked out."

Angie watched as she made her way past her and turned toward produce. The woman was a kook, but at least she wasn't running around town calling Angie a thief. She grabbed a bag of all-purpose flour, the spices she needed, and a smaller bag of cake flour, then threw ten pounds of sugar into her cart. At least the sugar was local. Nampa had a sugar beet factory where they extracted the white glistening powder from the unsightly roots.

She quickly finished shopping, threw the bags in her backseat, then put on her seat belt and got ready to head to the restaurant. All she had to do was get out of the parking lot without anyone stopping her to chat. She glanced in her rearview mirror. She wasn't going to be that lucky.

Pastor Tom was coming up alongside her SUV, his handsome face made even cuter with the wide grin he wore. "Angie Turner." He leaned on the windowsill of her vehicle. Now she regretted rolling down the window as soon as she got into the car.

"Pastor Tom. So nice to see you." Angie hoped little white lies didn't count in the Big Guy's book.

"I don't want to keep you since you probably have perishables in your grocery bags, but I wanted to tell you how nice it was to see you in the pews this last Sunday. I remember when your grandmother used to bring you into services. You were always such an adorable child with your black hair and piercing eyes." He paused for a moment, apparently thinking about what he was going to say next. Angie could see it in his eyes when he decided to take a chance. "You and Ian make such a lovely couple."

"Thanks. The sermon was interesting." Angie couldn't remember much of it since she'd been thinking about how to handle the Katherine thing.

"I don't think I've seen Ian with a woman friend since he moved here. I'm sure Allen and his wife are excited to have you as part of the family."

"Whoa, we're dating, not engaged." Angie didn't go into the whole story about how Sheriff Brown didn't like her dating his precious Ian in the first place. "And I haven't met Mrs. Brown yet. I'm sure Ian will introduce me as soon as he and I feel it's time."

"Look at me, jumping to conclusions. It's just when young adults reach a certain age and meet someone they're compatible with, wedding bells tend to follow."

Angie couldn't stop the comment. "Let me get this straight. You think my biological clock is ticking and I need a husband? Pastor Tom, I don't mean to insult you, but stay out of my business. I'm perfectly happy with my life. And I just opened a restaurant. No man, even if he is a saint who teaches Sunday school, needs to be tied down with someone who works too many hours and is always thinking about ways to make food better."

He quickly stepped back away from the SUV and almost hit the truck parked next to her. "Now I've offended you. I'm dreadfully sorry."

"No, you haven't offended me. I just wish people would stop trying to plan my life." She shook her head. "Sorry. I guess I'm a little worn out today."

"Well, I won't keep you, then. Tell Ian I said hello, and I'll be sure to get over to your restaurant sooner rather than later." He waved and stepped out between the cars.

Angie watched him as he went into the store, greeting people as they met, slapping one man on the back, bending down to talk to a little child. The man was personable. Nice, even. And she'd just jumped down his throat because he assumed she and Ian were more of a thing than she thought they were. She needed to get a grip. Maybe more coffee would help.

At the restaurant, she had a couple of hours before the kitchen crew would come in to test out next month's recipes. She would have liked to have Estebe there, but with the festival starting tomorrow, she knew he couldn't be spared. They'd just have to plow through without him. As she wandered through the kitchen, she poured herself a cup of coffee, then took it and the new recipes she wanted to play with to the table with a notebook.

That was where Felicia found her an hour later.

"Hey, girl, I didn't realize you'd showed yet." She poured herself a cup of coffee and sat next to her. "Why the doom-and-gloom face? Don't you like the menu?"

Angie pushed the notebook toward her. On it, she'd written *who killed Heather* on the top, and only one name hadn't been crossed off: Javier. "I'm trying to get this out of my head so I'm not a walking time bomb waiting to go off on people. I just yelled at the Methodist pastor a few hours ago because he insinuated that Ian and I might have a future. I'm sure he thinks I'm a looney."

Felicia glanced at the paper, then back up at Angie. "You know this isn't your problem. Sheriff Brown can handle it."

"Sheriff Brown hates me too. Well, I guess not anymore. He came to apologize and I gave him donuts." Angie rubbed her hands over her face. "He's just as stumped as I am, and he has all that fancy equipment and access to real reports and stuff."

"Angie, maybe we should call off today." Felicia put a hand on her friend's shoulder. "Maybe you just need to go home and relax."

"And watch Mrs. Potter glare at me? Did I mention she was ticked at me too? What am I doing to people? You'd think I was a living example of how to annoy friends and turn off people." Now Angie laid her head on the table. "You should get away from me before I say something stupid to you."

When Felicia didn't respond, Angie lifted her head and stared at her. Felicia had her arms crossed and was watching her. "What?"

"Are you done with your pity party?" Felicia waited a beat for Angie to nod. "Okay, so you might have spoken harshly to the pastor. I bet he gets more of that during his spiritual counseling of his flock on a daily basis." This time it was Angie's turn to stay quiet.

Felicia nodded. "Okay, so we're in agreement. I'll go on. The sheriff is concerned about his nephew and your relationship. That's normal. He's his only parental figure, from what I can uncover. He doesn't hate you."

"I guess maybe he's getting some of the same comments from people like Pastor Tom as I am." Angie's lips twitched in a small smile. "I can't blame him for being a little testy. I am."

"Exactly." Felicia sighed. "Mrs. Potter is just reacting to the fact that sometimes her life isn't her own. That sometimes other people make decisions for you that are in your best interest. You care for her. You didn't want to see her hurt."

"At least not until we actually knew something was wrong. I just felt like I was in the wrong with that one. I wanted to tell her." Angie sat up straighter and sipped her coffee. "You're right. I was just having a pity party."

"Sometimes people do things for other people that aren't right, but their hearts are in the right place." Felicia smiled. "Usually it's because love is in the mix."

Angie stared at the piece of paper. Now that she wasn't thinking with her logic brain but with her heart, maybe there were a few other names that needed to be on the list. She scribbled a few names, then slapped the notebook closed.

"No more thinking about that for a while. Maybe it will be like a set of lost keys. If I stop thinking about it, the answer will come."

Felicia sipped her coffee. "Or maybe you'll forget about the whole thing and just deal with those recipes in front of you?"

Chapter 20

The kitchen session hadn't gone as well as she'd hoped. Felicia had either forgotten Angie's direction or had gone against the advice and hired a temporary chef to help out in Estebe's absence. The guy, Ken, was a real jerk. He kept barking orders at Matt and Nancy, and he barely even acknowledged Hope. The only one he was even somewhat nice to was Angie, and that was only because she was the head chef. Apparently, Ken knew the chain of command and assumed he was above everyone but Angie in the kitchen. When he'd declined to participate in the family meal after his shift was over, Angie drew in a breath of relief.

Felicia stood by her as Hope and the others brought in the food. "You okay? You seem stressed."

"Any chance we can get a different temp for Friday and Saturday? I don't think Ken meets our requirements."

Felicia frowned. "The service said he'd been head chef at several restaurants around the state and had just moved here."

"He's an ass." Angie didn't use the term often, but it described this guy to a T. "I'd rather be one man down than put the team through two services with that guy. Besides, like I said before, all I need is a dishwasher. Hope will step in to help and everyone else will move up a slot."

"I get it." She straightened Angie's chef collar. "I'll call the service."

When they sat down at the table, Angie could see the tension on her team's face. She grinned. "Well, we lived through that."

"Angie, I know you're the head chef, but that guy, he's a tool." Matt took a serving, then passed around the platter of chicken with wild mushroom marsala to the server sitting next to him. "I'm just warning you, I might have to deck him this weekend. I'm laying bets on Friday about ten minutes into service."

"I don't think you'll last ten minutes." Nancy started the sweet potato hash around as well.

Hope took a sip of water. "I know you're not supposed to judge others, but wow. He isn't a very nice person."

"Felicia is working on getting us a replacement dishwasher. And Ken won't be back on Friday." Angie took the plate of hash and dished some on her plate. "Let's talk about everyone's month. What's been going on since we last had one of these?"

One of the servers shot up her hand. It was the left hand, and Angie could see the sparkling diamond from the other end of the table. She pretended not to see her hand. "No one has anything?"

That got a chuckle from the group.

Reba, the server, shook her head. "You guys are bad." She stood, held out her hand, and announced, "I said yes."

Cheers and toasts flew around the table, and Angie caught Felicia's gaze. This was the team they always dreamed of having. A group that worked together more like family than just coworkers. Who celebrated the ups and helped during the down times.

The idea of family and what someone would do for another family member nagged at her. By the time the family meal was over and she was helping Hope with the dishes, Angie had a raging headache.

"You look awful." Hope handed her a dish she'd just sprayed off for Angie to put into the rack. "Why don't you go home? I can finish up here and Felicia can lock up after me."

Felicia, who'd just brought in the last of the glasses from the meal, nodded. "You've been running yourself into the ground this last couple of weeks. I can't be missing both our head chef and the sous chef this weekend. Go home. You and Dom need some movie time on the couch. I'm sure he's been nervous having someone else in the house all week."

Angie wiped her hands on a towel and stepped away from the dish station. "I'm going. Besides, Estebe invited me to the opening ceremonies for the festival tomorrow, and I'd like to at least be able to make an appearance. If this headache doesn't go away, I'll be locking myself in a dark room for a couple of days."

"You're sure about not having Ken back?" Felicia studied her friend. "Two trained hands in the kitchen are better than none."

"Actually, no. He's such a distraction to the team it's like we don't have his hands." Angie picked up her tote. "If the service doesn't have anyone else, we'll make do. Having someone work against the team makes everyone's game off."

Hope shoved a tray of dishes into the washer and set it to run. "I don't like that guy one bit. I felt like he was judging me and I'd failed before I even opened my mouth."

"It's okay to not like someone." Angie gave her youngest team member a smile. "I think our subconscious lets us know who we can trust and who we should let into our lives."

"Well said. Now go home." Felicia gave her a little push toward the door. "Do you need to take food with you so you don't have to cook?"

Angie's stomach rolled at the idea of food. "No, if I get hungry, I've got soup in the freezer. See you Friday."

Felicia watched her walk toward the door. "You call and cancel with Estebe if you're still feeling bad tomorrow. And maybe get into a doctor."

Angie just waved away the suggestion and crossed the parking lot to her car. Out of the corner of her eye, she thought she saw someone standing in the alleyway, watching her. But when she turned her head, there was no one there.

"Leave me alone, Heather. I don't know what happened to you." Angie muttered as she started up the car. She needed sleep and home. And to not think about Heather or Javier or Mrs. Potter for a while. She didn't even turn on the stereo as she drove home.

* * * *

When she woke on Thursday, her headache was gone. The day was beautiful, and the festival would have amazing weather and probably crazy crowds. Estebe had warned her to be early if she wanted to park anywhere close to the street festival, so she finished up her chores and headed into Boise around ten.

Her phone rang as soon as she was in the car.

"Good morning, are you feeling better?" Felicia's cheery voice echoed in the cab.

Angie turned down the volume. "Much. I don't know what was going on with me yesterday, but I was in a funk."

"Maybe you were being attacked by negative energy. I met this psychic at a party last week who has a place in Boise. We should totally go and get your chi cleaned."

"Even if I knew what that was, I wouldn't do it. One, I have no time. And two, I don't believe in the supernatural." Angie shuddered a bit as she thought about the shadow in the alleyway yesterday. She'd told it to leave her alone and it had. "There's enough evil in the world that I can see and understand. I don't have to go all underworld to be scared."

"You really need to read more paranormal. It will open up your mind to the other side."

Angie shook her head. Her friend was persistent. "You know that's all fiction, right? Anyway, I'm fine, and thanks for checking in with me."

"I actually called to see if you'd completed the orders for this weekend. I know you turned that part over to Estebe, so I'm just checking."

Angie groaned. Her conversation with Mrs. Eisenhower about supply orders yesterday should have alerted her to the fact she needed to order, but no, she'd been so worked up about rumors she'd forgotten all about it. "No, I didn't. Can you review the menu and the pantries and see what we need to order? I'll stop by the restaurant on my way back from Boise and get it called in."

"I can do it if you review what I send. I'll let them know there may be additions when you come in. That way we won't miss the suggested noon deadline." Felicia shuffled some papers. "Their barn manager called as she was doing the weekly order processing over at Pamplona Farms and noticed we didn't have an order in. She's pretty on top of things. I told her it was coming."

"I can't believe they're still functioning without Javier."

Felicia laughed. "From what I've seen, I don't think the guy dealt with the actual business very much. This woman seemed to want to continue our relationship, even if we'd just started working with them. I think Javier must have been just the face of Pamplona Farms."

"A missing face right now. Have you heard anything? Has he reached out to this manager at all?"

"According to her, she hasn't heard from him for days. And she's worried. She didn't come out and say he was a bad manager, but she did say that he wouldn't have left the business just hanging. He apparently is pretty attached to the place."

"Well, let's hope someone finds him soon. It's got to be wearing on Estebe too." She paused. "Do you want anything from the festival?"

"Bring me a couple of cinnamon churros. I love those things."

As she made her way into Boise, Angie thought about Javier and Heather, Stephen and Kendra, Estebe, and the rest of the family. Could this be all about family? Stephen had been her choice of killer for a while until she found out he and Kendra were out of town that weekend. Brothers sometimes killed each other—it had happened in the Bible even. But it wasn't Javier who was killed. It was a woman he hadn't even really cared about.

As she pulled into the last street parking available on the road three blocks away from the event, she ran her fingers through her hair and glanced at herself in the mirror. Satisfied that her hair wasn't a windblown mess, she got out, locked the car, and joined the crowd walking toward the festival site.

She milled through the crowds, watching the children run through the blocked-off street with abandon. It wasn't every day you got to play in the middle of the street without risk of injury.

"Oh, to be young and foolish again."

She turned toward the voice. Estebe stood behind her, watching a group of boys and girls dressed in Basque costume chase each other through the crowded street. "Hey, thanks for inviting me today."

"I thought you might enjoy the ceremonies. The dancers will open it up in a few minutes, then Ander will talk. After that, the liquor and food flow until late tonight when they close down the street dance." He took her arm and led her toward the stage. "We'll have a good view from over here. How's the County Seat?"

"We had family meal for August yesterday. The dishes are great, but we missed you in the kitchen."

Estebe looked at her, his dark eyes troubled. "I don't understand. I thought Felicia was hiring a temp. You can't do service without another pair of hands."

"We'll see." Angie went on to explain how Ken wasn't a good fit with the team. As she finished up, she groaned. "I'd rather be without a dishwasher than invite him back to work with us. He made everyone uncomfortable."

He nodded, thoughtfully. "I suppose if you had met me a few years ago, you would have thought the same thing about me. I was arrogant, cocky, and didn't have much good to say about those who weren't at my level. Now I realize it's more about being nice and taking an interest in people." He sighed. "And that was one lesson my cousin never learned. I'm afraid not too many people are upset that Javier is missing."

"He didn't have to be loved by the masses. He's missing, and that's the problem. Has Sheriff Brown told you anything new lately?" Angie worried that the adage about the longer a person was missing, the more likely they'd be dead when they were finally found was going to come true. She saw the answer in Estebe's face before he spoke.

"No. Nothing new. The sheriff is a good man, but I'm afraid Javier has disappeared to somewhere he can't even imagine." He waved off the next question Angie started with a point to the stage. The performance was about to start.

"Thank you all for coming out to our annual San Ignazio Festival. We hope you will feel like family here as we celebrate, no matter where you're from. Today, you are all Basque." The woman blushed as a cheer came up from the crowd. "Now, we have a little change in our schedule. Papa Ander Diaz will speak now, and then our dancing troupes will entertain you."

She moved away from the podium, and a noticeably weak and tired man took her place. It looked like Ander Diaz had aged ten years since she'd seen him last weekend. He held a shaky hand up to the crowd, who cheered even louder. Finally, they calmed down and let him speak.

"I know there have been some rumors going around that I was thinking about stepping down as your leader this year."

The crowd started booing. This support seemed to strengthen him.

He waved his hand downward again and the crowd quieted. "Well, I've decided to hold off. I am not ready to hand over the reins of this lovely community even if I had someone ready to take over all the responsibilities of leadership." He smiled and winked to the crowd. "I guess you're stuck with me for a while longer."

The crowd went wild, and Papa Diaz stepped out on the stage and took in their love and affection. The emotion made Angie smile, but then as she watched, someone streaked across the stage toward Papa. As everyone watched, Papa Diaz was pushed from behind the podium and started to fall. He went down faster than Angie could imagine. A woman was on top of him, screaming. Then her wig fell off, revealing a bald head.

"What the heck? Hey, that's Carlotta Mendoza," a man closer to the stage said, then stepped forward. "Someone get her off Papa!"

He didn't have to worry because two men in suits, apparently Papa's bodyguards, were already pulling a spitting Carlotta off the old man. Angie moved closer to the stage and set her phone on video. Sheriff Brown needed to see this.

"You bastard," Carlotta screamed. They blocked her movements but let go of her arms. She reached up to straighten the wig that wasn't there anymore, and her face burned a brighter red. "Ander Diaz, you're nothing more than a dried-up old man."

Kendra came up from the side of the stage and tried to reason with her mother, who was being held back by the two large men as others help Papa up off the stage. She held out the cast aside-wig, and Carlotta grabbed it. "Mama, you need to calm down. What were you thinking?"

Carlotta's eyes narrowed as she pulled it on over her head. "I was protecting you. Stephen should have always been Papa's choice for a replacement, not that man-whore Javier. It's not fair."

Angie kept filming the ongoing train wreck. "Estebe, call Sheriff Brown and have him get over here. I think I know where Javier is."

Chapter 21

The gang gathered at the County Seat, waiting for news. Angie and Estebe made soup and a quick soda bread as the group talked about what had happened. Ian had come over as soon as they got back, and he helped chop vegetables.

"We'll make you a chef yet," Estebe joked as they spent the afternoon working together in the kitchen.

Ian grinned. "Wouldn't be the worst thing for me to learn. Right now, if I don't go out to eat, I make a mean bowl of ramen."

As the afternoon passed, others joined them. Felicia helped set up a buffet for people to eat when they felt like it with sodas, iced tea, and a wide arrangement of snacks and desserts. By late afternoon, Hope, Matt, and Nancy had shown up to support Estebe and wait for news.

It was after six when a tired Sheriff Brown came into the restaurant, with a disheveled Javier by his side.

"Cousin, it's nice to see you." Estebe hugged Javier tightly. "I was worried about you."

Javier slapped Estebe on the back. "I hear it was you and your friend who finally figured out that I was in Carlotta's basement. The woman is crazy."

"I hope you have her in custody. That way no one else will be hurt." Estebe stepped away from Javier and held his hand out to Sheriff Brown.

"Well, that's the thing. She's admitting that she took Javier." He sat at one of the tables and Felicia handed him a cup of coffee. "Thank you. I think I'm going to be up and working for a few more hours tonight."

"We have food." Angie nodded to Hope. "Go get the sheriff and Javier a bowl of soup and some bread."

"Thanks. There were a couple of boxes of protein bars and a couple of cases of water in the room when I woke up a few days ago. I'm starving for real food. We won't even talk about the restroom facilities." Javier sat at the table, taking the coffee Felicia offered. "She was crafty. She invited me out to Initial Point to talk about Stephen and ways to keep him from being Papa Diaz's choice. She said it would be bad for Kendra for him to get the position now."

"So you went out to meet her? How did you lose your wallet and phone?" Angie studied Javier as he wolfed down the soup Hope had just given him.

He tore off a piece of bread. "That was genius, right? I figured if something happened, you could track my calls and find me."

"Except there wasn't a call from Carlotta." Sheriff Brown smiled at Hope as she sat his dish on the table. "We ran all your calls."

"Maybe she called from a pay phone. Or someone else's phone. I guess I didn't think about that." Javier held the bowl back out to Hope to be refilled. His smile when she brought him more soup made Angie realize he wasn't done with his playboy days. Hope just ignored it and went over to stand by Angie. "Anyway, you found my stuff?"

"By accident," Ian added to the conversation. "You're lucky I'm a fan of historical sites."

"I know she kidnapped you to keep Papa Diaz from choosing you. Is that why she killed Heather?" Hope stepped forward, looking at both Sheriff Brown and Javier.

Sheriff Brown sat down his spoon. "She's claiming she didn't kill Heather. And there's no evidence in her house that has Heather's blood on it, and her prints don't match anything we've gotten so far from the knife."

"But she's crazy. That should explain it all."

Sheriff Brown sighed. "Actually, she's dying. I talked to her oncologist and she's been given a few months to live. I guess she wanted to see Kendra set up before she left this world. And having Stephen taking over for Ander Diaz would set them up."

"But she had to have killed Heather." Hope looked like she'd been hit with a cold wave of air. "This nightmare has to be over, doesn't it?"

Felicia stepped closer to the girl and put her arm around her. "Sheriff Brown will find out what happened, don't worry."

Hope let Felicia pull her into a hug, but Angie saw the fear still in her eyes. She glanced around the kitchen at the group that had gathered to wait. "It's late. You should go home and get some sleep. We're not going to find out anything else tonight."

After everyone had said their goodbyes and left, Felicia, Angie, and Ian sat around the table, drinking coffee. Felicia sipped her coffee. "Hope's pretty upset."

"I think this has been a roller-coaster ride for her. She's never lost someone to violence before, so when they found Carlotta had kidnapped Javier, it was easy for her to blame her for all the problems. Unfortunately, the world doesn't always work that way." Ian stood and grabbed the plate of cookies from the buffet.

"I could see her wanting to get Kendra taken care of before she passed on. According to the doctor that Sheriff Brown talked to, Carlotta has known about her diagnosis for about a year." Angie broke off half a cookie and offered the other half to Felicia.

"That's some strong motivation for killing someone." Felicia took the cookie. "Except Sheriff Brown says that Carlotta and Kendra had dinner plans that night, and as soon as they got home, she took a painkiller and went to sleep. Kendra confirmed it."

"Wait. Hold on a second." Angie ran to her office and returned with her notebook. She flipped through some pages and then stopped. "Someone said Kendra and Stephen were in Sun Valley that weekend. How can she be in two places at one time?"

"I know." Ian held up a hand. "Kendra is a secret twin and Carlotta has been keeping the second girl a secret all these years."

Felicia was the first to laugh. "I don't think that's within the realm of possibilities."

"Brainstorming means everything's on the table," Angie reminded her. "Let's add in aliens and time travel too."

Ian looked from one woman to the other. "I think you're all rummy and not thinking straight. But I am going to call Allen and ask him about this. It looks like you've found a hole in the story."

Angie watched as he walked out of the room. Leaning closer to Felicia, she whispered, "You know that means that all three of their stories are suspect."

"If we knew where they went to eat, we could ask about reservations." Felicia looked hopeful. "By the way, I found out who gave Stephen and Kendra that reservation the other night. It was Reba. She said she was just about to text me that one of the reservations had canceled, then Kendra called and asked if she could take it. I guess she's friends with the couple."

"But that's not what Kendra told me that night. She said we called her." Angie rubbed her face. "If she's lying about that, what else would she lie about?"

The women stopped talking when Ian came back into the room. "He's bringing in Stephen and Kendra for questioning and getting warrants to search their houses and vehicles. We might have an answer by the end of the day." Ian sank into his chair. "I hope that's true, for Allen's sake. The guy sounds beat."

"So what else can we do?" Angie looked at the other two. "Nothing?"

"Nothing. You look a little beat too. Why don't you go home and I'll let you know if we hear anything from Allen?" Ian stood and pulled her out of her chair. "Your investigation is over, at least this time."

"You really think there will be an answer sometime soon?" Angie laid her head on his chest and leaned in close. "I could use a nap."

"Go home." This time the words came from Felicia. She handed Angie her purse. "You could use some downtime. I've never seen you run this fast on a project."

"At first it was just trying to find out who killed Heather, but when Javier disappeared, I felt like I needed to figure it out faster. Before something happened to him. I know Estebe doesn't really like his cousin, but he is family." Angie closed the notebook. "I'm ready to crash, though. Call me if you hear anything."

Angie drove home and caught part of the news report regarding the rescue of Javier. A brief mention of Heather's killer still being at large made Angie shudder. If the killer was Stephen, he just got a clue that Sheriff Brown was still looking for someone. Sometimes Angie wondered if the easy access to news was a good thing or not.

A car was in her driveway. A pretty, newer model, cherry red sports car. When she pulled up, Kendra got out of the car and smiled one of her beauty queen smiles. Angie bet she'd been popular on the circuit. She had the ease to talk to anyone and make them feel welcome and important. As she climbed out of the car and went to meet her, something niggled in her head. Kendra was smart. There was no way her mother could have hidden this diagnosis for over a year. Not with someone in the house noticing her comings and goings, not to mention losing her hair. She glanced back at the car. She'd left her phone on the front seat.

Kendra took a step toward her and sighed. Then she pulled out a long knife from her designer handbag. "I was hoping we could get past this without me having to kill you. But I can see it on your face, you've already figured it out. What gave me away?"

"You're too smart not to notice your mother going through chemo treatments. Now, had you been away at college, I could maybe see a delay, but you knew, didn't you?" Angie stared at her.

"Of course I knew. I've been nursing her through those damn hot flashes for over a year. She didn't want anyone to know. She wouldn't let me hire a nurse to make her life easier. And when I got engaged, she swore she'd be at my wedding, no problem."

"I bet she wanted to be there." Angie tried to judge her chances of getting to either the car or the house without being sliced by that large knife. She didn't like her chances either way. Maybe she could talk Kendra into just leaving. "Your mother wouldn't want you to risk spending your life in jail."

"Now, you see, that's not going to happen." Kendra's smile was cold. "I'm heading out of this crappy little town soon."

Angie decided to push. "If you're going to make the border, you might want to leave soon. I hear Mexico just canceled their extradition agreement."

Kendra shook her head. "Sorry, I've got a couple of loose ends I have to clear up, like you."

"I won't tell anyone, I promise." Angie inched toward the car. She wasn't going to be able to talk her way out of this one. "Besides, I don't really know what happened."

Kendra jabbed the knife between Angie and the car. "I knew Mom was trying to set Stephen up, but it wasn't working. Papa Diaz wasn't seeing what an idiot Javier was at all. All I had to do was put Katherine into play."

"You know Katherine?"

"She was my sponsor for my last run at Miss Idaho. I should have won that one too, except the winner was sleeping with the judges." Kendra smirked, and for a second, Angie saw a glint of madness in her eyes. Then Kendra shrugged. "Mom said it wasn't my time to shine and God had other plans for me. I guess she was right."

Angie saw the way she looked at the knife. Like it was sacred and she was just fulfilling her god's wishes. The woman was crazy. She had to keep her talking, though. "So you asked Katherine to get Javier away from Heather?"

"I gave her my key to Carrie Sue's apartment. I'm supposed to be watering her plants. She was willing to take one for the team. I guess the guy's a pretty good lover. I know his brother is awesome. Isn't it funny that those things run in families?" Kendra got a dreamy look on her face. "I was trying to keep Stephen out of this, but I guess he'll work as a fall guy. It's not like I can't find another man. I might just go a little older next time. Someone who is already established."

"You actually think you're going to just walk away from this scot-free?"

"Of course I am. Really, no one ever suspects the pretty girl. I've gotten away with a ton of things in my life. You'd be amazed if we had time to really talk about them." She flipped her hair back and tapped her finger on her lips. "Where was I? Oh, yeah, Katherine. Then I was going to play supportive friend, and that guy shows up and messes up my plans." "The one your mother hired? Jerry Reno?" Angie hoped when either Felicia or Ian called, they wouldn't think she was sleeping when she didn't answer. Having them wonder and call the sheriff was her only hope. Worst thing would be if Felicia had decided to follow Angie home and had just got in her car and came out. If that happened, she'd have to wave her away. It might not save Angie's life, but at least Felicia wouldn't be part of the sacrifice. Who was she kidding? No one was going to notice she was missing until she didn't show up for work. Maybe living in Nona's house had been a mistake. At least in San Francisco people were closer.

"See, that's what happens when you keep secrets. If my mom's brain hadn't already been rattled by the chemo, she could have told me about that guy. Then I could have adjusted my plan and I wouldn't have been waiting in that dirty alley for so long." She looked at her watch. "Oops, I've overstayed my welcome. Time to get going. To finish the story, I waited for her to go to the bathroom, told her the guy was out back looking for her, and then I followed her out. She was blitzed. It almost wasn't fun. She went down fast."

Angie heard the crunch of tires on the gravel and, not waiting, dove for her car door. She got inside but didn't get the door completely closed. Kendra fell on it, trying to open it and stabbing the knife through the small opening. Angie held on and glanced in her rearview mirror. She didn't recognize the pickup behind her, but she did recognize Sheriff Brown and the officer who typically sat at the reception desk in the police station. She had just a minute to wonder why the guy who hated her would have volunteered to come out to save her, and then Kendra's knife sliced her arm.

Pain shot through her system and she released the car door. Kendra hadn't been expecting the release and she fell back, right into Sheriff Brown. After helping the sheriff cuff Kendra and moving the knife out of the way, the officer came over to Angie. He pulled out a napkin from his pocket and held it tightly to the cut.

"I should have waited and got my kit. You don't have any blood bugs in there I should worry about, do you?" He smiled as he looked into Angie's face. "You did great holding her off. When we got the call from Mrs. Potter, we weren't sure we'd get here in time."

Angie felt herself get woozy. "Mrs. Potter has blood bugs?"

He laughed, and the last words she heard before she passed out were "I guess I'll have to trust you on that."

* * * *

Angie awoke in a stark white hospital room. She glanced down at her arm, and it was wrapped in white gauze. She lifted it slightly and felt the ache from the cut again.

"Fifteen stitches. She got you good. That knife might be old, but it's still sharp as heck." Ian leaned forward into her vision.

"Hey, what are you doing here? I thought you were going to call." Angie let her lips curve into a smile.

"Ha ha. I always come when my girlfriend has been stabbed and rushed to the hospital. It's one of my charms. Are you all right?"

"And I bet you told all the nurses I was your girlfriend just so you could get in here." She glanced around the room. "I think she just cut me once, right?"

"Allen and Phillip got there just in time. Kendra's in a cage right now, but the girl is as crazy as her mother." Ian looked back as the door opened. "Someone else is here waiting for you to wake up."

Felicia came through the door with two coffee cups. She handed one to Ian, "Starbucks is on the first floor. And everyone was there, so the line was awful."

He took the other cup from her. "Someone woke up."

Squealing, Felicia pushed past him to Angie's side. "Oh my. You scared the crap out of me, missy."

"And that right there is why I took the second cup from you. I swear you two women get violent if someone comes between you." Ian came around the other side of the bed and set both cups of coffee down. "The doctors said you were just out because of stress and loss of blood. If you're feeling up to it, we're cleared to take you home any time you're ready."

"Home would be great. Did anyone check on Dom? What time is it?" Angie sat up quickly, then felt the head rush and fell back down. "And Precious and Mabel are probably starving by now."

"Erica called and said they checked in on Dom and fed the rest of the crew." He smiled. "Don't worry, we have your back."

"It's going to be challenging cooking tomorrow night with this arm." She glanced at Felicia. "But that doesn't mean we need Ken back. That guy was a disaster."

Felicia held up a hand. "I get it. I learned my lesson. I've hired a temp dishwasher to come in for the next couple of weeks while you get better. And with Estebe back next week, you should be able to take a day or so off."

"I'm not looking for a vacation."

Both Ian and Felicia laughed. Ian took her hand. "Seriously? You were just stabbed by a murderous prom queen and all you're thinking about is how to get back to work?"

This time when Angie sat up, her head felt clearer and she felt stronger. "People got to eat. I'll take it easy tomorrow and just expedite. I'll move Matt over to head chef for the night and have Hope fill in his spot. I promise I won't lift anything heavier than a plate."

"Well, then, let's get you out of here." A nurse was standing by the bed. Angie hadn't seen her come into the room but relaxed as she checked the bandage on her arm. "The doctor is reviewing your chart, and as soon as I get these tubes out of you, you'll be good as new. I'll bring in the discharge instructions in a few minutes. Who's your primary doctor?"

"I guess Dr. Ashley Blaine. I mean, that's who Nona saw, and that's the last doctor I had in the area." Angie hadn't even thought about setting up a doctor relationship.

"That will work. I'll make a note to have these records sent over to her office." The nurse busied herself taking Angie's vitals and making notes in her tablet. Finally, she smiled. "I'll send the doctor in as soon as he's available, then you're out of here. I've got reservations for the County Seat in a month. I've been looking forward to it."

"Make sure you ask for me, I'll come out of the kitchen to see you." Angie leaned back and smiled as the nurse left the small room.

"Not the best way to gain more customers, but you do know how to work a room." Felicia grinned, sipping her coffee.

Angie smiled but didn't feel the emotion. "I really can't believe this whole mess. What's going to happen to them?"

"Allen has Kendra locked in a cage, next to her mother. One more arrest and his jail will be completely booked. The district attorney is working on getting them transferred to Ada County. And don't worry, the judge already denied bail for both. Stephen has been quiet but I hear he's hired a good law firm for both of them." Ian sat on the side of the bed and held her hand.

"Supporting them must be hard since it's his family that they went after. I bet Javier is giving him a hard time." Felicia pulled out some fresh clothes from the tote she took off the floor. "I packed you fresh clothes before I drove in. These are my favorite yoga pants and T-shirt, so try not to bleed on them."

"Thanks." Angie closed her eyes. "At least the hard part is over for the family. Javier's back and not a suspect in Heather's murder anymore. The rest they can sort out with time."

"And the knife she used against you is apparently also from Papa Diaz's collection, although his collection is getting smaller and smaller since it's now part of the evidence chain against Kendra." Ian rubbed her hand. "I think this festival is going to be a little different for a lot of people."

Chapter 22

Angie was relaxing over a cup of coffee. She'd slept later than she'd expected, probably due to the drugs they'd given her. She'd have to watch the painkillers and only take them at night to help her sleep while the cut mended. This morning, she'd taken an over-the-counter product and although the pain was still there, it had taken the edge off so it was just an annoyance. She had to go into town soon and help the crew get ready for the County Seat's Friday service.

A knock came to her door, and before she could move, Erica peeked her head in. "Hope you're decent and up for visitors. I couldn't hold her back any longer." She stepped out of view and Mrs. Potter pushed her walker through the door.

She slapped at Erica's hands. "I can do this. You just go get that platter."

Angie started to rise, but Mrs. Potter waved her down. "You just sit, girl. I can't believe they let you out of the hospital yesterday. Did they not understand that crazy woman tried to kill you? I saw you come home. I can see the side of the house through my sewing room window. But I guess I didn't see her drive up. I was planning to come over and talk to you."

"Thank goodness you were watching for me. Ian said you called the police." Angie patted Mrs. Potter's arm as she sat next to her. "I'm so grateful. I'm not sure how much longer I could have held her off."

"I called the police right after she pulled the knife on you. I should have called sooner, maybe you wouldn't have gotten hurt." Mrs. Potter's gaze dropped to Angie's arm. "Is it bad?"

"Not really. I have stitches and I'll probably have a scar, but that just makes me interesting, right?" Angie nodded to the coffeepot. "Can I get you some coffee?"

"I'm done with coffee for the morning. Besides, tea goes better with what I brought over. I found it in my recipe book and thought you might enjoy having this." She pulled out an index card and handed it to her.

The card was old and stained with some sort of food spills, but Angie recognized Nona's handwriting instantly. On the top of the card, she'd written the words *Fried Green Tomatoes*. Angie's heart leaped. She glanced down the list of ingredients and nodded. She had forgotten a couple and had the wrong amounts for others, but this was her Nona's recipe. "I can't believe you found this."

"When you said you were working on the recipe, I wondered if Margaret had given me her recipe once upon a time. It took me a while to find it. The woman was always a better cook than I was. It made me want to hate her, if I hadn't loved her so much."

Erica came back in the kitchen with a covered platter. The smell of the food made Dom sit up in his bed. She set it on the table, then went to the cabinet to get plates and forks. "Ta-da!"

Angie lifted up the cover, and a steaming bunch of tomatoes battered and fried to a just right shade of brown sat in front of her. Two bowls of sauce flanked the pile of tomatoes. "This is perfect."

She speared several pieces onto her plate and drizzled first the spicy vinegar-based barbecue sauce, then the sour cream sauce. The smells mixed, and for a moment, she thought she saw her Nona standing by the stove smiling at her.

"Get some iced tea poured," Mrs. Potter instructed Erica, and Angie saw the smile widen on her Nona's face.

"Always the bossy one." Nona's words came to her as if she was really standing there watching the scene. Angie ducked her head to hide her grin and then took a bite of the treat in front of her and was transported back to a memory where Nona was standing at her old stove, talking to Angie about life and boys and being her own self. She'd been the one to transport Angie's career goals from fashion designer or career businesswoman to chef. This time Angie was in the kitchen watching and helping her with whatever was on the menu for them or the church picnic or a family in need.

"It's perfect," Angie said as she opened her eyes and realized both Mrs. Potter and Erica were watching her and holding their breath.

Mrs. Potter nodded. "Of course it is. I might not be able to make up recipes like your grandmother could, but I'm excellent at following directions."

Erica set a glass of tea in front of Angie and then sat and filled her own plate. "Tell us about the fight with a killer. Did she try to stab you more than once?"

Her neighbors stayed, polished off the fried green tomatoes, and chatted for at least an hour. After having her clean up the dishes, Mrs. Potter sent Erica out to feed Precious and Mabel and water the garden.

After the door closed, she turned to Angie. "I was wrong about Erica. You were right to try to protect me."

"No, I wasn't." Angie shook her head. "I should have trusted you to be strong enough to deal with a problem, even when that problem was out of both our control."

"She's very dear to me, and when I thought what might have happened? I swear my heart twisted in my chest. But you're also dear to me, and I hope my tantrum isn't going to affect our friendship." She smiled softly. "I treasured my friendship with Margaret. I hope we can have one just as strong."

Angie squeezed Mrs. Potter's hand. "We already do."

After they'd left, Angie went into the living room and added the recipe card to the pile of papers she was turning into Nona's Cookbook. The recipes were all her grandmother's, with a few tweaks from her in the side notes. It was like the two of them were writing the book together. She sat and reviewed the piles she currently had, sorting them into file folders by chapters. Desserts, appetizers, veggie dishes—she had piles for several but wasn't completely sure of the organization. If she added all of these, the book would be too long to publish. She needed to settle on a theme, so she took her notebook and pen and started brainstorming.

An hour later, she had the theme: Memories of Nona. Not just her memories, but Mrs. Potter's and Mr. Eisenhower's favorite potato salad. She could do little interview snippets from community members, and in one project, her Nona would live forever.

Pleased with the progress she'd made, she ran upstairs to take a quick shower, trying to keep her bandaged arm dry by tying on a small garbage bag. After a few false starts, she was ready to go into town. Since her arm was screaming, she took two more pills. By the end of the night, she'd be ready for the stronger drugs waiting for her on her bedside table.

* * * *

Saturday night was just about ready to go into the books when Felicia called her out to the dining room. "You have a guest who wants to talk to you,"

Instead of heading to a table, they went to the bar where Ander Diaz sat. Ian also sat a few stools away, and she met his gaze, then he nodded, letting her know that he'd wait to talk to her.

"Miss Turner." Ander turned toward her and stood as she walked up. He took her shoulders and kissed her on both cheeks. "The local Basque community owes you a big favor. You risked your life to protect the innocent, and that is a noble action."

"I was just at the wrong place at the wrong time." Angie shrugged, uncomfortable with the accolades.

"Carlotta was out of her mind from the stress she was facing. But Kendra, she always was a tricky one. Even in Basque school I would get reports of her being mean to others. Carlotta thought she grew out of her selfishness, but maybe that's just a stain on the soul you never grow out of."

He paused, looking at her. "But you, you are a good soul and a welcome visitor to our family any time."

"I appreciate it." She glanced around the dining room. "My family is here, in this restaurant."

"So we have a member in common. I am glad Estebe found a friend in you. He's a talented and thoughtful man." Anders glanced back at Ian. "I would make a case for him, but it looks like you are already taken."

Angie could feel the heat on her face. Glancing in the bar back mirror, even in the dim light, she could see the pulsing red on her face. She smiled in Ian's direction. "Yes, I guess I am."

Taking that as his cue to join the conversation, Ian moved next to her. Holding out his hand to greet the patriarch, he slid the other arm around Angie's waist. "Mr. Diaz, so good to see you."

Men, Angie thought. Always trying to show ownership of something that wasn't really to be owned by one person at all. It was a joint venture, a relationship, and she leaned into him to prove that as well.

"I was just about to invite Angie to the street dance tonight. With you as her guest, of course. We'll be closing up the festival with several bands the younger generation selected with the festival planners. I would have brought in some old-country singers, but I guess the world changes." He shrugged, amused at his release of the decisions.

"What about it, Angie? You feel up to some fun?" Ian stared down into her eyes. "You've had a pretty tough few weeks."

"It sounds wonderful. We just have a few more tickets to get out, and then Felicia and I will be ready to go." She grinned at Ian. "I can bring her along, right?"

"What's one more person?" Anders stood and gave each of them a big hug. He paused as he looked at Angie. "I want you to know that I owe you a great debt. Anything you want or need, you only have to contact me and it is yours."

Ian and Angie watched as Ander threw a twenty on the bar and made his way to the door, where his driver stood from the bench and opened the door for him.

"You know you don't have to go. I'm sure you're beat." Ian pushed a wayward strand of hair out of her face.

Angie caught sight of Felicia, who was helping clear plates and chatting with the few remaining customers. "I want to go. I think we all could use a little fun tonight. Wait here for me and I'll get this night closed up. You want me to make you something to eat?"

"I actually made my dinner before I came down tonight."

"You cooked?" Angie looked at him, speechless.

He squirmed under her watchful gaze. "Well, not really. I had a ham sandwich and a bag of chips."

"My offer still stands. You want some real food?" She paused, waiting for his answer.

He sat back at the bar and sipped what looked like a soda. "I'm good. I'll see you in a few minutes."

It took longer than a few minutes to get away from the restaurant, but soon the three of them were in Ian's truck, making the drive to Boise.

When they reached the street festival, the crowd was already filling the streets and the music rocking.

Felicia grinned and pointed across the crowd toward a corn dog stand near the band stage. "I can't believe Taylor is here. Now, there's someone I need to talk to. I'll text you if I need a ride home, but I think I'm good."

Angie glanced the way she pointed, but when she turned to ask who Felicia was talking about, her friend was already making her way through the crowd. Angie tried to watch to see where she stopped, but when Ian grabbed her arm, she turned back to him and lost her friend in the crowd. She leaned close, trying to hear his words. "What?"

Instead of answering, he pointed to a side street where Estebe stood, waving them closer. They finally made their way through the dancing crowd, and when Angie turned to see where Felicia had ended up, her friend was gone.

"Looking for Felicia?" Ian asked. The building they stood behind muffled the crowd noise a bit, and now she could hear him.

"She said she had a ride home unless she texted, but I hate just having her disappear like that. I hope she's all right." Angie pushed the thought away. Her friend was a survivor. She knew her way around, as she'd grown up in one of LA's tougher neighborhoods. "Where's Estebe?"

As if she called him, he reappeared with three cans of beer. "Sorry, we don't do bottles at the festival. Sometimes that's just not a good idea."

"No problem. This is cold and it hits the spot." Ian glanced around at the people sitting around tables in the area. "I didn't know you had this street set up too."

"We tend to spread out. The older generation likes to participate but not in the crazy crowd that's on the main street. Besides, we have our own band, and the food's better here." He led the way to a table that had a paper tent that was marked Reserved. "Have a seat."

"Did you enjoy your cooking experience?" Angie sipped on her beer, letting the icy liquid cool her throat. It had been a long night. Week. Month. Maybe she'd add in year, if she was going to be totally up front with herself.

"It was challenging, but I like feeding people. Besides, I enjoy telling people what to do. Now I know how you feel in our kitchen." He rubbed the back of his neck as he waited for an answer.

"I don't tell you all what to do. But I have to say, you've been training Hope well. We almost didn't miss you at service." She watched his reaction.

"She's a good student." He turned and looked up at someone walking by. "Mrs. Stockwell, so nice of you and your husband to join us. Do you want a chair?"

Angie turned to see Missy Stockwell gaping at the three of them sitting together and drinking a beer. Angie could just see the thoughts running through that woman's mind. She bit back the first sentence she wanted to say and instead smiled. "Yes, please join us. We were just talking about our next outing. Do you think Sun Valley is affordable this time of year for a getaway, or would you recommend something in the northern area?"

"I'm sorry, we can't stay." She glared at Ian. "I can't believe you are condoning this behavior."

"Estebe and I are friends, Missy. Nothing more, nothing less." He cocked his head sideways. "What exactly were you thinking I was condoning?"

She grabbed Herbert by the hand and aimed him toward the opening in the street and back out to the crowd.

Angie turned and looked at Ian and Estebe, who were both grinning. "You set that up."

"People shouldn't gossip." Estebe smiled. "Ian was kind enough to help me."

Heaven help her, she thought. Now the people in her life were collaborating on projects, even those that stopped a town busybody from gossiping. "You know, the rumors are just going to be more pointed now. She'll think we're all in a relationship."

"Maybe, but I'm sure she won't be telling her women's group about seeing us here tonight. She knows I'm well liked in that group. No one would believe her." Ian took her hand and kissed it. "It's nice to be boring again."

"I'll drink to that." Angie held up her bottle. "To boring days ahead."

They all clinked their glasses together and drank. Angie wasn't sure if it was making a wish or just wishful thinking. Either way, she hoped her toast would keep her out of the investigating business for at least a few weeks.

A note from the author:

As I'm writing the Farm-to-Fork series, my thoughts are always brought home to family. Angie and I have a lot in common when talking about connections of food to family. I grew up on the family farm with meals that were hearty and filling. We raised our own beef and pork and the freezer was always full of the season's bounty, even when the winter was long and the garden frozen over.

We didn't do Fried Green Tomatoes. Tomatoes were for canning to be used later for chilis, stews, and spaghetti sauces. Mom cooked a different summer treat, Fried Zucchini. Breaded and battered, the crispy treat made my mouth water, and even now I don't have much luck getting the appetizer on the table before the slices are stolen from the paper towel where they sit waiting to be plated.

Viola's Fried Zucchini
- One large zucchini—these are typically too small in the grocery store. Look for ones about 12 inches long and 3 inches around. But get them fresh, before the seeds harden. Wash the outside, then slice into fairly thin rounds.
- Make a breading station:

  ○ Three eggs beaten with ¼ cup of water in a flat bowl. Season to taste. (For me, garlic salt, pepper, and maybe some Season-All.)

  ○ Flour, seasoned as well. Also in a flat bowl or Tupperware. (If you want to fancy this up, you could use a third bowl of seasoned panko breading. But it's not needed.)

- Heat up oil in a cast iron skillet. (Mom used Crisco or lard, depending on what she had. I like the cleaner taste of vegetable oil.)
- Dip zucchini in flour, egg mixture, then flour again. Then place each slice carefully in the hot oil. You only need to cook these a few seconds on each side. The thinner the rounds, the faster the zucchini inside will cook. Get a nice brown crunch on the outside, take them out, and lay on a paper towel. Season with sea salt (my addition) while hot, and then serve.
- Repeat with the rest of the slices.

Enjoy. Fair warning: This is not diet food.

Lynn

ABOUT THE AUTHOR

New York Times and *USA Today* best-selling author **Lynn Cahoon** is an Idaho expat. She grew up living the small town life she now loves to write about. Currently, she's living with her husband and two fur babies in a small historic town on the banks of the Mississippi river where her imagination tends to wander. *Guidebook to Murder*, Book 1 of the Tourist Trap series, won the 2015 Reader's Crown award for Mystery Fiction.

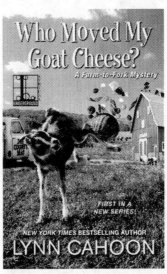

WHO MOVED MY GOAT CHEESE?
A Farm-to-Fork Mystery

**Angie Turner hopes her new farm-to-table restaurant can be a fresh
start in her old hometown in rural Idaho. But when a goat dairy
farmer is murdered, Angie must turn the tables on a bleating black
sheep...**

With three weeks until opening night for their restaurant, the County Seat,
Angie and her best friend and business partner Felicia are scrambling to
line up local vendors—from the farmer's market to the goat dairy farm of
Old Man Moss. Fortunately, the cantankerous Moss takes a shine to Angie,
as does his kid goat Precious. So when Angie hears the bloodcurdling
news of foul play at the dairy farm, she jumps in to mind the man's
livestock and help solve the murder. One thing's for sure, there's no whey
Angie's going to let some killer get *her* goat...

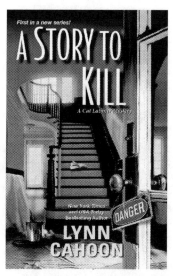

A STORY TO KILL
A Cat Latimer Mystery

Former English professor Cat Latimer is back in Colorado, hosting writers' retreats in the big blue Victorian she's inherited, much to her surprise, from none other than her carousing ex-husband! Now it's an authors' getaway—but Cat won't let anyone get away with murder...

The bed-and-breakfast is open for business, and bestselling author Tom Cook is among its first guests. Cat doesn't know why he came all the way from New York, but she's glad to have him among the quirkier—and far less famous—attendees.

Cat's high school sweetheart Seth, who's fixing up the weathered home, brings on mixed emotions for Cat...some of them a little overpowering. But it's her uncle, the local police chief, whom she'll call for help when there's a surprise ending for Tom Cook in his cozy guest room. Will a killer have the last word on the new life Cat has barely begun?

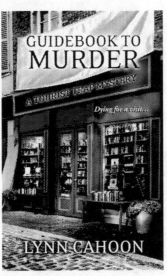

GUIDEBOOK TO MURDER
A Tourist Trap Mystery

In the gentle coastal town of South Cove, California, all Jill Gardner wants is to keep her store—Coffee, Books, and More—open and running. So why is she caught up in the business of murder?

When Jill's elderly friend, Miss Emily, calls in a fit of pique, she already knows the city council is trying to force Emily to sell her dilapidated old house. But Emily's gumption goes for naught when she dies unexpectedly and leaves the house to Jill—along with all of her problems...*and* her enemies. Convinced her friend was murdered, Jill is finding the list of suspects longer than the list of repairs needed on the house. But Jill is determined to uncover the culprit—especially if it gets her closer to South Cove's finest, Detective Greg King. Problem is, the killer knows she's on the case—and is determined to close the book on Jill *permanently*...